Petey the One-Eyed Rat

Petey the One-Eyed Rat

A Story for Animal Lovers of All Ages

KIM LAMPSON REIFF

Illustrated by Lynn Rosskamp

Copyright © 2016 Kim Lampson Reiff, PhD, PLLC.
Illustrations by Lynn Rosskamp

All rights reserved. No part of this book may be used or reproduced by any means, graphic, electronic, or mechanical, including photocopying, recording, taping or by any information storage retrieval system without the written permission of the author except in the case of brief quotations embodied in critical articles and reviews.

Archway Publishing books may be ordered through booksellers or by contacting:

Archway Publishing
1663 Liberty Drive
Bloomington, IN 47403
www.archwaypublishing.com
1 (888) 242-5904

Because of the dynamic nature of the Internet, any web addresses or links contained in this book may have changed since publication and may no longer be valid. The views expressed in this work are solely those of the author and do not necessarily reflect the views of the publisher, and the publisher hereby disclaims any responsibility for them.

Any people depicted in stock imagery provided by Thinkstock are models, and such images are being used for illustrative purposes only. Certain stock imagery © Thinkstock.

ISBN: 978-1-4808-2588-8 (sc)
ISBN: 978-1-4808-2586-4 (hc)
ISBN: 978-1-4808-2587-1 (e)

Library of Congress Control Number: 2016902543

Print information available on the last page.

Archway Publishing rev. date: 3/15/2016

To Dan, Chris, Krisanna, and Stevie
My husband and children who gave me the encouragement
I needed to persevere until I finished writing this book.

In memory of Petey
The loveable one-eyed rat who was the inspiration for this story.

In memory of Dr. Barbara Deeb
A gifted doctor of veterinary medicine unequaled in her
love for small exotic animals like Petey who was passionate
about providing them with the best care possible.

Contents

Acknowledgments
ix

Introduction
xi

Chapter One
The Journeys
1

Chapter Two
CarPet World
21

Chapter Three
Death Row
46

Chapter Four
The Mouse Bite that Changed History
65

Chapter Five
The Fight
83

Chapter Six
The Calm before the Storm
103

Chapter Seven
A Bad Dream Come True
124

Chapter Eight
The United Federation of Feeder Rats
140

Chapter Nine
Going Home
158

Chapter Ten
A Harsh Reality
175

Chapter Eleven
Dr. Beed
191

Chapter Twelve
Surgery
208

Chapter Thirteen
The Love of My Life
222

Chapter Fourteen
The Omen
252

Afterword
267

About the Author
269

About the Illustrator
271

Cast of Characters
273

Acknowledgments

I am filled with gratitude for the people who supported and encouraged me while I was writing *Petey the One-Eyed Rat*.

My loving husband, Dan, cheered me on when I felt discouraged. However, his greatest contribution that I appreciate so much was his willingness to support the operation of 3 Girls Rattery in our home for many years.

My son, Chris, believed that I could make my dream of writing *Petey the One-Eyed Rat* a reality. Knowing that he had faith in me gave me the confidence to continue writing and the determination to complete the book project.

If it were not for my two daughters, Krisanna and Stevie, *Petey the One-Eyed Rat* would have never been written. It was their idea to go to the pet store to adopt pet mice. We came home with two pet rats. The rest is history. Their help with editing the first draft of this manuscript was invaluable.

My parents, Mabel and Steven Lampson, taught me to love and respect all living creatures. They opened my heart to the joy of caring for pets. In turn, I have passed this love and respect for living creatures on to my children. When I was a little girl, my mother told me that someday I would be a writer. She was right.

I am so grateful for Mary and Keith MacDonald, who loved the idea of this book from the beginning, took the time to read the manuscript, helped twist my extremely busy illustrator's arm so that she would find time to do the drawings, and relentlessly asked, "Is the book finished yet?"

I value the exceedingly helpful contributions of Donell Frazier who was my consultant regarding the writing of the chapter about the United Federation of Feeder Rats.

Without the initial invitation extended by LeAnn Boardman, operator of Rattie Rascals Rattery, to attend a rat show, I would never have learned about the world of rat lovers and how enjoyable it is to participate in a rat show. I appreciate her friendship over the years and how much she has taught me about breeding, showing, and most of all, loving pet rats. Because of her, I have made many friends in RatsPacNW, our local organization of people who love rats.

My colleague Kristin Mauldin gave me the final push to move forward with completing the manuscript and publishing the book. Without her encouragement, *Petey the One-Eyed Rat* would still be a dusty document saved on my computer.

Last but not least, I want to thank my illustrator, Lynn Rosskamp, for her amazing drawings and her uncanny ability to capture Petey's personality in her artwork. In addition to being an exceptionally talented artist, Lynn operates a successful rattery called Rodents of Unusual Sweetness that has produced countless Best of Show rats.

Introduction

When I adopted Petey, I had no idea that one day I would write a book about his life. But, how could I not? Petey was an amazing rat. He impacted my life and touched the lives of many others with his gentleness and his disarming one-eyed face. Even people who had an aversion to rats softened after they met him and several actually overcame their fears of rats because of interacting with him. Just like he does in the book, Petey ran over to me when I called him, enjoyed riding on my shoulder, snuggled with me, loved being petted or scratched behind the ears, and was willing to do almost anything for some banana yogurt.

Petey

Originally I intended to write a factual account of Petey's life. Oddly enough, when I sat down to write, a different, more elaborate story told from Petey's perspective materialized on the computer screen in front of me. I found myself laughing as I wrote about his antics and crying as I penned the chapter about the plight of the feeder rats.

Petey the One-Eyed Rat is based on the true story of his life. Petey was a feeder rat with an infected eye when I adopted him. He lost his eye in surgery. Raspberry, Dusty, Huckle, Bailey, and Eddie were real rats. Dr. Barbara Deeb was an exceptional and gifted vet who was my inspiration for the character of Dr. Beed. Petey really did go to work with me all of his life and actually died in my arms while at my office.

However, only Petey can tell the story of what happened before I met him, and he does so in *Petey the One-Eyed Rat*. I hope that reading about Petey will change your life as much as knowing Petey has changed mine.

Chapter One

The Journeys

I WAS NOT ALWAYS CALLED PETEY. IN FACT, Mama and Pops named me Nicodemus after the leader of the rats in one of our favorite books, *Mrs. Frisby and the Rats of NIMH*. Just like the rats in that story, my family was educated and we could read. My parents thought that I would feel proud to be named after such a capable and highly intelligent rat, but I didn't. I remember how excited they were to show me the drawings of my namesake in the book. All I could focus on was how odd and scary Nicodemus looked with only one eye. I felt afraid of him.

You see, I was not always a one-eyed rat. When I was born, I was a normal, healthy rat with two round, dark ruby eyes. Life was good and I was happy. Then, things began to change and my eyes were opened to a darker side of life. I had no idea that a seemingly innocent conversation with my father would be the first event in the chain reaction that turned my life upside down.

"You are going to be a show rat, my son," my father told me, his deep voice confident, his sparkling eyes filled with pride. My dad paused and looked me over very carefully. "Yes, you are a handsome rat. Best of Show, I'll bet! A chip off the old block," he said, winking at me and grinning.

"What's a show rat, Pops?" I asked in my young, four-week-old voice that was so high and shrill it sounded like the squeaky wheel in our cage.

Right after I asked that question, something amazing happened. As if on cue, bright rays from the late-afternoon sun began streaming through the window in our breeder's home, lighting up my back. It was like a big spotlight in the sky found me and magically changed my tawny fur to the color of spun gold.

This particular afternoon my father and I had awoken early. Being the only two rats stirring, Pops decided to teach me how to search for the hazelnuts that our breeders hid in the rat room for us to find. Hazelnuts taste so good. They are like candy for rats. I was torn. I wanted to focus on my father's words, but I also wanted to crack open my hazelnut. I had been struggling to chew through its hard, chocolate-colored shell for a long time.

"Well," replied my father between bites of nut meat. "A show rat is an especially talented or attractive rat who competes against other rats for ribbons. The judges are humans who are trained to evaluate us, usually breeders of exotic rats. The honor of Best of Show is awarded to the rat with the highest score, and the Best of Show ribbon is magnificent!"

I noticed a wistful look in his shiny black eyes. Something about that look made me move closer to him, my small brown nut slipping to the floor, momentarily forgotten.

It seemed to me that my dad was remembering a very important moment in his life. I concentrated hard for a moment trying to figure out what it might be, and then a thought suddenly occurred to me.

"Did *you* ever win Best of Show, Pops?" I blurted out, excited that I might have solved the puzzle.

I squinted at my father, waiting expectantly for his answer. It was hard to see his face because the bright light was shining right into my eyes as the sun dropped lower in the sky.

Pops shifted his weight from one hind paw to the other. Then he moved a little to the left, his body shading me from the blinding light of the sun. I watched, holding my breath as my father looked down and then cleared his throat.

"Well, not exactly, my son. Almost. I won Reserve of Show. That's second place. It was a very close finish. The rat who won was a striking fellow with pure black fur. We had a tie score, but the judges decided to award him Best and me Reserve."

I watched Pops stare at the floor so long I wondered if he was looking at a bug. Then I heard him sigh. I sighed too.

There was an awkward silence. I hesitated, not knowing what to say. I cleared my throat just like my father had and then asked, "Well, isn't Reserve of Show really good too, Pops?"

I waited for my father's reaction, not knowing if I had said the right thing.

"Yes, Nicodemus, Reserve is really good too. Unfortunately, no one in our line has ever won Best of Show, so I was hoping to be the rat to bring that honor to the family." Pops sighed again.

I watched him very closely. He paused. Then I saw his expression change. It was a night-and-day difference. His face brightened, and his whiskers moved faster like he was excited about something.

"So, my son, it will be up to you. Yes, that's it. I know you can do it. I will teach you everything I know about being a show rat. You will be the first in our family to win Best of Show. I can just feel it." My father was so stirred up that he was almost dancing on his hind legs.

My eyes opened as wide as saucers, and my mouth got as dry as the fresh bedding in our cages. I opened my mouth to speak, but no sound came out. I shut it again, not knowing what to say. Because I admired my father so much and wanted to bring honor to my family, I finally stammered, "Okay, Pops. I'll do it! I'll win Best of Show for our family."

Inside, I was scared. What if I couldn't do it? Why didn't he pick one of my brothers or sisters instead?

I picked up my hazelnut and started chipping away at its shell again. At first, thinking about the nut distracted me from my fears, but then I became frustrated with myself. How could I ever think about being Best of Show if I could not even make a hole in a nutshell? Pops came and stood beside me.

"Son, let me help you. Your tiny young teeth are no match for this tough shell," Pops said as he took the nut in his larger paws and began gnawing, making a familiar grinding sound.

I watched as my dad skillfully wore down the hard shell with his sharp, adult teeth until the nut looked a little lopsided because of the small hole he made in its side.

"Here, Nicodemus. I think you can take it from here," Pops said as he handed the nut back to me.

I held the nut in my front paws and started gnawing. Now I could actually break down more of the shell myself since my teeth fit perfectly into the small hole my father had made. I was totally in awe of my dad. Not only was he a master at chiseling a hole into a hazelnut and a very wise father, but he was also a famous show rat.

Show rat. All my worries about being in a rat show came back to me. My whiskers began moving a little faster, and my ears perked up as I concentrated on what question to ask next.

"Uh, Pops?" I began. "When you were in the rat show, what did they judge you on?"

Pops answered in a majestic voice that reminded me of an English nobleman addressing his court, "Standards, my son. Standards."

I learned about British royalty when my father read a book to me about an animal that wore boots and stood before the king. Sadly it was a cat.

Pops continued, "The judges begin by evaluating your appearance—the size of your eyes, the spacing and shape of your ears, the quality of your fur, the arch in your back, and the length as well as roundness of your tail, things like that."

When I heard this list, I naturally became curious about my own suitability as a potential show rat. While Pops paused to swallow the remaining bit of nut in his mouth and to wash his face with his front paws, I decided to look myself over.

I craned my head around with an owl-like move so that I could

Pops shares words of wisdom with his young son.

inspect the quality of my fur and the roundness of my tail, the hazelnut once again parked on the floor.

Pops must have been watching me. "Nicodemus," he said. He waited until I brought my head back around to face him. He was smiling at me lovingly as if he was amused by my self-scrutiny. "You do not win Best of Show on looks alone. Personality counts as well. The judges call this temperament. You have to let the judges hold you without squirming too much or biting. You need to smile. You must not squeak even if you are scared; and you must definitely wait until the judges have put you back in your show box to go to the bathroom. You are a prime specimen of a rat, my boy, and you will do very well!"

I smiled but my smile felt like a mask. Underneath the mask was fear. The pressure I felt to win Best of Show for my family made me feel older. At that moment, I no longer felt carefree and young. I treasured this time alone with my father when we discussed my future, but it was changing me.

I picked up the nut without really thinking about what I was doing and began chewing on it. Then I stopped chewing, holding the hazelnut motionless in my paws, and stared at my father as though seeing him for the first time.

Pops was highly intelligent and well respected in the rat community besides being a very handsome rat. I looked at him intently, remembering the standards he had outlined for me.

His brown fur was ticked with reddish blond tips, a color combination called agouti. When the sun shone on his back, it highlighted the lighter fur so that it glowed like the newly minted copper pennies we *borrowed* from our breeder's pockets. His fur was thick, smooth, and even. His tail was long and round. His ears were smooth with no folds or wrinkles. His eyes were large and shiny, and his back had an enviable arch.

I knew Pops had what it took to be a Best of Show rat.

I was worried. I did not look like my father. The most obvious difference was fur color. I was a fawn rat. This meant that my fur was honey beige with reddish tips. At first glance my eyes looked black, but in the sunlight they were the color of a ripe Bing cherry, a dark ruby red. My fur was splotchy, and my tail was short. I could not tell if my back arched, and I had no idea about my ears.

I did not want to disappoint my father, but I had to tell him what I was thinking. My young voice sounded sad and shaky when I said, "But I don't look like you do. How could I ever win Best of Show?"

Pops answered my question without hesitation, looking at me with love and pride shining in his twinkling black eyes, "It does not matter if we are different, Nicodemus. I want you to be yourself, not a carbon copy of me."

"But Pops, I'm worried about my eyes. I don't have black eyes like yours, and I've heard that humans don't like to look at rats with red eyes. Isn't that right?" I asked.

"Well, there is some truth to that, Nicodemus, but it is usually the pink eyes that bother the humans. They remind them of rats in scary movies or something. Your eyes are so dark red they are almost black. I think you will be fine," Pops replied confidently.

"But my fur color is not even, and my tail is so short," I protested.

Pops reassured me by saying, "You are still very young, my son. So your fur will thicken, and the color will even out. Your tail will get longer as you get older. Don't worry about these things. Your looks are good, but even more than that, you are smart, kind, and lots of fun. Remember, appearance is not what is most important. The way you treat other rats is what really counts!"

"Okay, Pops, I will remember what you said. And you know what else?" I asked. The bubbly enthusiasm of youth was returning, eating up my fears just as quickly as a hungry rat scarfing down a hunk of cheese.

"No, what?" Pops answered, gazing into my face with genuine interest.

"When I grow up, I *am* going to be a Best of Show rat, and you will be so proud of me!"

I spun around in circles so fast I almost fell over. I could not tell if it was because I was nervous or excited, but it did not matter. It felt good to move around like that.

"Nicodemus, I am already proud of you and will always be proud of you whether you are awarded Best of Show or not," my father responded.

His voice was serious, and I could see the pride in his eyes. My father said exactly what I wanted to hear, but I chose not to believe him. I felt I had to win Best of Show, or my father would never be proud of me again.

Although I was too young to comprehend the implications of all that Pops had said to me that day, I had listened very carefully, intuitively knowing he was telling me some very important things about life.

Without realizing it, I took his words and stored them away for a later time just like the squirrel that lived in the tree outside our window hid chestnuts in the fall so that she would have food during the cold, lean days of winter.

Thinking about nuts reminded me of my neglected hazelnut. I put it up to my mouth and sawed on the shell a little more with my teeth. Finally, I broke through to the tender meat inside. The flavor was unbelievably good.

I was so absorbed with my snack that I did not notice my brother Templeton, an agouti rat with a white patch on his belly, sneaking toward me until he jumped on my back, interrupting my man-to-man talk with Pops. We rolled over and over, tousling on the floor. Pops watched, laughing, holding his belly with his front paws, bemused by our antics.

The room suddenly darkened when the sunlight left the window and the sun slipped lower in the sky. The dim light remaining cast interesting shadows as we rolled around the room. Templeton touched my shoulder and then ran off, initiating a game of tag-and-tackle.

I did not chase after him right away like I usually did. I hesitated and looked at my father, unsure if our conversation was finished. He spoke as if he could read my mind, "Nicodemus, go play with your brother. We have had enough serious talking for one day."

I did not need any more encouragement. I ran off after Templeton, who had just darted behind the small silver storage can that contained our food. Like animal tracks in a fossil, my father's words were etched in my memory forever.

When I was five weeks old, Mrs. Hamsterford appeared at the rattery. She was a tall, skinny woman with curly, reddish gray hair that was a color unlike any rat fur I had ever seen. Large black glasses circled her big green eyes giving her an owlish appearance that spooked all of us. Even though most of the rats were sleeping when she arrived, we all opened our eyes as if on cue when we heard the clicking of her shoes as she walked in our direction.

Feeling a sense of foreboding, my brothers, my sisters, and I huddled close to Mama and Pops. It was as though the wicked witch of the west had just flown in on her broomstick and landed in front of us. There was a collective intake of air as we simultaneously inhaled. We waited expectantly.

Mrs. Hamsterford was not evil. I once overheard Annabelle, our breeder, refer to her as a pet broker. Mama explained that she was the person who contacted breeders to find baby animals and birds for local pet stores.

Since she had been here many times before, all of us knew what her arrival meant. It signaled that it was time for another litter of baby rats to say good-bye to the rattery and move to a pet shop.

We watched as Annabelle and Mrs. Hamsterford walked across the room, hoping and praying that they would walk right past us, but they did not. Annabelle stopped directly in front of our cage and said, "Here they are, Mrs. Hamsterford. This is a particularly desirable litter. Wonderful temperament and great colors. If you stand over here, you can see the two fawn babies hiding behind their mother."

Annabelle was pointing toward my sister, Rose, and me. The loud clanging and churning sounds of a garbage truck outside the window made it hard for me to hear what they were saying. I strained to listen, hoping Mrs. Hamsterford would decide we were not the kind of rats she wanted.

"Oh, yes, I see them. Gorgeous fur!" she said as she peered into our cage.

Mrs. Hamsterford's tone was matter-of-fact and businesslike in sharp contrast to the warmth and friendliness of Annabelle's voice. "Just what I am looking for. Pack them up."

The garbage truck's sounds faded as it pulled away. The relative quiet allowed me to hear her pronouncement loud and clear. I found myself involuntarily shrinking back toward the far side of the cage. Even though my parents had prepared me and my siblings for this day from the time we had first opened our eyes, I was not ready to go anywhere.

I liked my life—the familiar routine of feeding in the morning and evening, the excursions during free-range days in the rat room, the reading lessons, the family huddle with our bodies piled all over each other as we slept, and the nightly stories read or told to us by Mama and Pops.

"Where are we going, Pops?" I whispered, my little body trembling. I was scared.

I knew what he was going to say.

My father whispered back in his soothing way that calmed my fears and helped me feel strong, "To a pet store, I think. It is time to leave home and seek your fortune. You are a very talented rat, Nicodemus. You are good-natured and handsome just like your dad."

I could tell he was trying to make me laugh so I would not be afraid, but I noticed his voice wavered as he spoke, betraying his own emotion. He spoke quickly, as there was no time for lengthy good-byes, and then he winked to reassure me. This simple blinking of his eye reminded me of our talk about my future when we were hunting hazelnuts together.

I sighed.

Pops spoke again. "Don't worry, my boy. You will be successful in life and will make a fine father when you grow up. I bet you will win Best of Show just like we talked about the other day. Farewell, my son. Remember that your mom and I love you now and will love you always."

His voice cracked, and not afraid to show his feelings unlike most other male rats, Pops let a tear roll down his face. I watched it drip onto the floor of the cage and disappear into the bedding, winding its way through the particles of wood like a tiny river.

I felt my own eyes welling up with tears, as I, too, experienced an odd mixture of intense emotions. There is no doubt that I, in keeping with the adventurous spirit characteristic of rats, was excited about the prospect of a new escapade, even if it was merely going to a pet store.

In stark contrast, I felt a sick, all-too-familiar, anxious feeling growing in the pit of my stomach at the thought of separating from my parents. The bond between us was very strong. My heart began to race as I panicked. I felt I lacked the confidence that I could survive this big change.

This was not the first time that I had been frightened about something. I remember feeling afraid to drink water from the water bottle in our cage. I know it sounds silly, but the shiny, silver metal ball that turns around in the waterspout scared me. Somehow I got the idea that licking the little ball would turn it into a monster that would chase me and bite my tail.

I was so embarrassed about this fear that I kept it a secret. As I think back, I know it would have really helped me if I had talked to somebody about it. Instead I watched. I watched Mama drink from the water bottle. Then I watched Templeton. Then I watched Rose. To my surprise, no monster came out and chased them or bit their tails. The fact that nothing bad happened was a mystery to me.

I felt pressured to get over my fear because my brother Stuart kept pestering me.

"Hey, Nicodemus, try this water with me. It's really fun. See that little ball. It spins around when you put your tongue on it. It is so cool. Come on," Stuart encouraged, confused by my reluctance.

I did not know how many more times I could say, "I'll do it later, Stuart. I'm just not thirsty right now."

Finally I ran out of excuses. With my growing thirst as motivation, I gathered up my courage, marched up to the waterspout, and licked it. My tongue recoiled from the small metal sphere as fast as if

I had licked a hot stove. I immediately sprinted away as though I was in a relay race, tagging base, reversing direction, and racing toward my team.

When safely back in our nest, I timidly turned around and looked toward the object of my fear. To my relief, there was no monster following me. I checked my tail, and there were no bite marks. The little ball had not changed one bit, and best of all I was still alive. To my surprise, the tiny droplet of water that landed on my tongue felt cool and tasted quite good.

After that, I had no problem drinking from the water bottle. Well, that is not exactly true. I did look over my shoulder the first few times I took a drink just to make sure.

Unfortunately the memory of overcoming that fear was not enough to stop this panic. My heart was pounding like a drum, and I felt a strong need to defecate. Rats do that, you know, when they are scared. We are actually very private about our toilet habits and have considerable control. However, when we are afraid, that all goes out the window, and we have an uncontrollable urge, well, to put it bluntly, to poop.

Mama sensed that I was having a hard time and gave me a few licks on the fur just behind my ears and tidied my whiskers just as she had done hundreds of times before. This time she added words to her actions. "Take deep slow breaths, Nicodemus. Like this." I watched her chest move up and down, very slowly.

Mama was demonstrating how to calm down so that I could copy her and learn how to do it. "Count with me. In ... one, two, three, four. Out ... one, two, three four."

"Okay, Mama," I said. At first, my breaths were shallow. My chest felt heavy like it did when Templeton and I were wrestling and he flipped me over and sat on top of me. There simply was not enough air to breathe. With Mama's help, I could soon breathe more deeply again. I felt the rhythm of my heartbeat slowing down like a train chugging more slowly as it went up a steep hill.

Mama spoke from her heart, "Nicodemus, I want you to look at me." My tiny dark ruby eyes gazed into her beautiful black ones. "I can tell that you are scared. I remember how upset I was when I left home for the first time, so I understand."

Mama glanced up at the ceiling for a moment, a faraway look fleeting across her misty eyes. It was as though she had changed into that little girl rat who knew exactly what I was feeling. Then the moment passed, and she was the adult, focusing on the needs of her children once more. Knowing Mama understood helped me so much.

My mom peeked over her shoulder to see if we had more time to talk. Mrs. Hamsterford was engaged in an animated discussion with Annabelle. In the background, I could hear the dishwasher making its familiar gurgling and swishing sounds as the water swirled around the dishes.

I'm going to miss that noise. How odd that the sound that used to irritate me as much as a rat running on a squeaky wheel had suddenly become a fond reminder of home.

Mama spoke again, her strong, gentle voice empowering me, her front paw gently stroking my back. "Just like generations of rats before you, Nicodemus, you have to face the transitions of life with courage. I know you well, my son, and I am confident that you will be okay. I am so proud of you, sweet one, and I will always love you. Even though we will be apart, we can keep the memories of the good times we have had together with us forever ... in here." She pointed to her heart and then kissed my head.

Annabelle and Mrs. Hamsterford finished their conversation and pivoted around to face us. As Annabelle opened the door of our cage, Mama turned away as though she could not bear to watch. I saw my father reach out to comfort her.

"George, turn off that dishwasher!" Annabelle yelled to her husband. There was a short whirring noise, and then the sound abruptly stopped. I did not want it to stop so soon. I wanted to listen to it a little longer as if in some magical way, the clanking of the dishes could postpone my departure.

"Okay, little guy, you're first," Annabelle said to me, the lightness in her voice betraying that she had no idea how upset I was.

She gently picked me up and held me cupped in the palm of her hand as carefully as if I were a fragile china ornament rather than a live creature.

"Look, Mrs. Hamsterford. Isn't he cute?" Annabelle crooned, beaming with pride.

Mrs. Hamsterford, a woman of few words, looked more owlish than ever as she peered at me over the top of her glasses and repeated, "Gorgeous fur."

Annabelle lowered me onto some soft gray material in the bottom of a small cage. I watched my parents say a quick good-bye to my two brothers and two sisters. Then I felt the warm bodies of my siblings drop down one by one beside mine. We huddled together, not so much to get warmth but to quell our fears. Then I heard it—a soft, almost imperceptible sound. Peony, my youngest sister, was crying.

"Flight attendants, prepare for arrival." Karin's eyes popped open. The booming voice of the captain startled her, snapping her out of the semiconscious state so typical at the end of a long plane flight. Karin glanced at her two daughters, Claire and Sarah, sitting beside her. They were looking out the window at the ever-enlarging scene below as the plane descended into the Seattle area.

This had not been a good flight. Karin had been irritable and short with her daughters, and that only made her feel worse. She was angry. It seemed like nothing could fill the hole in her heart created when her father died.

Her heart was perforated a year and a half ago when he was first diagnosed with colon cancer. During the months that he was sick, the hole kept growing just like the cancer until it had quadrupled in size by the time that he died.

Karin desperately missed her father. No matter how many times she told herself to be grateful for all the years they had spent together, the pain did not lessen. The feelings were too new and too raw for anyone to console her, even her husband and children, whom she loved so much. When they tried to make her feel better and failed, she felt

Karin, Claire, and Sarah about to land at SeaTac airport.

guilty that she could not respond. She wanted time alone to hurt and feel sorry for herself, but she also wanted to stay present enough to be a good wife and mom. Her own mother was too grief-stricken to advise her and there was no manual to instruct her regarding how to strike a balance between these two strong inner conflicting desires.

Her two young daughters were hurting too. They had been very close to their grandfather, whom they affectionately called Papoo, the Greek word for grandpa. It was their first experience with the death of a family member, and Karin wanted to be able to comfort and help them through their grief. At this moment it felt too hard to help anyone else, even her daughters, but she was determined to try.

Still lost in her thoughts, Karin was jolted back to the present when United flight 852 made a rather bouncy landing at Seattle-Tacoma International Airport. Karin watched groggily as harried passengers pulled suitcases down from the overhead bins and streamed off the plane like sheep herded from behind by the flight attendants.

Although happy to be going home, Karin did not feel like stirring. She was tired, and the effort it took to stand was too much for her to muster. As the passenger line moved on, she forced herself to gather her belongings and straighten up, stretching her arms out in front of her and yawning. The stretch seemed to help. Karin now had enough energy to help her daughters.

"Claire, don't forget your violin," she reminded her eleven-year-old daughter who was struggling to maneuver the carry-on bag that had been stowed under the seat in front of her. With a final twist, Claire managed to right the bag and move it into position to wheel it off the plane.

"Sarah, look under the seat to make sure you don't leave anything behind," Karin instructed her youngest child, who was almost seven.

Karin sighed. Her daughters, especially the younger one, had had so few years to spend with their grandfather. She wished they could have seen the pride in his warm brown eyes when they graduated from high school.

Sarah grabbed several marker pens and a piece of candy that had fallen out of her backpack. After she stuffed the pens into an outside pocket of her jacket, she popped the candy into her mouth. Karin glanced at her, a less-than-pleased expression on her face. Sarah had already had way too much candy for one day.

Does it really matter? Maybe it helps her feel better. Let it go. Karin smiled at Sarah, who smiled back.

As she walked off the plane, Karin spotted her husband, Doug, and her son, Charlie, waiting for them. Doug and Charlie flew home the week before right after the funeral. She and the girls stayed longer to help Karin's mother. Charlie, a college graduate who was no longer living at home, had been keeping his dad company while the girls were away.

Karin hoped that seeing familiar faces would ease the difficult transition from the intense time in New Jersey to the familiar activities of their lives in Seattle. She noticed Sarah waving a hand to catch her father's attention as she tried unsuccessfully to wriggle through the bustling crowd to connect with him.

Doug was excitedly scanning the faces of the passengers leaving the plane, looking for his family. It was so good to see him again. When his eyes met hers, he smiled, his grayish blue eyes brightening. His smile gave her hope that she would heal. Karin could see how eager he was to have his family all together at home and this warmed her sad wounded heart.

"Papa, we're home!" Claire and Sarah exclaimed, giving him a big hug while Karin greeted Charlie. Karin joined in the embrace, sighing with relief that they had made it safely back to Seattle.

"It's so good to see you and Charlie. How are things at home, Doug?" Karin asked.

"Fine. Everything is under control. The cats are healthy, and the rhododendrons are in full bloom," Doug explained as the family made its way toward baggage claim. "How was your mom when you left?"

Karin sighed and then spoke, "Not very well. She was so close to Pa. They did everything together, you know. I'm really worried about her. I hope she's going to be okay. She seems so lost and sad without him."

On the ride home, Karin and Doug discussed the events of the past few weeks. Karin expressed her fear that she and the girls would have difficulty jumping back into the routine of work and school after such a sad occasion. Charlie, Sarah, and Claire joked and laughed in the backseat, finding humor to be a great distraction from the sad memories.

A month passed. To Karin's surprise, returning to the predictable pattern of school, work, and after-school activities seemed to comfort her family. The good feelings associated with the fond memories of Papoo when he was alive were taking the place of the intense feelings of loss that were so pronounced when the family first came home. Karin was less on edge and more giving, but the hole was still there.

One Thursday evening Karin and Claire were doing the dinner dishes. Claire picked up a clean plate and then stopped moving, the large plate in her motionless right hand suspended midway between the dishwasher and the closet. Claire looked at Karin, who was working at the sink, and asked, "Mama, could Sarah and I get a new pet? One for each of us?"

Karin, slightly tilting a salad dish so she could maneuver the uneaten portion into the garbage, stopped scraping the dish and turned to look at Claire. Oblivious to the fact that the angle of the dish had shifted when she faced her daughter, she was unaware that the remains of the salad had missed its mark and dropped to the floor instead.

Karin, momentarily taken aback by a question she had not expected, recovered quickly and stalled for time to think by asking, "What kind of pet are you thinking of, Claire?"

When she noticed the spilled food, she quickly scooped it up and tossed it into the garbage, wiped up the floor with a paper towel, placed the dish into the dishpan, and then picked up a pot that had been soaking in the dishwater.

"Well, something we could take care of ourselves without your help. Claire hesitated. Then speaking with a soft, timid voice, she posed the question without looking at Karin. "Ummm," she began, followed by a long pause. "What about a mouse?"

Claire glanced up at her mother, a hopeful smile on her face, her robot-like arm suddenly moving again as if someone had pressed a button that controlled its motion. She added the dish to the stack of dinner plates on the left side of the closet, holding her breath as she anxiously awaited her mother's response.

Karin hesitated for a few moments, pausing in the middle of scrubbing a stubborn spot on the pot used to cook the thick pasta sauce they had eaten for dinner. Something stirred inside her. The loss of her father had left a sad place in her heart and the hearts of her children. The idea of new life and an animal to nurture appealed to her, and she thought it might be good for them too.

"Well, I guess a mouse would be okay," she said tentatively, "but I'll have to check with your father. You do realize that—"

"I know," interrupted Claire, who was now sorting the silverware as she put it in the drawer. "We have to be responsible for feeding them and cleaning their cages."

"That's right," said Karin as she dried the pot and put it away. "Maybe we can go to CarPet World, that big pet store that just opened near our house."

Karin was thinking aloud, "If your dad agrees, we can go on Memorial Day weekend. That way there will be three days for you and Sarah to spend time with your new pets before you go back to school."

"Really? That's next weekend! I'll go tell Sarah." Claire could hardly contain the excitement in her voice.

The silverware dropped out of her hands and fell onto the counter with a series of staccato clinking noises as she took off in a flash, disappearing down the stairs as she ran to find her sister.

"Claire, wait! You haven't finished the dishes yet—" Karin's voice trailed off as she realized that the sound of her words faded away without ever reaching Claire's ears.

Karin walked over to the top of the stairs and listened, eavesdropping on the conversation between her two daughters. She smiled as she overheard Claire's young voice, full of a level of enthusiasm that had been missing in the past few months, saying, "Sarah, Sarah, Mama said we can go to CarPet World and get baby mice next weekend."

Karin slowly walked back toward the kitchen. Yes. A couple of baby mice might be just the thing our family needs right now.

Chapter Two

CarPet World

"SNUGGLE UP WITH ME, PEONY," I WHISPERED as I positioned my body next to hers and curled my tail around her tail like always. We started sleeping like this when we were two weeks old.

"It's going to be okay. I'll take care of you. Just like the generations of rats before us, we have to face these transitions with courage," I said, repeating Mama's words with a feigned air of confidence.

I felt like a cross between a puffer fish who pretended to be very brave when it was really very scared and Franklin Delano Roosevelt. Pops read about Mr. Roosevelt in a history book he found at the rattery and explained that, a long time ago, he was president of the United States. During a particularly dark moment in history, FDR told the disheartened people of his country, "You have nothing to fear but fear itself."

Just as I imagined it was for this famous man, my advice to Peony was intended as much to convince myself as it was to convince her.

My stomach did a summersault as someone lifted our cage upward, carried it a short distance, and then plopped it down on the front porch of the house with a thud. It was raining outside. It was a strong, steady, spring rain that was long overdue. I looked out between the bars of our carrier. The drooping flowers and the parched trees flecked with the pale green of new spring growth could really use a good drink.

A few raindrops bounced off the wires of the cage onto my fur. Although I had heard rain beating on the roof of our house, this was the first time I had actually felt it. It was wet. I licked one of the drops on my fur. It tasted surprisingly refreshing and delicious.

We could see Mrs. Hamsterford through the narrow bars of the cage. The beam of the porch light gave her reddish hair an odd hue that reminded me of cheese puffs. After a brief discussion and exchange of cash with Annabelle, the rat broker slowly navigated the front steps, carefully carrying our cage in both hands like an overflowing bag of groceries. As she looked sideways around the cage in order to see the location of the next level, she gingerly moved down the staircase one step at a time.

"Over here, Marge," came a man's voice booming out of the dark shadows. A shiver ran down my spine as I imagined an exterminator, a scary rat killer lurking in the dark. Mama had told us all about them.

"I see you, Joe," said Mrs. Hamsterford.

As I peered through the bars of the cage, I could make out a bright red van with big zebra-striped letters on the side. Since there was no picture of a dead bug on the side of the van, I relaxed. This was not an exterminator. A man I had never seen before was standing beside the open door at the back of the van, talking into a cell phone. He was a tall, lanky, middle-aged man with sandy brownish gray hair, a rat fur color called lilac, and horn-rimmed glasses. He actually looked friendly.

"Here, let me take them from you," the man called Joe said. I watched him extend one hand toward our cage while he stuffed his cell phone into his back pocket with the other hand. Mrs. Hamsterford pushed our cage toward him, seeming more than ready to hand us over to Joe. He took the cage from her and held it up at eye level and then smiled at us. I looked back at him and found myself smiling despite my anxious state of mind. He seemed like a nice man. "Wow, these rats are as cute as can be. Bet they'll be gone by the end of the week." I had no idea what *gone* meant.

Mrs. Hamsterford cleared her throat and then commented, "I'm sure they will. They're all yours now, Joe."

Joe carefully lowered our cage into the roomy back of the van and then gently shut the door. We heard him say good-bye to Mrs. Hamsterford as he opened the driver's door, climbed inside, and started the engine. Then he addressed someone we could not see, "Hey, Fred, turn on the ball game. Should be about the seventh inning by now, don't you think?"

As the van slowly inched backward, I heard a funny beeping sound that stopped when the van stood still. The van jerked as it changed direction, and we started traveling forward, picking up speed rather quickly. The trip to the pet store was underway, the windshield wipers tapping out a rhythmic cadence that reminded me of the dishwasher.

I felt exhausted. It was not the tiredness that comes from physical exertion but the tiredness that comes from weathering intense emotions. It seemed like a tornado was tearing around my brain, tumbling my thoughts, and generating a whirlwind of strong feelings.

I had known leaving home would be hard, but not this hard. The more I thought about being away from Mama and Pops, the more scared I became. My heart started beating as fast as a hummingbird's wings. My chest felt as tight as the springs that latched our cage doors. I wished I were not so prone to panic attacks. None of my siblings seemed to get as worked up as I did when they felt nervous about something new.

I wanted to know where we were going. What if Joe and Fred really were exterminators and we were not going to a pet store at all?

Breathe deeply and slowly. Pretend Mama is sitting right there, telling you to breathe slower. Okay, I can do this. It helped. I felt a little calmer. Not knowing what else to do, I lay down and curled up in the corner of our cage, using my front paws as a pillow. I shivered, so I wrapped my tail around my body like a very skinny blanket, but it was too small to provide any warmth. After another parade of uncontrollable shivers, I got up and lay down next to Peony, comforting myself by entwining my tail in hers. The warmth of my sister's small sleeping body next to mine felt soothing, and the shivers subsided, leaving me as still as a leaf on a windless day.

I listened to the voice of the baseball announcer on the radio rise and fall as he called the strikes, balls, runs, and outs in the baseball game. It made me more homesick. Annabelle and George were avid baseball fans, so listening to baseball was a nightly event at our rattery. Once in a while, just as our breeders did, Joe or Fred made a comment about a particularly exciting play. I sighed, the sad feelings hissing out of my body like air from a bike tire going flat. I had the odd sensation that I was floating, observing my life from a distance.

I felt like I had been reading the story of my life and slammed the book shut when we left the rattery, too scared to read any more.

"Hey, Fred, let's unload these rats and then head out for dinner," Joe suggested as he pulled up to the employees' entrance to CarPet World. He jammed on the brakes so hard that his glasses slipped down his nose.

Unload? What does that mean?

"Right," agreed Fred as he stepped out of the van, stretched like a sleepy cat, and then pulled on the hood of his raincoat to shelter his balding head from the light drizzle that was so typical of Seattle weather. Stroking his beard, he lumbered past the large zebra-print letters toward the rear door of the van.

Not wanting to be the only one awake, I nudged my four siblings who were, to my surprise, sound asleep. How could they sleep at a time like this?

"Wake up, everybody. We're here," I announced.

They stretched and yawned. My brothers, Templeton and Stuart, as well as my sisters, Peony and Rose, looked drowsy and confused. By the time Fred opened the door to the van, all were fully awake. I peered out of the cage and glimpsed a short, stocky man with a little bit of dark brown hair framing his face, a thick graying beard hiding his chin, and deep-set olive green eyes staring back at me. Startled,

I immediately recoiled, pulling my head out of his sight like a turtle going back into its shell.

"Where are we, Nicodemus?" asked Peony, standing on her hind legs to catch a better view of our surroundings.

All I could see was the front of a huge rectangular building. There was a large neon sign plastered on the wall closest to us with zebra-striped letters exactly like the ones on the side of the van. I squinted until I could make out the words *CarPet World*.

"I think a place called CarPet World, Sis. At least that's what that big sign says," I answered as I pointed my right paw toward the identifying letters. I tried to sound brave, but the shakiness was creeping back into my voice with the persistence of a squirrel stealing seed from a bird feeder.

CarPet world. Is that a carpet store? What if they are going to kill us and use our fur to make rugs just like they do with bears and sheep?

An involuntary shiver ran down my spine.

On the other hand, maybe the place really *is* a pet store. After all, the word pet *is* in the name.

"What a cool sign. I can't wait to see what's inside," Peony responded with enthusiasm.

I was surprised to hear the eagerness in her voice. Although I pretended to share in my sister's excitement, the truth was that I was worried. The possibility of another panic attack made me even more anxious.

This was ridiculous. I had just gotten myself to calm down a few minutes ago, and here I was, revving up my engine all over again. Okay, Nicodemus. Chill. You need to keep it together to help your brothers and sisters. Remember how you overcame the scared feelings about the water bottle?

Yes, but that was different.

I must be going crazy. I am actually arguing with myself. But it *was* different. When I was afraid of the water bottle, I could watch my parents and siblings and see what they did and then take my time in building up the courage to try it myself. Here, there was no one to watch, no example to follow, no parent or sibling to show me what to do. The water bottle was scary, but it was a known quantity. CarPet World was not.

"Nicodemus! Are you listening?" Peony was tapping me on the shoulder with her front paw.

I forced myself to focus my attention on her and push my own thoughts aside for the moment. "What happens if there isn't a human who wants to adopt me?" she asked. The excitement had vanished from her voice. She was looking at me with fear in her eyes that mirrored my own.

"Of course someone will want you, Peony. You are so loveable. If no one does, well ... let's not think about that right now," I answered, not sure what to say next.

Her questions were my questions too. If no human chose me to take home, I would never reach the two goals I had for my life—to be adopted into a nice, loving family and to win Best of Show. Frankly I had no idea what would become of me if I stayed at the pet store my whole life. Pops and I had not discussed that.

Peony and I stopped talking when our cage began rocking from side to side like the wheel in our cage did after we stopped running on it. This minor earthquake occurred when the man called Fred clumsily lifted our carrier out of the van. I saw him for the first time.

He was a large human with brownish patches of curly fur around his ears and a little on the top of his head. There were some rats with fur like that at our rattery. Mama said they were called double rexes.

"Hey, Joe, you didn't tell me we were delivering rats. Here, you carry them in," Fred said in a surprisingly shaky voice as he held out the cage to Joe.

"I don't want them," shuddered Fred, arms outstretched, stiff as a board, holding our cage as far away as he could. He reminded me of Annabelle when she would discover a smelly, rotten potato in the back of her pantry, make a sound of disgust, and then race past us to the garbage can, arm extended so the smelly potato was as distant from her as possible.

"What did you think we were picking up at Annabelle's rattery, Fred? Goats? Of course we're delivering rats. What's the matter with you? You're not afraid of them, are you?" asked Joe, walking around the truck to face Fred, his glasses reflecting the light from the zebra-print letters on the neon sign.

"Of course not," lied Fred, biting his lip. "Are you, Joe?"

Fred reined in our cage a little closer to demonstrate his bravery. Not a good idea.

Accidentally positioning the cage so that one side touched the bottom of his coat, Fred unwittingly provided me the opportunity to use my paws and teeth to draw a little of the fabric into the cage.

I smiled.

"He wants to eat me!" screamed Fred, looking at me with an expression of pure terror. "Look, Joe. He's got my coat. Help!"

Despite my anxiety, I found myself laughing, and the laughter helped me relax a little. Rats do have a great sense of humor, and at moments like these, that sense of humor dampens fear like water on a smoldering fire.

"Don't be ridiculous, Fred!" said Joe, stifling a laugh. "Here, give me that cage! I can't believe that you, a grown man, are afraid of a few baby rats!"

He took our cage from Fred with one hand and closed the door to the van with the other. The rain had stopped. Bits of blue sky were peeking through the rapidly dispersing gray clouds. Joe turned, and with an air of importance, he began striding toward the big building like someone carrying a shipment of gold bullion.

The journey from our transport vehicle toward the back door of CarPet World had begun. Fred, his heart still pounding, locked the van and meekly followed his coworker, stroking his beard and muttering something about what his mother would think if she ever found out that he was delivering rats for a living.

It has never ceased to amaze me that a human man could be so afraid of me, an animal who is just a fraction of his size. I tried to imagine what it would be like if I were afraid of an ant.

Pops and I talked about the fact that many humans are afraid of rats. He told me it was our tails that got to them. He explained that some humans thought they looked like earthworms. I was shocked.

My tail bears no resemblance to a worm! First of all, it is warm not cold, and secondly, it has a soft covering of hair that makes it smooth not slimy.

Fred held the door open as Joe carried us across the threshold of CarPet World and ushered us into a room bigger than the whole backyard at the rattery. The store was like nothing my brothers, my sisters, and I had ever seen. I saw lots of animals and reptiles in glass containers, some fish in small box-shaped lakes, birds in cages similar to ours at the rattery, and a bunch of cars parked in the center of the place.

I was most interested in the pet sections, of course, but I could not stop looking at the many cars and trucks prominently displayed in the middle of the store. I recognized vehicles of all sizes ranging from tiny cars to huge vans. They were all shiny and clean like they were dressed up to go somewhere special. It might seem odd that I knew so much about them, but it was only because Pops had showed us a magazine filled with images of all kinds of cars and trucks. After looking at a few pictures, we had a great time chewing the edges of the pages and then ripping them apart so we could drag selected pieces around the rattery.

At CarPet World, the pet section was separated from the car section by a large circle of six red minivans with the familiar zebra-striped letters spelling CarPet World painted on their sides. They formed a protective barrier around the cars and trucks that were for sale just like Mama and Pops did for us when they made a warm circle with their bodies to shield us from harm when we were very small.

We were very close to one of these red minivans, so I craned my neck to see what was inside. This was not difficult because the doors were gone, so the van looked like a bean on wheels with the inside all hollowed out.

Instead of the steering wheel and seats that I expected, there was a desk with a computer on top, a chair behind the desk, and two chairs facing the desk. When I read the sign above the opening to the van that said, "Deals on Wheels," I realized that the inside of the van had been scooped out to form a private office where the car salespeople and car buyers negotiated their deals.

In addition to all the creatures and automobiles, there were people everywhere. The room was buzzing like a beehive. Customers were bustling about the store, looking at cars and pets. The salespeople, speckled among the customers, gave the room a red polka-dotted look since all of the employees at CarPet World wore the same bright red T-shirt with the words *CarPet World* written across the front in zebra-print lettering and the CarPet World logo on the back.

"Bring them over here, Joe," yelled a big man who stood about six inches taller than most humans, wildly waving his arms in the direction of a sign that said, "Rodent Pavilion." He was a good-looking man with a shiny completely bald head that shone in the bright lights of the store. The thick gold necklace that he wore sported a small solid-gold jaguar pendant that bounced around on his chest as he walked. Despite his unique appearance, the distinctive CarPet World red tee that he wore helped him blend in with the other employees.

When the tall man turned around to walk toward the rodent pavilion, I saw the CarPet World logo up close for the first time. There was a picture of a convertible with a dog behind the wheel and a variety of animals stuffed into the passenger seats. A parrot was sitting on top of the windshield. A rat with a top hat and tails was leaning against the hood, and an aquarium full of fish was strapped to the trunk.

I turned around when I heard Fred's high-pitched voice.

"Hey, Joe!" Fred's hand was shaking like a leaf as he pointed to the left. "There are tarantulas over there. Big, hairy buggers. Some guy was holding one!"

Fred shuddered for the second time that afternoon and began stroking his beard so hard that I was afraid he was going to pull it off.

"Take it easy, Fred," said Joe. Then he muttered, "Excuse me," to a lady who was leaning over to peek inside a new cherry red minivan on the showroom floor.

Three children were tugging at her coat and saying, "Look, Mom. Those men have rats! Can we go see them please, please?"

They were pointing at us. She gave Joe an irritated look.

"I like the big light brown one," said the little boy. He was looking at me. I smiled and chattered my teeth.

The CarPet World Logo

"Hey, Joe," shouted Fred, pointing in my direction, "That beige one is grinding his teeth like he's hungry or something. Better keep your fingers away from the bars of the cage."

How Fred could hear my relatively quiet noises above the din of CarPet World was beyond me. Joe squinted at Fred. His glasses had slipped down on his nose, so he was looking over them rather than through the lenses, and he responded, "Fred, don't you know anything about rats? That's called bruxing. Rats do that when they are happy."

"Yeah, right," Fred responded in a dubious tone. "Why would this rat be happy?"

He gave me a very skeptical look. Because he was not watching where he was going, he had to stop short to avoid walking smack into the big man with the bald head.

"Slow down, dude," the big man said, chuckling as he directed Joe to his left. "You can put that cage right here on this shelf, Joe. See those two bins to your right? We'll be moving the boys, called bucks, into one and the girls, called does, into the other. Got to have a health check first," he explained as he pointed to two large boxes made of glass.

Extending his huge hand to Fred in a welcoming gesture, he announced, "Name's Arnold Jaguar, but you can call me Jag for short. Kind of funny since I'm so tall." He laughed, amused by his own joke. It was a warm, friendly laugh that gave me the same kind of good feeling inside as I felt after I ate a big hunk of cheese. "I've met your pal, Joe, but I don't think I've seen you before."

"Name's Fred, uh, Jag. Hey, I get it. That little animal around your neck matches your name!" Fred grinned as he pointed to the miniature jaguar with a look of accomplishment on his face as if he had just figured out the winning answer on a game show.

At that very moment, a prospective automobile buyer decided to test the brightness of the high beams of a sports car located in the automobile section of the store. The light rays shone toward Mr. Jaguar, reflecting off his pendant so that it glinted like a golden coin in a pirate's chest. The little jaguar sparkled and looked as though it were winking back at Fred.

"That's right! Mr. van Goat hired me on the spot when he heard my name. Said I was one of the few people he had ever met who shared the distinction and good fortune of having a last name that was both a car and an animal." He laughed again as Fred stared at him, apparently at a loss for words.

I studied Mr. Jaguar for a moment, intrigued by the fact that he had no hair on his head. I had heard of hairless rats, although I had never seen one. I concluded that this must be a hairless human. His skin was a warm brown color, and his eyes were a deeper brown that reminded me of the delicious chocolate Pops used to sneak into our nest whenever he could find some.

"What a good-looking group of rats! Might take one home myself!" Mr. Jaguar said in his warm, deep voice.

Mr. Jaguar smiled, reached in our cage, and picked up Stuart, my younger brother. The man stroked his back, and then with a well-practiced motion, he deftly deposited him upon his shoulder.

Stuart, a handsome black rat with white paws, teetered precariously for a moment like a tightrope walker might at the circus. Then he regained his balance and looked down at us from his high perch.

"Fine specimen of a rat," Mr. Jaguar observed, stroking Stuart's shiny black fur as he opened the top of the bin he had prepared for the rest of us. "He's going home with me tonight."

I watched Stuart carefully positioning himself on Mr. Jaguar's shoulder as his new owner bent down to add some fresh food to the food dish. Stuart and I chose this moment to make eye contact, his big black eyes so like our dad's meeting my dark ruby eyes. We were making the best of the only connection available to us. An *eye hug* was better than no hug at all.

I felt a sudden wave of sadness flood over me when I realized I would most likely never see my brother again. When we were very young, Mama and Pops told me that it was unlikely that I would live in the same human home as my brothers and sisters when I grew up, but this separation from one of my siblings was happening a lot faster than I had expected. I thought we would at least have a few days together at the pet store before the inevitable parting. We squeaked our farewells, communicating with the high-pitched sounds rats make that humans are unable to hear.

Once again I felt the sensation of things happening too quickly like a movie playing on fast forward, a new scene appearing before I had time to take in the one before. I wanted to press a pause button and stop everything from changing so fast, but there was no such button to press.

A few minutes later, I turned as I felt a big hand gently pick me up. Mr. Jaguar carefully examined me as he said, "Got to make sure you are healthy, little guy."

He listened to my breathing, pushed on various parts of my abdomen, looked at my eyes, toes, nails, teeth, and tail, and then pronounced his verdict. "You are fine! Welcome to CarPet World!"

Mr. Jaguar's touch was kind, and I intuitively knew I would be treated well here. Still holding me in his hands, he turned toward Fred. When Mr. Jaguar spoke, his manner commanded so much respect that I half-expected his employees to salute and say, "Yes, sir!"

This is exactly the impact he had on Joe and Fred when he barked their orders, "This is ER 22. Write his name down on the clipboard outside the bin, would you, Fred? Here, Joe, would you hold this rat for me while I do the health check?" He handed Stuart to Joe.

"Yes, sir. Did you say ER 22?" repeated Fred with a questioning look. He picked up a pencil lying on a nearby table and then lifted the clipboard off its hook beside the bin as he took a few steps back away from me.

"That's right," Mr. Jaguar replied. "ER stands for exotic rat, so ER 22 stands for exotic rat number twenty-two. Got to have a way to keep track of all the little critters. Got that? Okay, then write *fawn buck with standard ears* right next to his name."

In case you are wondering, rats can have two kinds of ears—standard ears like my family members have or dumbo ears. Standard ears sit more toward the top of the rat's head and are shaped like an oval. Dumbo ears are positioned more toward the side of the head and are a little bigger and wider like Dumbo the elephant's ears. Both kinds work equally as well for hearing sounds. They just look different.

"Yes, sir," Fred nodded as he scribbled something on the paper, holding the clipboard out in front of him as if he were about to read a proclamation before an ancient king. When this recording process was completed, Mr. Jaguar tenderly lowered me into the bin that was to be my new home.

I listened as Mr. Jaguar assigned numbers to my remaining brothers and sisters—ER 23 for Templeton, ER 24 for Rose, and ER 25 for Peony. Something about the name ER 22 made me uneasy, but I could not pinpoint the source of the feeling. I decided to wash my fur, hoping that the familiar process of cleaning myself might rinse the uneasy feeling away.

I had just twisted around, so I could scrub the lower part of my back with my tongue. Then all of a sudden, something slammed into my side. The force of the impact knocked the wind out of me. I rolled over onto my back, momentarily stunned.

When I regained my upright position, I scanned the bin. My eyes found two other eyes looking right back at me. They belonged to a large, odd-looking rat with a dazed look on his face who was squinting at me from about six inches away. He had dumbo ears, a white face resembling that of an opossum, and several grayish splotches splattered on the white fur of his back.

"Good grief! Watch where you're going!" I shouted as I quickly regained my composure.

"Sorry, buddy. I didn't mean any harm. Are you okay?" he asked as he walked toward me, looking as startled by the unexpected encounter as I did.

His voice was higher than mine, and he spoke so fast that one word hardly ended before the other began. This manner of speaking had the effect of blending his phrases together so they sounded like one long, complex word. "You see, it's just been me and those three over in the corner, ER 002, ER 4, and ER 19 in this place for a week. I didn't see you come in. Name's ER 17." He paused as he nodded toward the rats in the corner, and then he continued, "But they call me Hoover. I know, weird name. Don't ask. What's yours?"

Hoover extended his paw in a gesture of friendship. Still a little dazed, I stared at him intently for a moment and then slowly extended mine with about as much enthusiasm as if I were about to stick my paw into an electric light socket. He pumped my arm about five times. Then he let go, smiled at me, and patted me on the back. I could not help but smile back, although to be honest, it was more from amusement than friendship.

Although neither of us knew it at the time, this rather awkward, accidental meeting was the beginning of what was to become a very special, close friendship.

"My name is Nicodemus. Well, that's what it used to be. I guess ER 22 is my new name now. I just arrived. My brother, Templeton, I mean ER 23, came with me." I answered while I washed my ruffled fur to smooth it into place.

I glanced toward the far corner of the bin, and Hoover noticed my perusal of the other rats.

"They name us by number when we come in, but we hate that. Makes us feel like lab rats, so we either name ourselves or give each other nicknames," Hoover explained matter-of-factly. "Do you want to keep Nicodemus then?"

"Sure, works for me."

"See that rat who is chewing on the rat block? That is ER 4. We call him Sketch," he explained with as much disinterest as one giving a weather report.

I noticed that Sketch was an agouti bareback rat, which meant that he had brownish fur on his head and white fur on his back.

"That guy next to him washing his fur is ER 19. He picked the name X-Con," continued Hoover with the same detached tone.

X-Con was a blue Berkshire. The fur on his back was a beautiful grayish blue color framed by a white tummy, white gloves on his paws, and a white tip on the lower third of his unusually short tail.

"Now the third one, that one staring in our direction, is ER 002. He hasn't picked a name yet. He couldn't decide between El Diablo, Mack the Knife, or Killer, so we still call him ER 002." Hoover's voice was noticeably different. There was an ominous crescendo in its sound as he mentioned this third rat in the group.

ER 002 was an unusually handsome rat with a long tail; shiny slate blue fur; and a perfectly symmetrical lightning blaze, a striking, jagged white streak that ran from the top of his head to his nose. He was about a head bigger than the other two rats. It was clear by the way Sketch and X-Con positioned themselves that ER 002 was, without a doubt, the leader of the pack.

Hoover described the unspoken understanding the rats had developed. "Those guys keep to themselves. Not a particularly friendly group. I just ignore them, and they leave me alone. Works just fine for all of us." He shrugged and then added as an afterthought, "Welcome to CarPet World."

"What exactly *is* CarPet World?" I asked Hoover as we walked over to his nest.

The unusual mixture of cars and pets in the same big building confused me. I knew it was a pet store, but I had not pieced together in my mind why there were cars there too.

Hoover spent the next hour answering my questions, and this is what I learned.

A rather unique place, CarPet World is the only store in the world that sells new cars and new pets under the same roof. Despite the fact that people scoffed at the idea when Mr. van Goat first opened the doors, CarPet World has been extremely successful. Rumor had it that Mr. van Goat envisioned owning a store like CarPet World shortly after he purchased his last car, a traumatic experience he tried to repress forever without success.

What happened was this. While he and his wife were haggling over various and sundry extras on the new car they would soon buy, they made a strategic error. They momentarily forgot about their three children, ages five, seven, and nine, who had come with them to the car dealership. Their children, however, being typical kids, saw this memory lapse on the part of their parents as a golden opportunity. Seizing the moment, the three children made a beeline for the new cars on the showroom floor and entertained themselves by sitting in the driver's seats. They grasped the steering wheels and then drove the cars with the confidence and recklessness of a seasoned race-car driver.

One particularly ambitious underage driver happened to shift into neutral and then released the parking brake on the brick-red SUV that, as circumstances would have it, was parked on a very slight incline just above a tiny, extremely expensive sports car. Well, to make the long story short, Mr. van Goat left the dealership that day with a much larger bill than he expected.

However, as is often the case in life, painful experiences are fodder for creativity energy. This was definitely true for Mr. van Goat. About a year after this dreadful indoor car accident, Mr. van Goat, with all the fanfare befitting any grand celebration, announced the opening of CarPet World.

Much to Mr. van Goat's relief and to the annoyance of the owners of the other local car dealerships, CarPet World soon became a thriving, very successful business that received national attention for its uniqueness.

At other car dealerships, children are still *driving* the cars on the showroom floor much to the chagrin of all the adults (buyers and salespeople alike). At CarPet World, the children wander around happily entertained by their prospective pets.

Now as you probably know, children are very good observers and mirror adult behavior with unnerving accuracy, sometimes a little too accurately. It should come as no surprise that the children at CarPet World learn to be masters of negotiation by listening to the dialogues between prospective automobile buyers and car salespeople. It should also come as no surprise that many bargains are struck between parent and child to the tune of "I'll buy you a new pet if you will be good at the dealership" or "I'll be good at the dealership if you will buy me a new pet."

Each day a stream of families leaves the store, driving off with a new car full of pets, big smiles on everyone's faces, and a complimentary red T-shirt for each family member stuffed in the backseat. Each shirt, of course, sports big zebra-striped letters saying *CarPet World* on the front and the famous CarPet World logo on the back.

"You know, Nicodemus, there are all kinds of animals here," Hoover went on to explain. "The rats end up in the rodent pavilion. It is in the small animal section with the guinea pigs and hamsters and gerbils." He pointed to the sign that said, "Small Animals."

"Then Mr. Jaguar sorts us into groups like piles of dirty laundry. None of us really know how he decides who goes in each group." Hoover scratched the soft white fur behind his ears.

"We know that the males and females are split up as soon as we turn five weeks old. Mr. Jaguar is clear that he does not want any litters born here. Then some of us go into the exotic rat group and the rest in the feeder rat group. That bin over there is exotic females." Hoover smiled as he pointed to his left.

"The name of every exotic rat begins with ER followed by a number, and every feeder rat's name begins with FR followed by a number. Does that make sense?" Hoover looked at me intently.

"I guess so. Let's see. I am ER 22. That means I am in an exotic rat bin, right?"

Hoover nodded and then said, "I'll show you around."

With as much pride as if he were giving me a tour of the White House, he gave me a tour of the bin that was to be my new home. This took about ten seconds since all there was to see was a communal water bottle, communal food dish, a wheel for exercise, and a magenta plastic dome that humans engineered to serve as a sleeping place for rats.

"That sleeping dome looks pretty cool," I said.

"Yeah, but none of us males like sleeping in there. We need our space. The does over there use their dome sometimes," Hoover explained, pointing toward the bin where the female exotic rats lived.

I glanced in that direction and noticed that their dome looked empty at the moment, too. Two females were looking over toward me. I averted my gaze, suddenly feeling self-conscious and shy.

I turned back to Hoover and thanked him for giving me the tour and for relating the history of my new home. He nodded, stretched, and then yawned. I followed suit. My brother, Templeton, joined us.

We clustered close together in one small corner of the bin and spent the rest of the afternoon napping.

If there was one word that could sum up my life at CarPet World, it would be *routine*. Everything happened at the same time in the same order every day.

Each morning a red-shirted crew arrived at 9:00 a.m. The highlight of my day was when Catherine, the person responsible for our food and water supply, arrived. She was called Cat for short, which was no surprise. She fascinated me. When I first saw her, I had the odd sensation that I had seen her somewhere before. Puzzled by this, I searched my memory until I finally remembered.

At the rattery, there was a painting hanging on the wall just above our cage. The artist had used his brush to tell the story of a man who had been injured so badly that he could only lie on the ground, unable to move.

A beautiful angel with huge translucent white wings was hovering close to him, ministering to his needs. Below the painting was the inscription *Everyone has a guardian angel.*

Cat looked so much like this angel that I was convinced that she had come straight from heaven to take care of us. Cat's eyes were so blue that they looked like the sky on a cloudless, sunny day. This was the first time I had ever seen blue eyes and I thought they were beautiful. Her long hair was beige and cascaded down her back like a waterfall. Sometimes she wore it in a thick braid that swung back and forth as she walked. It reminded me of my tail.

I often wondered how humans survived without tails. I could not imagine life without one. We rats use our tails to help regulate temperature. Between our tails and our fur, we manage a wide range of temperatures without the need for clothes.

Shortly after Cat arrived each day, she gave us clean water in our water bottles and then said, "Okay, boys, time to line up for breakfast!"

Now as you may recall, rats are nocturnal creatures preferring to go to sleep about eight or nine o'clock in the morning and waking up about eight or nine o'clock in the evening. This makes our schedule exactly opposite to that of humans. That means that what our caretakers call breakfast is actually a middle-of-the-night snack for rats.

So needless to say, many of us who have just gone to sleep for the night are rather irritable at this time of the day. Even under the best of circumstances, rats are not particularly excited about or adept at lining up for anything. We tried to make the best of it, so we lined up and waited.

However, rats are even less skilled at waiting patiently. Cat handed each of us a rodent block, a small rectangular chunk of highly nutritious food that tastes like cardboard. Frequently there would be a scuffle, as a more impatient rat would steal a block from one ahead in the line.

Cat would calmly say, "Now, boys, there is no need to fight. I have one for each of you." Her reassurance did not make any difference. Every morning we did the same thing.

After breakfast, we spent the day alternating between dozing off and being entertained by drowsily watching a parade of parents and children passing by our bin.

At around five o'clock, early for rats since we prefer to eat around midnight, we roused and listened expectantly until we heard Cat's singsong voice pronouncing the magic words, "Dinnertime! Come and get it, ratties!"

As soon as we heard those words, we ran over to the food dish like a pack of hungry dogs, anxiously awaiting our evening meal. We adapted so quickly to this schedule we should have been stars in an operant conditioning video. Experimental psychologists figured out years ago that rats really enjoy eating. I hate to admit it, but it is true that rats will do almost anything for food.

Our evening meal began with a mixture called *rat food*. Rat food consisted of various seeds, grains, and small multicolored chunks of something that tasted good, although none of us could figure out what it was. We were hungry, so we ate it.

After the rat food, Cat gave us dessert. Cat absolutely loved us, so she went out of her way to make us happy. Tonight our treat was corn on the cob carefully cut into thin round slices.

"I snuck in some fresh corn from home for you guys tonight," she whispered as if it was a very important secret.

We listened intently to what she was saying as we gathered around the food dish, looking up at her as though we had front-row seats in a performance hall and were anxiously awaiting the start of a ballet.

"Okay, guys. Come on over, and I will give each of you a corn wheel!" Cat added as she picked up the first cross section of the ear of corn to give to us.

As I have already mentioned, lining up for food is not something rats do very well, so we approached her in what looked like a moving mosh pit.

Sharing is not a rat's forte either. When we rats find food we really like, we have a tendency to grab it in our teeth as fast as we can and run to a secluded place to eat it with the hope that no other rat will notice and we can eat it in peace.

However, often en route to the secluded place, another rat will run over and grab all or part of the tender morsel for him or herself. The original owner then can either fight to regain possession of the treasure or return to the food source and look for more.

This scenario played out several times as we were acquiring corn wheels. I had mine swiped twice before I ended up with one to eat and enjoy. Eventually we each had a piece. I was in heaven. Each kernel tasted like candy to me, and best of all, it was something other than rat food!

After Cat and Mr. Jaguar went home, a young human named Moose took over. He spent his time helping the customers interested in adopting small animals. After the store closed, he cleaned the rodent pavilion.

Moose was an interesting guy. He seemed younger than the other employees and his hair was colors I had never seen on any human head before. It was blue and purple! I liked it. He always had white things that looked like yogurt drops in his ears, but unlike yogurt drops, they made sounds. A thin cord connected them to a shiny rectangular

Cat serves the exotic rats a favorite treat, corn wheels.

object that stayed in his pocket. I knew they made sounds because of what happened the first night it was my turn to ride on his shoulder while he cleaned the cages.

Intrigued by these white objects, I put my head really close to smell them, and to my surprise, I heard music coming out of the tiny dots. The cord reminded me of dental floss.

When I was very young, my breeder would carry me around in her robe at night while she was brushing and flossing her teeth. Observing that she put the long, thin, white string in her mouth, I grabbed the part dangling down by me and put it in my mouth too. It had an unusual minty taste. She never objected, so I thought I was doing the right thing.

When I saw Moose's white string, I assumed it was dental floss, grabbed it with my paws and got ready to put it in my mouth. That was a mistake! Moose went berserk. It was like he had just seen an owl or a snake.

He almost threw me off his shoulder as he grabbed it out of my mouth, and shouted, "Dude, don't chew that. Those are my earphones!" I froze, dropped the earphones, and decided I would never touch them again.

I stayed motionless on his shoulder for the rest of the might. When he put me in the bin, he said, "Don't worry, man. We're good." I nodded.

Every evening at 10:00 p.m., Moose said, "Good night, rat dudes," as he turned out the lights. We were on our own until the next morning when the routine started all over again.

Hoover and I often talked about life.

"You know, Hoover, this life really is not bad. But it's kind of boring," I complained one lazy night.

"Yeah, I know. It sure is a lot better for me since you came, Nicodemus. My life used to be really dull. What was your life at the rattery like this?" Hoover asked while he ran on the wheel.

"Well, we got a lot of time to run around. I felt free even though I was not outside. The wheel looks like fun, but it is just not the same," I said and sighed. "I sure hope someone adopts me soon."

"Yeah, me too. I just can't see living here for a long time," Hoover agreed, a little out of breath.

"I thought for sure that that last family who came by would have adopted one of us. They ended up with hamsters. Can you believe that? Want to try the wheel?" He flopped down to rest. I thought about it, but decided not to, feeling tired and unmotivated.

"I know. Why would people want hamsters when they could have rats instead? Beats me. I watch everyone who comes in, hoping to get picked." Hoover washed his tail vigorously.

"Me too! But you know, I actually do like living here, except for one thing." I paused to wash my face.

"Yeah, what's that?" Hoover asked, his head resting on his front paws.

"Well, it's ER 002. He really has something against me, and I have no idea what it is. He either ignores me or glares at me. Sometimes he makes snide comments. One night he actually nipped at me and then stole my food. He even pushed me aside with the side of his body, trying to start a fight," I explained as I settled down next to Hoover.

"I think I know why, Nicodemus. Before you came, he was the most handsome, healthiest male rat at CarPet World. Now it's you. I don't think you meant to take his place, but you did. He's jealous, man." Hoover nodded emphatically.

I stared at my friend. "Are you kidding me? No way! I'm not handsome." I was shocked.

"Yeah, you are, dude. ER 002 is jealous," Hoover said confidently.

"Well, I thought he and I had an understanding, but now I'm not sure what to think," I said uncertainly.

"Don't worry about it. We'll get adopted soon and it won't matter anyway. Let's go see what Templeton is up to," Hoover said while washing the fur on his back.

"Good idea, " I replied.

Other than these occasional incidents when ER 002 was openly aggressive, it seemed that we had established a peaceful coexistence, or so I thought ... until an unexpected twist of fate resulted in things taking a decided turn for the worse.

Chapter Three

Death Row

THE DAY I LEARNED ABOUT DEATH ROW BEgan like every other day in the rodent pavilion at CarPet World. The familiar sound of raindrops falling on the metal roof of the store served as background music for the daily activities.

Red-shirted employees arrived early to prepare the store for opening. Greetings, jokes, and pleasantries were shared, and then the routine tasks of organizing papers, polishing cars, and feeding animals began.

However, that day something special was going on in the auto department. Car salespeople were peppering the showroom with red, white, and blue balloons that hovered above the cars just like seagulls floating above the ocean. I watched with interest, my attention riveted by the bobbing motion of the colorful orbs.

Just after the last balloon was blown up and hung, Mr. Jaguar and Cat came in and walked over toward us, already engaged in an animated discussion about ways to rearrange the rodent pavilion. Joe and Fred breezed by with a new delivery of guinea pigs.

Cat served us our breakfast as always. We spent the day dozing, now and then rousing enough to observe any new or interesting occurrence at the store. Hoover, Templeton, and I shared a space in one corner of our bin, and diagonally across from us, ER 002, Sketch, and X-Con slept in the opposite corner. The magenta plastic sleeping dome in the center of the bin stood empty.

We all came together at feeding time, but the remainder of the day, we hung out in two groups. It was midafternoon, and I was sleeping, dreaming about a delicious meal of Swiss cheese, tuna fish, and yogurt drops when the sound of a loud, angry voice woke me. There was a young man with a wild look in his eyes, yelling at Cat, demanding to speak with the manager.

Alerted by the man's angry tone of voice, Mr. Jaguar strode toward him and then stood protectively between Cat and the disgruntled customer.

"Excuse me, sir. Direct your words toward me. I am the manager," commanded Mr. Jaguar, his authoritative voice like that of a general leading his troops in battle.

Mr. Jaguar extended his hand in a friendly greeting and then asked, "How can I help you, sir?"

The man did not extend his hand in return. He held up a box instead. Something was scurrying around inside the box. "Here! Take this rat. I don't want to ever see him again," he said with some difficulty since he was panting like an exhausted marathon runner.

As if he were passing off a hot potato, the man quickly thrust a shoebox with small air holes poked in the top into Mr. Jaguar's outstretched hand. Then the man yelled, "I bought this creature here at CarPet World as a feeder for my sweet baby, Jimmy, and he almost killed my buddy."

Mr. Jaguar stood motionless, the box in his hands. The man paused for a moment, his voice cracking with emotion. He pulled out a tissue from his back pocket with a hand covered in bandages, dabbed his eyes, and then went on, "If you know what's good for you, don't try to sell him as a feeder a second time!"

The man paused again, pulled out another tissue from his pocket, vigorously wiped his eyes, and then blew his nose with a loud snorting sound.

The man was crying. Mr. Jaguar opened his mouth to say something, but before he could, the man had pulled himself together enough to go on with his tirade. "Don't bother with a refund. I don't want to ever touch anything that is from CarPet World again, not even money! I will never set foot in this store for the rest of my life, and I will make sure that none of my friends do either!"

He wiped his hands against each other as best as he could despite all the bandages covering one of them. It seemed like he was trying to scrape off some undesirable sticky substance.

When he finished, he turned abruptly and stormed out of the store. Mr. Jaguar stared after him, dumbfounded, still holding the small box in his hands.

As this drama unfolded, the rats in my bin migrated to the right wall of our container to get a better view of what was happening. Six pairs of small, round eyes watched the man leave, no clue what he was talking about. Then lining up against the glass as though watching a parade, we turned our gaze back to Mr. Jaguar and watched expectantly as he slowly lifted the lid off the box and peeked inside.

He broke into a big smile, the little crinkly lines at the corner of his eyes fanning out in a way that enhanced his expression, and said. "Hey, FR 89, you're back!"

We stared in disbelief, feeling confused by this highly unusual turn of events. Once rats left CarPet World, they simply did not come back.

I turned to Hoover and whispered, "What did he mean by *a feeder?*"

"I don't know." He replied, in a hushed voice, as though talking about something secret. "None of us know."

That night we learned the shocking truth from the returned rat.

It turns out that FR 89 was a huge, all white, young male rat who looked like a stereotypical lab rat except that he had black eyes instead of the usual pink. Apparently Mr. Jaguar took the man's advice, because he did not put him back into the feeder bins. Instead he rather unceremoniously introduced him to the rats in my bin.

"Here's a new buddy for you guys," Mr. Jaguar told us, his eyes twinkling. I could tell he really liked FR 89. Then he spoke directly to the white rat in his hands. "Guess we have to give you a new name.

How about ER 89? I know it's not much of a change, but it works for me."

He lowered ER 89 gently onto the shredded aspen bedding on the floor of our bin, muttering to himself, "I have to remember to make a note of that."

Mr. Jaguar closed the lid to the bin and walked away, shaking his head and chuckling as he murmured something that sounded like, "Snakes zero, rats one."

Next thing we knew, ER 89 was milling around with us, exchanging sniffs in silence, the way that rats do when they are meeting and greeting each other.

The pounding of the rain on the roof grew louder. A storm was upon us.

ER 002 was the first to speak. "Hey, Pillsbury Doughboy, have you been rolling around in a sugar bin?" he sneered, poking fun at ER 89's white fur.

Sketch and X-Con joined in the laughter, obviously admiring the wit of their leader.

Our new bin-mate, unabashed by ER 002's attempt to insult him, retorted, "Yeah, man. Made me pretty sweet. Just call me Sugar! That's what they called me in the feeders."

The name stuck, and from that moment on, we did exactly that. I invited Sugar to join Hoover, Templeton, and me in our nest since we were drowsy and ready to go back to sleep. The remainder of the day passed uneventfully with the rhythmic sound of the raindrops making sleep come easily.

It was a few hours later that Cat fed us our dinner followed by a special treat of cantaloupe squares. All the rats in my bin clustered around the food dish, thoroughly enjoying this delicacy, their heads facing the dish, their tails pointed outward like spokes on a wheel.

Pausing with half of the tasty orange morsel held gingerly in his paws, Hoover asked Sugar to tell us his story, "Hey, dude, what happened? You didn't cut it as a pet rat?" asked my buddy between bites of cantaloupe.

"No, man, that's not it at all! Pet rat? Are you kidding? Don't you know what happens if you are in the feeder bins?" Sugar stared at Hoover in disbelief, his black eyes wide. His voice, which was usually so strong and confident, was suddenly shaky.

I noticed that he was trembling. It was something so uncharacteristic of male rats that we drew closer to him as if we were pulled by a giant magnet. Hoover dropped his piece of cantaloupe. We instinctively knew that what he had to say was very important.

"No," I whispered, not quite sure why I had lowered my voice. "Tell us."

Sugar walked around in a semicircle. He would sit in one spot and then get up and move to another as though he were trying out chairs in a furniture store, looking for the most comfortable one to buy. We arranged ourselves in two rows like an audience in a theater and watched him expectantly, waiting for him to begin. He stopped at the food dish and picked up a piece of rat food, nibbling it intently as though he needed the extra nourishment before he told his story.

In characteristic fashion, he visited the water bottle, took a few sips, and then washed his impeccably clean white fur. We sat still, facing him, waiting expectantly, as curious as a bunch of cats. No one, not even ER 002, said a word. The only sound was the drumming of the raindrops as they pounded out their never-ending cadence on the roof above us.

After what seemed like an eternity, Sugar finally settled down. He spoke as a survivor who was reliving an extremely traumatic event, his voice hushed but strong, "Feeders, my friends, are rats who are sold at a very low price to snake owners who serve them to their reptiles for dinner."

As if cued by an invisible choir director, we all took in a sharp breath at the same time. There was a loud, collective gasp followed by dead silence.

Sugar narrowed his eyes and continued, "No cheese! They feed you to a snake when you are totally awake and see it all!"

"Are you serious? How'd you find out?" I asked, aware that my whiskers were starting to twitch agitatedly.

"Well, it didn't take long. A few hours after we got to his house, this guy who bought me picks me up by the tail and brings me over to Jimmy, his pet yellow rat snake, and dangles me in front of the stupid reptile. Then he says, 'Here, Jimmy, old boy, come and get your din-din.'

"I couldn't believe what was happening, but I figured it out fast enough. My guard hairs stood up, in position for a fight. I tightened my stomach muscles, curved my body upward, and took aim. I bit the idiot as hard as I could on the soft part of his hand.

"He gasped and then yelled, 'Ouch!' and dropped me. I landed on a table and was pretty disoriented, so I ran right into a lamp, knocking it over. It fell to the floor with a loud crash, shattering into pieces. The guy started swearing at me. I knew that was a bad sign, so I made a beeline for the couch, hoping to hide underneath it.

"'You crazy rat. Get over here!' the snake dude yelled. He was so mad that he chased me across the room and then tackled me like he was a linebacker playing football for the Seahawks. He pinned me to the floor with his hands just before I could get under the couch. Man, he was fast for a human. I couldn't believe he caught me.

"He scooped me up, blood dripping down his arm. The guy glared at me then yelled, 'Dumb rat, what do you think you are doing?'

"Muttering more to himself than to me, he added, 'Never had a rat do this before,' and then with a look of renewed determination in his eyes, he headed toward Jimmy once again, gripping me like a vice.

"We were both really fired up. I turned my head and glared right back at him. Then I shot daggers with my eyes at Jimmy, who by the way was a really ugly snake."

Sugar paused and took a moment to wash his face, drawing his paws down over his eyes as though he could wipe away the image that was so vivid in his mind since the event had just taken place yesterday.

We sat facing him, motionless and silent, as if the drama of the story he told had turned us into statues. Stunned, we waited for him to continue, our minds reeling as we tried to make sense of what we had just learned.

Sugar began speaking again in a hoarse whisper. "The guy was determined not to let me go this time. Held me so tight I could hardly breathe. Then he dangles me right above the huge glass aquarium where the snake lives and says, 'Take a good look, bud, 'cause this is the last stop for you!'

"By now he's so mad that his hands are shaking, and he can hardly open the door to the reptile house. He finally manages to lift the lid and throws me in with Jimmy. Then he says to me, 'See how you like that, you stupid rodent!' Then in a totally different, sickeningly sweet voice, he says to Jimmy, 'Here's your din-din, little Jim-Jim.' I wanted to throw up when I heard this.

"The snake dude picks up this huge board and bangs it down on top of the lid of Jimmy's container to make sure I can't get out. Then he storms out of the room, holding the bleeding hand with his other hand, and slams the door behind him.

"I was furious that I had been put in this situation and knew beyond a shadow of a doubt that I was not ready to die. For those first few moments after the snake dude left, there was absolute silence. Instinct told me that I had about as much time to think of a plan for survival as a bird who looks up to see she is about to be pounced upon by a cat.

"Then I heard it, an almost imperceptible sound like something slippery gliding across a sheet of ice." Sugar's eyes narrowed into slits as he recalled the moment. He resumed his account after a shiver ran through his body.

"I took a deep breath and then turned toward the sound and faced my nemesis. He instantly froze into a statue shaped like a backward letter S lying flat on the ground, perfectly still except for the two beady eyes. His tongue kept moving in and out. It was so weird. Looked like a fork. Then there was his tail. It moved back and forth so fast that it was a blur.

"At first Jimmy and I just stared at each other. Then he coiled his body, raised his head, and started swaying, moving slowly from side to side like a pendulum, his tongue flickering in and out of his mouth. I had never seen a snake before, but I knew exactly what he was doing. He was planning how to kill me and eat me for dinner."

Sugar paused again and began washing his back. We just sat there, waiting. It was as if we had been watching a horror movie on TV that

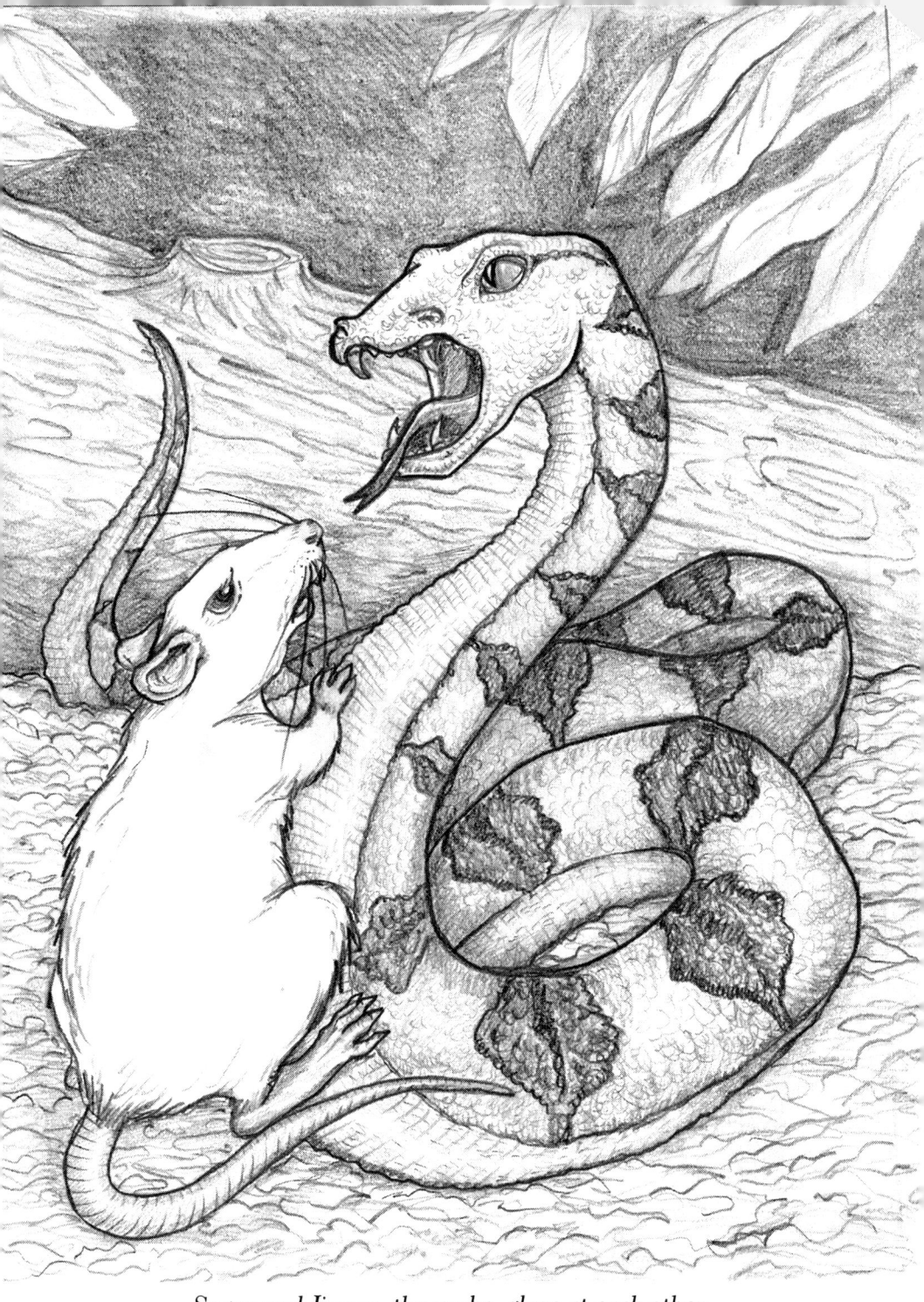

Sugar and Jimmy, the snake, glare at each other.

had been interrupted at the scariest moment by a commercial. The suspense was killing me. The rain was so loud now that it was like a drumroll.

Hoover broke the silence, "Hey, Sugar, could you take the bath a little later? We're all dying to know what happens next."

I think Sugar felt a little pleased that his story was having such an impact. He glanced at us for a moment, licked his back one more time, cleared his throat, and then began talking again.

"I instinctively knew that *Jimmy* wanted to sink his sharp fangs into my flesh and would move with amazing speed. I was ready. Like a bolt of lightning, he struck, aiming for my neck. Because I had anticipated the strike, I was waiting and ready for him. I maneuvered to the side and over the top of his scaly body. Then just like I did with his human friend, I bit him as hard as I could as he slithered forward.

"His flesh tasted so awful that I thought the taste alone would kill me. I wanted to bite his head off, but he was too fast for me, so I made my mark somewhere in his long belly instead."

Sugar paused once again and took a long drink from the water bottle. We waited silently, listening to the clicking sound of the little ball in the waterspout accompanied by the pounding of the rain.

ER 002 was the impatient one this time. "Okay, Walt Disney, get a move on with the story!" he quipped, referring to Sugar's ability to capture an audience with his recounting of the events that had taken place.

Sugar laughed at ER 002's comment, but the rest of us did not. We were too engrossed in the story to smile. It was as though our faces were frozen in an expression of shock and disbelief. Sugar went on.

"Well, go figure, the stupid snake hissed so loud I thought a steam engine was coming toward me. I knew he was angry and guessed that pain was revving him up.

"A split second later, the crazy snake comes at me again, but this time I could tell he was getting ready to put on the big squeeze. I had nothing to lose, so I went after him with every ounce of energy that I had, preparing to fight to the death if necessary.

"Believe me, we fought. We must have looked like those dogs

and cats you see on cartoons, rolling over and over on the floor of his container with my paws wrapped tightly around his body as if I were shimmying up a tall, skinny tree.

"He managed to throw me off, and I landed pretty hard on the floor. But I hoisted myself up and lunged toward him again. After I jumped on his back, I dug my claws in and hung on for dear life as he flopped around, biting his scaly flesh wherever I could. That darned snake moved so quickly that I could not bite deep enough to make a difference. "It must have been something to watch."

Sugar got a faraway look in his eyes as he relived this moment. Then he took a deep breath and went on with the account of the battle.

"Thrashing around with me clinging to his back, Jimmy was desperately trying to coil his body around mine to kill me. He managed to smash me against the side of the bin so hard that it knocked the wind out of me, and I actually saw stars.

"That was a strategic error on his part because it made my blood boil. I got my second wind.

"The snake looked at me and paused for an instant, just long enough for me to take aim. I dug my teeth deep into his flesh just below his head, feeling sickened by the awful taste.

"He hissed the most venomous hiss I have ever heard. My guard hairs bristled, and I was prepared for retaliation. But to my surprise, it didn't happen. It was like he was one of those electric guitars, and someone had pulled the plug. The music died. The snake stopped fighting. He was just lying there completely still on the floor of the cage."

The big white rat stopped talking for a moment, then continued, "I backed away a few inches and then crouched down in front of him. I watched and waited. Nothing happened. I thought I had killed the slimeball. Then I saw his eyes flicker. He wasn't dead."

Sugar puffed out his chest a bit at this point, feeling proud of his accomplishment. Then he added, "You know, it was the weirdest thing, but that snake and I never said one word to each other."

We waited to make sure he was finished and then cheered for a long time, giving him many pats on the back. After a while we became quiet again, as if on cue. I think we all needed time to ponder the implications of his story for our lives and those of our fellow rats in the feeder bins.

After what seemed like a long time, ER 002 broke the silence and verbalized the question that had been forming in my mind, "I don't get it, James Bond. How did you end up back here?'

"Well," Sugar continued, beckoning us to move a little closer, his pink eyes taking on an eerie glow in the dim light. He threw a furtive glance over each shoulder as though he wanted to make sure no one else was listening.

"A few minutes later, the snake dude comes back to see his little sweetie, Jimmy, and finds me gloating over my victory. He says, 'You crazy rat ... you hurt my snake!'

"He picks up Jimmy and cradles him in his arms like a baby. It was pretty clear that Jimmy was hurt really badly. But you'll never believe what took place next. The guy starts to cry.

"The dude sits down on the couch and holds that snake for the longest time as though it was the most precious thing in the world, tears running down his face. I'm looking over there, studying him, and I see furrows as big as the Grand Canyon form in his forehead like he's in deep concentration. I guessed he was trying to decide what to do to help Jimmy. Not knowing how else to pass the time, I sat there washing myself, waiting.

"After what seemed like forever, he rushes out of the room with Jimmy, leaving me alone. I figured that he had taken the snake somewhere to get him some help. I feel asleep. I have no idea how long it was before he returned.

"He glares at me with pure hatred in his eyes and says, 'Do you know where I have been? At the reptile doctor! All because of you! Do you know what else? It's going to cost me over two hundred dollars to get my snake fixed up. Two hundred dollars!'

"Of course, I didn't know it would cost two hundred dollars to fix Jimmy, and frankly I didn't care. He went on, 'So now it's your turn. You're coming with me.'

"Still glaring at me with his squinty eyes, he says, 'I'm warning you, you little scoundrel, if you bite me again, I'll kill you with my bare hands, which I probably should do anyway, but I'm too nice a guy to do that.'

"To be perfectly honest, I had been entertaining the idea of sinking my teeth into his other hand, but at that moment I decided that wasn't a good idea. I actually think he meant it when he said he would kill me if I bit him again."

"He grabbed me by the scruff, shoved me into a small box, and took me for a ride in the car, and next thing I knew, I was back here. Guess they decided it wouldn't be good for business to put me in the feeder bins again," Sugar said and chuckled. "So I'm with you guys now."

We took turns giving Sugar more pats on the back and repeatedly congratulated him. I had stashed a vanilla yogurt drop, one of my favorite treats, in the corner of our bin, waiting for a special occasion to bring it out. I decided that this was the time, and I dashed to get it. After I returned with it in my mouth, I dropped it at Sugar's feet.

"Here you go, buddy. Let's eat this in honor of your return," I suggested.

Sugar winked at me, and we enjoyed our treat. Between bites, he looked around and said, "I can't believe I'm back at CarPet World! You know, I'm a changed rat. Coming that close to death has made me happy just to be alive. Treasure every day you've got, my friends."

We thought about what he said for a few minutes. Then Hoover, not one to be serious for too long, changed the subject and said, "Hey, Sugar, could you tell us the story one more time?"

Sugar was more than happy to do so and told the second rendition with gusto, embellishing things a little more this time around.

After the second telling of the story, the elation about Sugar's victory over our common enemy, the snake, was replaced with a sense of sadness that spread quickly throughout our exotic rat bin like spilled cranberry juice spreading across the face of a dry paper towel.

I spoke first. Something had been bothering me ever since Sugar first mentioned the true nature of the feeder bins. "Sugar, do you know why some rats are put into the feeder bins and some into the exotic rat bins?"

"Sure, I know, and it's not pretty. The feeders are like second-class rats. They are the ones who are sick or disabled or not beautiful enough or handsome enough. Seems like some human decides that the ones who become feeders would not fetch the higher price of an exotic rat, so they dump them into the feeder bins. I guess they figure that the snakes don't care what their dinner looks like or if it has a cold or it walks funny. Pathetic, isn't it?"

Sugar's pink eyes flashed. His guard hairs bristled, and his tail swished back and forth as anger at the injustice of the situation surged through his body.

My eyes widened in shock and disbelief, and I could feel the fur on my back bristling too. I was shaking my head with disgust as I replied, "I was afraid you were going to say that, Sugar. It's just not right. All of us rats deserve equal treatment regardless of our health or appearance. I just can't believe this is actually going on in the world today."

My words, dripping with conviction, came out so forcefully that several rats turned in my direction. "So you know what this means guys?" I was facing them now, almost yelling the words as my emotions intensified. "It means that any one of us could end up in the feeder bins if we become sick enough or injured!"

"That's right, doll face. Better hang on to those good looks as long as you can!" ER 002, his sarcasm masking his fears, tossed out his comment as he walked past me. I had not even noticed he was listening.

It was at that moment my brother Templeton, a rat of few words, stepped forward, cleared his throat, and then began to speak. "Guys, now that we know what the feeder bins really are, I think we need to give them a new, more fitting name, a name that will remind us of the death sentence that each of our fellow rats who lives there faces every day. I propose that we call them Death Row. What do you think?"

Six pairs of eyes looked back at Templeton. Almost immediately, six heads nodded in affirmation of his idea. There was no need for discussion. We all felt the same way. From then on, the feeder bins at CarPet World had a new name, Death Row. The meaning was unmistakable.

The thought of Death Row struck terror into our hearts. We realized that any of us could become seriously ill or injured, and then it would be only a matter of time before we got booted to the feeder bins. I shuddered at the thought.

We needed some time to process what we had just learned. ER 002 slunk off to one corner with Sketch and X-Con trailing behind. My brother and Hoover went off to another corner while Sugar and I stayed together by the water bottle and talked a little more.

I was still engaged in conversation with Sugar when Hoover came bounding over to me. "Sorry to interrupt, guys, but I have got to tell you something important, Nicodemus," Hoover said, beckoning me to follow him.

"Excuse me a minute, Sugar. I need to see what he wants," I explained, reluctant to stop talking to Sugar but curious to find out what Hoover had to say.

"Hey, no problem, man. Catch you later," Sugar said, strolling over toward Templeton. I stretched and yawned and then slowly walked across the floor of our bin until Hoover and I were standing side by side.

"Look, I know you're still really upset about Sugar's news, and I am too. But something good just happened. I thought it might lighten things up a little if I told you. Do you want to know what it is?"

Hoover was treading water with his words, trying to figure out if I would be receptive or not. I thought for a minute. Not wanting to wallow in the depressing feelings I had been having, I decided to go for it.

"Sure, Hoover, why not? I could use some good news right now," I replied, watching Sugar settle down next to Templeton.

"You'll never guess what I just overheard. You know ER 12, Willow? That really cute Siamese female with the pink eyes and dumbo ears who lives in the exotic rat bin next to ours?"

I nodded. Of course I knew Willow. All the males knew Willow. What made her so irresistibly attractive was that her inner qualities were even more desirable than her outer beauty. Not only was she very smart and quick-witted with a great laugh, but she was compassionate and loving too.

In addition, she had absolutely gorgeous cream-colored curly fur, striking points, engaging eyes, a really long tail, and very alluring dumbo ears. Siamese rats look similar to Siamese cats in that they have dark fur on their noses, just above the tail, and on their paws that contrasts with the creamy white fur on the rest of their bodies. These dark patches are called points.

Hoover went on, talking even faster than usual in his excitement, "Well, she was talking to your sister, Rose, who lives with her in the bin next to ours. She didn't know I could hear, and she was talking about you!"

"She was?" I asked nonchalantly, trying to hide the excitement in my voice. I immediately started washing my face and ears to cover the fact that I was blushing.

"Yeah. Well, she said that she had had a crush on ER 002 until—" Hoover was speaking in a whisper, not wanting to catch ER 002's attention. Then he paused as he scratched a bothersome spot on his head for what seemed like an eternity.

I waited with baited breath. Even though I tried not to, I couldn't help myself from hoping that he would say that the wind had changed and now she liked *me* instead of him. Although I felt foolish, I had the sensation of being a contestant in a talent show, anxiously awaiting the determination of the judges, mentally prepared to lose but desperately wanting to win first place.

Hoover lowered his voice so much I had to strain to hear him, "Until you came. She said that you were the kindest, smartest, strongest, most handsome rat she had ever seen!"

"She did?" I asked incredulously.

I could not believe my ears. It was as though he had said, "And the winner is … Nicodemus!" Why would she be saying all those wonderful things about me? I thought of myself as a pretty average guy who was not a particularly good-looking rat.

"And that's not all! Every day she sits in her bin and watches you. She said she can't stop thinking about you and wants to hang out with you but doesn't know how to make it happen," Hoover blurted out.

Hoover was so worked up that he was speaking at warp speed. I could barely understand him. His black eyes framed by his white possum face were bright with admiration for me.

A few seconds later, speaking at a more normal speed, he added with a sigh, "You are so lucky, dude. I wish she had said that about me."

My heart was hammering in my chest so hard that I thought I was going to have a heart attack and die on the spot. From the very first time that I had laid eyes on her, I thought Willow was the most beautiful rat I had ever seen. Hoover did not know this, but I had been secretly watching her too, sneaking glances in her direction whenever I had a chance.

A couple of times our eyes had met, but she looked away so quickly that I thought she was not interested in me. I was unbelievably happy about the news, but not to the point of being oblivious to Hoover's last comments.

"Hey, buddy, your turn will come. I know you're going to meet a doe someday who thinks you're great ... because you are, so don't give it a second thought."

I truly meant what I said. Hoover was the best friend I had ever had.

Not one to stay in a depressed state for more than a few minutes, Hoover immediately brightened. Agreeing with my assessment, his black eyes danced with excitement for me once again.

"You're right, Nicodemus. My turn will come. So let's start planning how you guys can ... well, you know, get better acquainted."

Before I could respond, I was startled by a sharp, unusual sound, "Sssshhhnick!"

I turned in the direction of the strange noise and saw Sketch washing his face with his front paws as he recovered from a sneeze. When he saw me looking at him, he froze. Standing right next to him, X-Con and ER 002 were looking at me with that deer-in-the-headlights look on their faces. ER 002 was definitely not pleased that I had noticed them.

It suddenly dawned on me that my conversation with Hoover had so absorbed our attention that we had completely missed the fact that despite our efforts to be quiet, the three other rats had been listening to every word we had said.

"Shut up, you moron!" ER 002 sneered at Sketch, reprimanding him for his indiscreet sneeze.

The big rat's slate blue fur was bristling so much that he resembled a stiff, fat brush used to clean toilet bowls. ER 002 side swiped his henchman hard enough to knock him off balance. Then he shifted his focus to me and Hoover.

"Well, if it isn't Batman and Robin?" he taunted.

We stared back at him. I wanted to respond with a clever retort, but no witty words came to mind. Once he knew that he had my attention, he unleashed his fury on me.

"She's mine, Blondie!" he hissed, pacing back and forth, his white blaze standing out against his blue fur, his tail twitching as he spoke. "Everything was fine around here until you showed up. No one messes with ER 002 or his girl without paying big time. I will get you for this, Sir Lancelot, if it's the last thing I do!" His voice was vicious, and his beady black eyes burned with hatred. If I were Lancelot, he was definitely no King Arthur!

Like a quarterback whispering the next sequence of plays to his teammates, ER 002 huddled together with Sketch and X-Con, his front paws touching their backs.

"Come on, boys. I have an idea. Let's go plan a nice surprise for Saint Nic," he said in a voice that made my blood run cold.

He beckoned to the others. "We'll leave the pretty boy and his little sidekick alone ... for now!" They slunk off to the corner.

"Let's go, Nicodemus." Hoover was pulling at my front leg. I was glad that he did that because I felt unable to budge. It was as if my paws were glued to the floor.

ER 002's outburst was so unexpected that I was in shock. I forced my legs forward; however, I felt like they were buried in mud, and I was walking in slow motion. Somehow I finally made it over to our

ER 002's hatred grows as he jealously watches Willow flirt with Nicodemus (also known as Petey).

corner of the exotic rat bin, and Hoover and I tried to make sense out of what had just happened.

I felt as though I had spent the evening on an emotional roller coaster. Too much had happened too fast. First there was the intense pride and joy about Sugar's victory. Second there was the equally intense anger at the injustices in Sugar's story and the realization of what really happens to the feeder rats on Death Row. Third there was the elation at the thought of Willow's feelings for me. Adding the shock of ER 002's unexpected tirade on top of these three caused my brain to short circuit.

I felt numb. Hoover was not doing well either. After I pointed out to him that he had washed the same paw five times, he stopped and looked at me with a quizzical expression and said with an uncharacteristic edge to his voice, "Well, what else do you expect me to do?"

"Sorry, buddy," I replied. "I didn't mean to give you a hard time. I sure wish we had a TV."

"What?" Hoover was looking at me incredulously as if that was the last thing he had expected me to say.

"Well, at my old home at Annabelle's rattery, I observed the humans a lot. Sometimes they would turn on the TV and just stare at the screen when they felt stressed or tired. Getting lost in someone else's life seemed to help them forget their own problems. That's exactly what I'd like to do right now." My voice sounded detached and mechanical.

"Yeah, sounds good to me," Hoover agreed. "Then when we felt better and had more energy, we could deal with our real lives again, right?"

"Exactly," I mused.

However, the reality was that we did not have a TV at CarPet World. I sat by Hoover and stared, not at a screen but into space, waiting for the dawn of a new and hopefully less emotional day. There was an eerie, unsettling silence in the store.

It had stopped raining.

Chapter Four

The Mouse Bite that Changed History

THE RAIN RESUMED ITS FAMILIAR PATTERN, breaking the silence of the night. It drummed out a symphony of staccato notes that could be heard on both the metal roof of CarPet World and the cedar shake roof of the home of Doug, Karin, Claire, and Sarah.

Karin looked outside. She frowned. Even though she had lived in Seattle for many years, Karin had not adapted to the cloudy, rainy climate. She missed the East Coast weather. Oh, well. Even though it was raining, it was a special day. She was taking Claire and Sarah to CarPet World.

It was a short ride to the huge store. Just as Karin pulled her beige minivan into a parking spot, the rain intensified. Great.

"Come on, you guys. It's pouring!" yelled Karin as she held her jacket over her head like a makeshift umbrella while she ran into CarPet World.

Claire and Sarah followed closely behind in single file like baby ducks chasing after their mother. Once inside, the three looked around. There was a lot to see. A red-shirted car salesperson immediately descended upon them with the deliberateness of an eagle swooping down upon its prey.

"Hello. Welcome to CarPet World. My name is Jason and I would love to show you our newest minivans. You three look like you would be so happy in one of our luxury models. Maybe a blue one like this beauty right here?" He pointed to a light blue vehicle to his right.

Jason inhaled, then continued, addressing his remarks to Claire and Sarah. "They all come with tablet and cellphone holders now, you know! Video screens, too. And, amazing sound systems!"

He lovingly stroked the side of the blue automobile but then paused and smiled expectantly, waiting for a response.

"Where are the mice?" asked Sarah, a quizzical expression on her face, her large brownish green eyes scanning the expansive showroom as she spoke.

Jason stared at her without replying, flabbergasted, his mouth twisted into an odd shape. She might as well have asked him to eat a whole lemon, including the skin, while he had to stand on his head. Karin stifled a laugh.

Claire, who was growing impatient with Jason, decided to take matters into her own hands. "Over there," she replied to Sarah, pointing to a sign behind the row of sports cars that said, *Rodent Pavilion*.

Claire took the lead as they made their way to the other side of the store, winding in and out around the crowd of shoppers and red-shirted CarPet World employees. Sarah looked back over her shoulder and saw Jason still standing there, his mouth slightly open, gawking at them as they walked away.

As they approached the small pet section, they could overhear an animated conversation between a short, thin woman with curly brown hair and black-rimmed glasses and a tall man with a bald head.

The man was shaking his head back and forth and saying, "No, ma'am, I'm sorry, but we don't sell rugs. Didn't you see the sign over the door as you came in? It says CarPet World."

"Of course I saw the sign," she snapped indignantly, one hand on her hip, the other pointing to the sign. "It says C-A-R-P-E-T, Carpet World, so what else would you sell? You know, rugs, carpets, floor coverings? If your sign says carpets, you should sell carpets. All I see are a bunch of cars and some hamsters."

"Oh, I understand." Mr. Jaguar nodded his head and smiled. "You thought the sign said Carpet World. It's CarPet World. Like the two words *car* and *pet* combined together, not the one word *carpet*! Sorry for the confusion, ma'am, but I'd be happy to show you some of my small pets. We have gerbils, rats, and mice, as well as hamsters and guinea pigs."

The short woman made an exasperated sound, did an about-face, and marched out of the store, the tall, bald man, Karin, Claire, and Sarah staring after her.

The man rolled his eyes. "I don't get it. There must be ten people a week who come in here and ask for carpets or rugs. People just aren't as smart as they used to be when I was a kid," he muttered more to himself than to his new customers.

Karin laughed out loud. She liked this man.

He smiled and then frowned. He gazed intently at the three new customers and asked, "You're not looking for rugs too, are you?"

"Oh no!" Claire reassured him as she walked over to the mouse bin and peered inside, Sarah following closely behind. "My sister and I want to adopt a pet mouse."

"Thank goodness," he said and sighed, looking visibly relieved. "That is something I can help you with. I think we have the best mice in the world. By the way, my name is Arnold Jaguar. I am the manager of the small pet section of our store."

"Nice to meet you, Mr. Jaguar," Karin replied. "My name is Karin, and these are my two daughters, Claire and Sarah."

"Pleased to make your acquaintance, ma'am and young ladies. What do you say we go meet some mice?" Mr. Jaguar's enthusiasm was contagious.

"This one is so cute. I want this one," said Sarah, pointing to a gray mouse who was washing his face with both front paws. She turned to Mr. Jaguar and politely asked, "Can I hold the tiny gray one please?"

"Sure, little lady," Mr. Jaguar responded as he smiled again, his brown eyes full of warmth, while slowly opening the lid to the bin and reaching inside. Sarah looked up at the man's friendly face and smiled back.

He took out the gray mouse and handed it to Sarah as gently as if the mouse were made out of thin, very fragile glass.

Unbeknownst to the family, I was intently watching this whole scene. My reaction alternated between disgust and curiosity like a pinball pinging back and forth, stuck between two obstacles. First I was disgusted by the fact that these people wanted to adopt a mouse. Then I was curious to learn more about them. Then I felt disgusted again that they wanted a mouse. Then as I was listening to them talk, I became curious again. And so on.

What bothered me the most was that these humans who wanted to adopt a mouse and not a rat looked like decent people. They must be misguided.

The mother had greenish eyes and curly reddish blonde hair, similar in color to mine. She was a velveteen, the word that rats use to describe curly fur or in this case, hair. The older sister had wavy brownish hair and brown eyes. Her hair was the color of Pop's fur, agouti, but hers was curlier than his was. The younger sister had straighter and lighter brownish hair with brownish green eyes. In the rat world, her hair color is called cinnamon, and the shiny, straighter texture of her hair is called satin.

When I first saw them, I immediately sensed that they were safe people, and I started to preen my fur to attract their attention, hoping they had come to adopt a rat. When I heard the younger velveteen say, "Mouse," I felt discouraged. Every day I hoped and prayed that someone would come in to CarPet World and want to adopt me, a rat, and take me home. Every day I was disappointed.

In the past when it became clear that the human shoppers were not looking for a pet rat, I lost interest and went back to sleep. But today for some unexplainable reason, I felt compelled to continue to watch them.

My eyes widened, and my ears perked up when I saw the mouse the girl was holding glare at her and then deliberately bite her on her finger. Typical mouse. I grimaced as I heard the one called Sarah scream, "Ouch! It bit me!"

Mr. Jaguar raced over to Sarah, a frown darkening his usually smiling face.

"Are you hurt?" he asked while he grabbed the little gray fur ball.

I noticed that the mouse was smirking. It was EM 3 (Exotic Mouse Number 3). The mice here, especially this one, were known for being grumpy when they were awakened out of a sound sleep.

"No, I'm okay. It just stings a little," she said while she closely inspected her index finger. "It's not bleeding or anything."

Not wanting the reputation of CarPet World to be tarnished in any way, Mr. Jaguar held the agitated mouse up so that they were face-to-face and reprimanded him, "That is not the way to treat our customers, EM 3. You should know better than that!" EM 3 stared back at him and blinked, nodding slightly. He understood but showed no remorse.

Mr. Jaguar closed the lid to the mouse bin and then said, "You know, girls, I have an idea." His deep voice was cheerful again.

He motioned with his hand for them to follow him. Mr. Jaguar took a few steps, and to my surprise, he stopped right in front of my bin. I felt disheartened when he reached into the exotic rat bin next to mine and extricated a black-and-white male rat that I recognized as Snake Eyes (ER 51). Then he held him out for them to see. If only he had reached for me. I sighed.

"Rats are much better pets than mice," he said with the confidence born of personal experience. "They rarely bite, and they are much smarter! I think you might be happier with a pet rat."

I smiled. My smile was so big that even the Cheshire cat could not have held a candle to it at that moment. Historically there has been no love lost between mice and rats.

"A rat?" He might as well have suggested they adopt a unicorn. They sounded so surprised. They moved cautiously, peering curiously at the little creature in his hand as tentatively as Jack, who climbed the beanstalk in the English fairytale, approached the sleeping giant.

"Can I hold him?" asked Claire, gingerly extending her hand toward Snake Eyes.

"Sure," replied Mr. Jaguar, his bald head shining in the bright lights of the store, his eyes twinkling. "Do you know how to hold a rat?"

"Well, not really," admitted Claire. "Can you show me?"

"Of course," Mr. Jaguar said, grinning down at her. His huge smile instantly lit up his face.

Claire smiled back as Mr. Jaguar explained, "The little guy likes it better if you hold him close to your body like this."

Mr. Jaguar showed her how to cradle the rat in her hands so he would feel secure. "He might want to snuggle up by your neck and then crawl inside your sweatshirt. We let our rats do that all the time, so they are used to being carried around that way."

Snake Eyes illustrated the point by climbing up to Mr. Jaguar's shoulder and perching there.

"Okay," said Claire as she extended her hands again, this time more confidently. "I'm ready to give it a try."

As Mr. Jaguar handed him to Claire, Sarah, who had been watching and listening very intently, exclaimed, "He's so cute!"

After less than a minute passed, she added, "I want one too. Can I hold that one?" Sarah was pointing to another black-and-white rat in the bin.

"Of course, you can," Mr. Jaguar answered as he opened the bin and picked up Fritz (ER 54), the rat she had indicated, and then he carefully placed him in her hands. "See how these rats have a black head and black stripe down their backs but the rest of their fur is white? They are called black hooded rats."

Sarah nodded, but her attention was focused on the little animal exploring the inside of her jacket.

Unnoticed by the two girls, I had been watching and listening very intently. I felt a little ashamed of myself, but I must confess that I kept hoping they would look at me and say, "Wait a minute, Mr. Jaguar. I just spotted that adorable little beige rat over there. Could I hold him please?"

But they did not do that. They really liked Snake Eyes and Fritz. Truth be told, I was envious. Why did they choose them over a fawn-colored rat like me?

Usually I felt just fine about my appearance, but I have to admit that sometimes I wished I had a blaze or stripe down my back like these guys did. Humans definitely seemed more interested in rats with unusual markings.

Karin had been looking at cages, small mouse sized cages. She missed the entire turn of events and subsequent conversation. She walked toward her two children.

Claire ran over to tell her mother, so excited that her words bubbled out effusively, "Mama, guess what? A mouse bit Sarah, so this man said we should get a rat instead! Can we get these baby rats, Mama, please?" Claire pleaded while stroking Snake Eye's fur.

"Rats?" asked Karin, a confused expression sweeping across her face. It seemed as though she was having a hard time adjusting to the idea of a pet rat. "Well, you know, the thought of adopting a rat just doesn't seem the same as the thought of adopting a sweet little mouse. What will your father say? How big will he get, Mr. Jaguar?" she asked, asking questions to stall a bit so that she had more time to contemplate this new development.

"Oh, about six to nine inches long, about the size of a large baked potato, plus four to six inches for his tail," said Mr. Jaguar while he directed another customer to the ferret gazebo.

I winced. *Baked potato?* I never thought I resembled a potato. How insulting.

Karin held her fingers about six inches apart to try to visualize a potato with a tail, but she was distracted when Claire and Sarah began poking her arm to get her attention.

"Can we get these baby rats please, Mama? Look how cute mine is!" Sarah exclaimed with a huge smile on her face as she held Fritz for her mom to see. "I'm going to name him Raspberry."

I saw Fritz flinch for a moment when he heard his new name.

Claire placed Snake Eyes on her shoulder as comfortably as if she had done it a thousand times before and said, "I'm going to name mine Stardust. Dusty for short!"

I could sense the mother warming up to the idea of pet rats. She stood still with a contemplative look on her face. I guessed that she was trying to decide if it would be okay to bring two rats home.

After a few minutes passed, she shifted her focus outward and looked over at my bin. Rather unexpectedly, our eyes met, and to my surprise, she pointed a finger toward me. I felt a flurry of excitement, and my heart started beating a little faster.

"What about a beige one, girls? I really like this one's color. There's something special about him." I smiled.

"No, Mama," Claire stated emphatically. I frowned. "We are already bonding with these."

I could see Snake Eyes, now perched on her shoulder, his tiny face peeking out through a cascade of long hair.

My hopes dashed, I sighed a long, deep, discouraged sigh. The velveteen stared at me for a few minutes longer and then turned away. I decided to go back to sleep. Curled up close to Hoover hoping for a dream of eating delicious cheese to obscure my waking disappointment, I felt restless, unable to stop thinking about that lady. I knew it was silly, but I wanted her to come back and take me home with her.

"Okay," said Karin, capitulating in the face of her daughters persistent pleas. "Let's buy the supplies and food we need for them and take them home. Can you help us find what we need, Mr. Jaguar?"

"Certainly," Mr. Jaguar replied. "Let me show you the cages first. How about this luxury model?"

Mr. Jaguar could have been describing the most expensive car on the lot at CarPet World. "It has two levels, an easy-to-open front door, a built-in wheel for exercise, and an easy-to-clean plastic pan to hold the litter." Mr. Jaguar paused for a moment and then added, "I could even throw in a bag of rat food compliments of CarPet World if you decide to take it."

I wondered if Mr. Jaguar had been a car salesperson before he took the manager job over on the pet side.

"Oh, Mama, let's get this one," Sarah said, pointing to a smaller aquarium style container. "It is so cool! Raspberry and Dusty will love it!" She was sold on the idea.

"Looks fine to me. I've never bought a rat cage before, so I really don't know what to look for," Karin commented.

Still a little disoriented by the recent turn of events, Karin spoke

Sarah and Claire hold their newly adopted rat kittens, Dusty and Raspberry.

tentatively like a rat tasting a new kind of cheese for the first time, unsure if she would like it or not.

Their voices faded as they walked toward the section of the store where food dishes, water bottles, bedding, rat food, and other supplies were sold.

I let out a slow, deep breath. There was no denying it. I was really disenchanted with the whole pet shop life. I knew it was my own fault. I should have stayed asleep like Hoover, and then I would not have gotten my hopes up. When would I learn?

Frustrated with myself, I decided to wash my fur. I had just licked my front paws in preparation for cleaning my face when ER 002 appeared out of nowhere.

"Didn't want you, did they, Oliver Twist?" he said and laughed, making fun of my longing to be with a family. "Got to wait your turn, Blondie. I've been here four weeks, and no one has picked me yet! Do you really think you'll get adopted before I do? Maybe you think so because you stole my girlfriend. Is that it?" He glared at me. I was speechless. This was the last thing I needed right now.

He laughed again, but it was a sardonic laugh, one dripping with sarcasm and hatred. His tone suddenly became more ominous as he quipped, "Would have been much, much better for you, Martin Luther King, if they *had* taken you home with them instead of leaving you here with me."

I stared at him, mouth open, shocked by his outburst. Once he saw that he had gotten to me, he was satisfied. He turned away, swaggering over toward Sketch and X-Con with his head held high, like a bully who had just sucker-punched a kid on the playground.

ER 002 *had* gotten to me. I felt troubled by the viciousness of his comments and unsure of what he meant by his parting remark. Usually I found his nicknames funny, but this time was different. The allusion to Dr. Martin Luther King was particularly worrisome. I knew ER 002 had not called me that because he admired my courage, conviction, and nonviolent approach to life. I think he called me that because Dr. King was dead, murdered by someone who was cruel and angry.

I remembered one night back at the breeder's home when Pops read a story about Dr. King's life and mentioned his speech the night before he was killed. That man was amazing. He said he had seen the Promised Land and was ready to die if he needed to. I sure didn't feel that way. I hadn't seen any promised land and certainly did not feel ready to die.

I felt confused. ER 002 hardly knew me, yet he hated me. I was too tired to think, so I curled up in the corner next to Hoover and drifted off into a restless, uneasy sleep. That night I had a dream, not the kind of dream Martin Luther King had but a nightmare.

It began in a dark forest. I am not sure how I got there, but I was not alone. Willow was there with me, her creamy white fur reflecting the moonlight. She was huddled next to me because she was scared. Actually she was not just scared. She was terrified. I could feel her body shaking with fear.

"Please, Nicodemus, find the way back to CarPet World. We should never have come here," she said, her words broken by sobs, pleading with me to save the day.

I wanted to make everything all right and to be her hero. I felt stupid and embarrassed because every attempt I made to find the way home lead to a dead end. The bottom line was that I had no clue what path to follow.

I was lost.

In a feeble attempt to comfort her, I spoke words of encouragement that I myself did not believe, "I don't know where we are, but don't worry, Willow. I'll get us home."

She looked at me with hope and trust in her beautiful pink eyes. They had a soft glow in the dark shadows.

I tried desperately to find the way back to CarPet World, but I could see no landmarks. Surrounded by thick brambles, prickly blackberry vines, and tall, leafy trees, there was no path for us to follow.

Suddenly three dark shapes loomed in front of us. It was as though they materialized out of thin air. At first, I thought they were rats, but I soon realized that they were grotesque monsters with huge, ugly heads, thick necks, and short bodies. They stood upright on two legs, but they had four arms swinging at their sides that reminded me of a spider's legs.

One of the creatures grabbed Willow with all four arms and picked her up like a bag of groceries. She screamed. I tried to save her, but another one brushed me aside as easily as if I were a speck of dust.

I heard them laughing as they ran off with their prize, Willow's muffled screams punctuating their laughter like a series of commas in a complex sentence.

I struggled to my feet, frantically searching for Willow, but she was gone. A pathway littered with large irregularly shaped iridescent blue stones suddenly opened up in front of me. The stones were so close together that it was impossible to move forward without stepping on or touching one.

I tentatively touched the closest stone with my front paw, and it immediately morphed into a huge rat dressed in an unusual, oddly familiar costume. It wore a funny turban-like blue hat, a pink vest, pink shorts, gray leg warmers, and a big sash at the waist from which hung a scabbard that housed a large sword.

I jumped back in fright, and the massive rodent lunged toward me. My guard hairs bristled, making me about twice my normal size, but it still towered over me.

I remembered where I had seen a rat like this before. It was in *The Nutcracker* ballet. When I was very young, my whole family had the opportunity to watch the fight scene.

I need to interrupt the telling of my dream for just a minute to describe how this happened. One night our breeder accidentally left a window open in the rattery. It happened to be free-range night for our family, so as typical rats who could not resist an open door or window, we snuck out.

Pops led us to a nearby building called McCaw Hall. After we entered through a small hole hidden behind a concrete staircase, we ran along the walls of a long gray corridor, up endless stairs, across a cold tile floor, and then past a dark billowing curtain.

"Shhh! We are in a famous theater and about to go backstage!" Mama whispered.

I had no idea what that meant, but I followed her instructions. There were humans running around everywhere, some dressed in black with earphones on their heads and others in very fancy costumes. Loud, beautiful music was playing, and I could see some of the humans taking turns dancing on the stage.

"We are here to watch my favorite ballet, *The Nutcracker*," Mama stated as matter-of-factly as if she was telling us that we needed to wash our faces after dinner.

"There are rats in this ballet. That is why we want you to see it, children," Pops explained. "The humans call them fighting mice, but who are they kidding? We know they are really rats. It's just that humans think that it's more suitable for a ballet to have fighting mice rather than fighting rats. What a shame. Now quick, come over here. I want you to see the fight scene!"

We slunk along the side wall of the theater, hidden by the shadows backstage. Crossing over to the wings so that we were close enough to watch the ballet was much more challenging, but somehow we managed to do it without anyone noticing or stepping on us. Being stepped on by a dancer wearing pointe shoes would have been the end for me or my siblings.

The music was so loud that I could no longer hear anything my parents were saying. The sounds crescendoed, becoming louder and louder, mirroring the level of excitement on stage.

I could see small humans dressed like soldiers dashing across the stage. They were not very tall, and I realized that they were children. The red circles painted on their cheeks caught my attention. I liked them.

Then came the most exciting part of all, the rats! First came the leader with the blue turban, and then the other fighting rats followed. They brandished their swords at the soldiers and leapt high in the air.

I knew they were humans with masks on, but I was fascinated by them. Whenever one died and was dragged off stage, I felt so sad. The mouse king almost trampled us when he ran on stage.

The end of the fight was tragic. The rats lost the fight, and their king died. That was hard to watch, but I loved every minute of it.

Mama and Pops take the family to see the fighting "mice" in The Nutcracker *ballet.*

For some unknown reason, it was the fighting rats from *The Nutcracker* that invaded my dream. As my nightmare continued, their numbers increased. Whenever I tried to move forward, I brushed against blue stone after blue stone. Each time I touched one, it immediately turned into another huge fighting rat fiercely waving a sword until there were so many that I was surrounded by them.

I could feel myself becoming increasingly anxious. I turned around, hoping to run back the way that I had come. I saw a space between two of the rats that was wide enough for me to escape, so I decided to run for it. I had to get away so that I could save Willow.

To my horror, I could not move. It was as if my legs were stuck in cement. They would not budge no matter how hard I concentrated. The rats were coming closer, swords held high. They were laughing.

I began to panic. I struggled to move my feet, but they would not stir. I could feel the hot breath of the rats as they drew even closer. My heart was beating so fast that I was sure it was going to pop out of my chest. I felt like I could not breathe.

Then one rat raised his sword and cut off my tail. The pain was intense, and I felt nauseous at the sight of my tail lying on the ground, detached from my body. I tried to scream, but no sound came out. Another rat approached, grabbed my back, and shook me so hard that I thought my head was going to fall off.

"Nicodemus! ER 22! Wake up!" I thought I heard a familiar voice, but it sounded fuzzy and far away like someone was shouting to me from the other end of a long tunnel. "Nicodemus! Wake up! Open your eyes. You're having a bad dream!"

"What?" I could hear my own voice, which really surprised me because a moment ago I could not make a sound. I struggled to open my eyes.

"Nicodemus! You keep thrashing back and forth. You're dreaming." The familiar voice was louder and clearer now.

I stood up with a start and found myself staring into the eyes of my friend Hoover.

"Where's Willow?" I demanded in a panicky voice, my eyes wide with fear, searching for her.

Hoover looked at me intently with a bewildered look on his face. He answered with a question, obviously befuddled by my agitation. "What are you talking about?"

"Willow," I repeated, "Where is she? Is she safe?"

"Yeah, man, she's fine. Willow's over in the doe's bin, sleeping," Hoover replied, still somewhat dazed by this unexpected interrogation.

"So she's safe. Thank goodness," I muttered more to myself than to Hoover and breathed a sigh of relief. "Then where did they go?" I asked in a calmer but confused voice as I glanced from side to side, straining to see past Hoover's back.

"Where did who go? What are you talking about?" Hoover was trying to be patient with me, but exasperation was beginning to creep into his voice.

"The fighting rats. Where are they?" I asked him with such conviction that he began looking around as though maybe he had missed something.

"I don't see any fighting rats. I think they must have been in your dream," Hoover said with a bemused expression.

My head was beginning to clear, and the familiar surroundings of CarPet World were becoming sharper and sharper. It was as if I were turning the focusing dial on a pair of binoculars until finally everything became clear around me.

A new wave of panic struck me as I remembered that a sword wielded by one of the fighting rats had guillotined my tail. I immediately twisted my head around to see if my tail was still there.

"What a relief!" I exclaimed. "I still have my tail."

"Of course you have your tail. What are you talking about?" Hoover began to laugh. "I have no idea what you are going to say next, Nicodemus."

By now I was awake enough that I was able to laugh at myself too, and I was able to relax. "Hoover, I have never been happier to see you," I stammered. Hoover had positioned himself a few inches away from me, looking a little shell-shocked. I added, "I think I owe you an explanation, so I'll tell you what happened in my dream."

"That would be very helpful," Hoover responded as he settled himself into a comfortable position and listened.

"Well," I began, "You were sound asleep when ER 002 walked over and threatened me. That's why I felt very troubled right before I fell asleep. I guess that's why I had this weird, scary dream."

I recounted the dream in detail, and we both shuddered a bit as I described the big fighting rats. "Do you think the dream means that I am afraid of losing my tail?"

Hoover gazed at me for a few moments, looked away as if in deep thought, washed his back with great vigor, and then began speaking in his rapid-fire style, "Well, I'm not Sigmund Freud, but I think that dream means that you are afraid that ER 002 is going to find a way to punish you and Willow for liking each other and that everything you do will only make things worse."

I stared at the rat. What amazing insight! "You know, Hoover, I think you hit the nail on the head. I *am* afraid that ER 002 is going to do something bad that will hurt Willow and me. Do you think the dream means that will really happen?"

"Well, you have to remember that it was only just a dream," Hoover said in an attempt to reassure me. "I've had lots of scary dreams in my life that have never come true."

"You're right, buddy. So have I." I was feeling better now and less afraid.

Hoover yawned, his dumbo ears lying flat as his head tilted back a little. "What do you say we go back to sleep?" He yawned again.

"Sounds good to me," I replied. We rearranged some of the bedding in the bin and then settled down to resume our sleep.

After all, it was the middle of the night for us. I was worried that the nightmare would start all over again when I closed my eyes, but much to my surprise, it did not.

I actually slept pretty well and woke up quite refreshed that evening. The night was uneventful, which was fine by me since the night before had been quite a ride. I thought a lot about that dream. It was so vivid that I was constantly looking at Willow to be sure she was definitely safe. I kept watching the floor of our bin, expecting to see blue stones appear in front of me. For the whole night, I felt disoriented and unsettled, unable to shake the sense of foreboding that followed me with the tenacity of a lion stalking its prey.

Chapter Five

The Fight

THE NEXT NIGHT THERE WAS A NEW MOON. No light filtered in through the skylights. It was dark in CarPet World except for the faint celestial glow emitted by a constellation of randomly placed fluorescent security lights scattered across the ceiling of the store. Dimly lit, they looked like long, skinny stars.

I could barely perceive the outline of the slightly illuminated cars in the center of the store. Their huge gray shapes resembled the irregularly formed rocks that loom off the coast of Washington state.

I saw pictures of them in a geography book Pops showed us one night. "This is where we live," he had said, pointing to a place between two big rows of mountains. "And over here is the Pacific Ocean. Look at this picture."

Pops was showing us a photograph of a rocky beach. "This is where our ancestors arrived by boat many, many years ago. They were great sailors." He beamed with pride.

As I stared at the cars, I suddenly flashed back to my dream. The huge gray shapes of the cars triggered my memory. Random images of the frightening blue stones and the large gray fighting rats danced before my eyes one after the other like a slide show on shuffle.

My heart started beating faster. Oh no, not again. The panicky feelings started coming in one after the other like ocean waves.

Calm yourself, Nicodemus. It was only a dream. I forced myself to slow down my breathing. In ... one, two, three, four. Out ... one, two, three, four. I did not want to go back into those feelings, not now. What could I think about instead?

Suddenly it came to me. There was a scene in *The Nutcracker* ballet where the soldiers climbed out of a large box. I imagined myself opening the lid of this box, stuffing the disturbing memories inside, slamming it shut, and then watching as the box disappeared off stage.

Believe it or not, I actually felt better and exhaled slowly. Mama always helped me when I was upset. She would say, "Look around you, Nicodemus. Listen. What's going on here? Now?"

I tried this on my own. The dogs and birds were sleeping. The nocturnal creatures were as busy as bees. Wheels were spinning. Water bottles were clicking. Food was crunching, and squeaks were filling the air. I chuckled. The snoring of the dogs sounded like background music for all of the other activity. It was against this backdrop that Hoover approached me to begin our nightly game of tag-and-tackle.

"You're it!" The minute his paw touched my shoulder, he scurried away, glancing over his shoulder to see if I had taken the bait.

I had. I chased after him, welcoming the distraction. I overtook him and tackled him, bringing him down like a linebacker rushing the passer. He howled with laughter and we rolled over and over on the floor like tumbleweed. When we stopped rotating, I was lucky and ended up in an advantageous position.

"I give up! Raise the white flag! Uncle! Uncle!" squeaked Hoover, lying on his back, pinned down by my paws. I laughed. We had played this game so many times, but each time his reactions were so funny that he made me hoot with pleasure. I jumped up and darted behind the sleeping dome. Hoover raced after me, chasing me around the bin, scattering particles of bedding as he ran.

Without warning, I stopped and stood still so abruptly that Hoover plowed into me.

"Hey, dude, why did you—" Hoover stopped midsentence when he noticed the expression on my face and felt the tension in my body. My guard hairs were standing out straight in porcupine-like fashion, and my whiskers were twitching so rapidly I was afraid they would fall off.

The presence of danger was so strong I could feel it closing in around me like a thick fog rolling in from the sea in the early morning. I squinted into the semidarkness in an attempt to pinpoint the source of my feeling, but I was too late.

Within seconds I felt the wind knocked out of me as two large rats pushed their bodies into my side so hard that I collapsed under their weight. Since I had not seen them coming, I had no time to defend myself.

The shadows obscured their faces, but my whiskers told me the identities of my attackers—Sketch and X-Con. I winced as I felt one of them slash my left shoulder. It was not a deep wound, but it hurt.

A moment later I heard Hoover scream in pain. That sound fueled my mounting anger in the same way that a dousing of gasoline ignites a smoldering fire. I was enraged. It was one thing for ER 002 and his boys to come after me, but no one was going to hurt my innocent friend and get away with it.

Adrenaline surged through my body, kick-starting my survival instincts. I whirled around to face my attacker, my paws clenched with anger. The white fur on his back was glowing in the dim night light of CarPet World, but the shadows hid his dark head. He looked like a cotton ball with legs. It was Sketch.

I had never wanted to hurt another rat before, but I did now. He lunged at me a second time, but this time I was ready. It was his mistake to make the first move.

I gashed his face with my toenails and then jumped on his back. I rode that sucker like a horse, sunk my teeth into his back just below his neck, and then dismounted, leaving him writhing in pain. Some of his fur remained in my mouth, and I spit it out in disgust just in time to see X-Con move swiftly toward me despite the fact that one of his hind legs was dragging and his breath was coming in loud gasps. His leg was hurt. That must have been Hoover's work. Good job, buddy.

When he came close enough that I could smell his sour breath, X-Con changed his posture. He turned his body sideways, moving forward flank-first like a driver positioning a car in an auto chase so that it could sideswipe another car and push it off the road.

Rats use this sideswiping maneuver to back their victims into a corner to gain the advantage in an attack. In order to outmaneuver my attacker, I flattened my body and darted to the side.

I nipped his tail, hoping to distract him. It worked. X-Con could not resist looking back to check on the condition of his tail. Rats take great pride in their tails, and any threat of damage to that part of the body is very distressing.

That gave me just enough time to perform my favorite offensive move. I jumped on his back. All that practice playing tag-and-tackle with Hoover was paying off.

X-Con was a more formidable opponent than Sketch. We tousled, rolling over several times. I hung on with relentless tenacity until I felt him tiring. I slipped off his back to his side and used my body weight to push him over onto his back. He did not struggle to get up. By maintaining this submissive posture, he indicated that he had accepted defeat.

I could have mortally wounded him, but I chose not to. I just wanted him to be in enough discomfort that he would leave me and Hoover alone, so I bit his nose and then let him go. Blood spattered all over me as he shook his head from side to side. His face contorted with pain, and he curled into a ball like a roly-poly bug and held his bleeding nose with his front paws.

Now it was my turn to breathe heavily. The struggle had exhausted me. Plus I had lost some blood from the wound in my shoulder, and the throbbing was intensifying. Unsure of what to do next, I began to wash X-Con's splattered blood off my face, and then I abruptly stopped, my paws stalled midway down my cheeks.

Two black eyes full of hatred were beaming at me like the headlights of an oncoming car on a pitch-black road. I froze. I was the proverbial deer caught in those headlights. There was only one rat I had ever seen look at me with eyes like that, ER 002.

We glared at each other in silence, staring at each other like two gunfighters with hands on their guns, waiting for the other to make the first move. ER 002 lunged at me, but I managed to dodge his attack. He turned and came back toward me. I reared on my hind legs, and so did he. We stood eye to eye in this posture, indicating extreme aggression.

ER 002's eyes were so angry that it felt as though they were burning holes in my head. He lunged at me again, and I blocked him with my front paws. I dug my claws into his skin while pushing sideways, using all of my body weight to knock him down.

He staggered backwards and stumbled, but recovered quickly. As he righted himself, his ear brushed against my face. I grabbed it with my teeth. He twisted his head and pulled to loosen my grip. I felt the delicate skin of his ear tear as he backed away.

I gagged when I realized that a piece of his ear had found its way into my mouth. I found the ear skin with my tongue and thrust it out onto the floor. Even so, the bitter taste of his flesh remained behind and nauseated me. I felt such revulsion that I almost became the first rat in history to successfully throw up.

The injury to his ear ignited a new level of rage in ER 002. He made a deep guttural sound and then reared on his hind legs and lashed out wildly with his paws like a tiger in the circus who had been teased one too many times. What happened next changed my life forever. One of his paws found my face. I winced in pain as he sank in his claws and scratched.

I felt searing pain in my right eye followed by the unmistakable sensation of warm blood trickling down my neck. The pain pushed my rage to the boiling point. Anger danced in my brain, short-circuiting any capacity for rational thought. I was not a killer, but at this moment I hated ER 002 so much that I wanted him to die.

I stared at him. All I wanted was revenge. He looked smug. "Not going the way you hoped, General Lee?" he taunted, his words alternating with heavy, labored breaths.

He obviously thought I would be conceding the fight, or he would not have referred to me as the general who surrendered, ending the Civil War.

Well, I was not one to give up so easily. I said nothing and watched, waiting for him to once again make the first move.

ER 002 launches his attack.

After what seemed like a year of silent staring at each other, he lunged at me. I was ready. I jumped over his head onto his back, bit him as hard as I could, and hung on with my teeth. He screamed a loud, piercing shriek that unnerved me enough that I released my grip. Then I flipped over onto all fours again and faced him, crouched down low and ready for his next maneuver.

He started toward me, and then abruptly without warning, he stopped moving. To my surprise, he glared at me before he turned around and backed away, his legs unsteady enough that he moved in a zigzag pattern. I could hear him chuckling softly to himself.

I stood there staring at the rat, confused and disappointed. Why was he walking away? I thought he would want to fight to the death, but obviously he did not. Apparently he had had enough.

I panted hard, gasping and trying to catch my breath, my shoulder hurting every time I inhaled. A wave of nausea crashed down on me. The taste of his blood was strong and vinegary when I swallowed. I was alive, but I could not move. Although my body was still, my thoughts continued to race. I kept reviewing the fight in my mind, going over every detail, attempting to put together the sequence of attacks and defenses in a way that made sense.

This is not the way it is supposed to be. The good guys are supposed to win, right?

I sighed. Not this time. This can't be true. It's not fair.

Although my body was motionless, my thoughts were racing. Something about the way ER 002 walked away was bothering me. Sure, I did not understand why he had stopped the fight before one of us had obviously beaten the other, but it was more than that. You see, ER 002 did not walk away as one defeated. He held his head high like one who had accomplished a great feat.

It was almost like once he knew that he had hurt me, he was satisfied, so satisfied that he snickered with glee as he slunk away to join his two buddies despite his own serious wounds.

He reminded me of a football player who is injured on the final play of the game but still manages to run the ball through the opposing linemen to score the winning touchdown. When he collapses in the end zone, the crowd goes wild, the sacrificial injury making the victory even sweeter.

I was puzzled. Why did he give up so easily? Was this part of his plan?

Of course, it was! The impact of this illuminating insight was so great it was as though a thousand light bulbs suddenly switched on in my head. How stupid I had been!

ER 002 had not given up at all. He had scored in exactly the way he had wanted. His goal was to disfigure me, not to kill me. He wanted me alive but maimed.

He wanted me alive so that I would have to endure Willow's rejection, which he assumed inevitable if I lost my attractiveness. He wanted me alive to feel the pain of the jealousy I would feel if she left me and went back to him.

I was distracted from my thoughts by the barely audible sound of someone walking toward me. Another rat was approaching. Panic surged through my being because I knew I did not have the energy to fight again. I tried to raise my head enough to look around, but the effort made me dizzy, so I laid it back down on the bedding.

My guard hairs, apparently the only part of my body still able to move, instinctively bristled, and I stiffened until my keen sense of smell told me that this rat was friend, not foe.

Hoover, my best bud, was slowly making his way over to me despite his own wounds. The first thing he did touched me so deeply that I still think about it with wonder. Without a word, he began carefully licking my wounds, not wanting to hurt me. This act of unselfish kindness reflected the depth of his devotion to me.

I could feel him examining every inch of my body with his whiskers, trying to assess the damage. When he finished, he cleared his throat and then broke the silence.

"Uh ... Nicodemus, can you hear me?" he asked in a tentative, strained voice. His voice seemed muted and faraway just like it had been when he was talking to me after my nightmare.

"Is that you, Hoover?" I whispered in an odd, muffled voice I did not recognize as my own. I sounded like I was trying to talk with a bunch of hazelnuts stuffed in my mouth.

"It's me, dude. Don't worry, man. You're going to be all right. How do you feel?" His words were encouraging, but his tone was anything but convincing.

"Terrible!" I moaned. The simple act of speaking, normally effortless, was enough to cause my breathing to become more labored. "What about you? I heard you scream. Are you okay?" I choked out each word, my voice a hoarse whisper.

"Yeah, one of them crunched my tail, but it doesn't look too bad. It bled a lot. Might be a small chunk missing, but it seems okay. It was that big bully X-Con. He bit me, and I screamed like one of those baby monkeys they had here the other day. It didn't hurt that much, but I wanted to freak him out. Guess it worked. He was rattled so much that he stopped biting me. That gave me the chance I was waiting for. I jumped on his back and held on like a vice." Hoover was so agitated that he was speaking at hurricane speed.

He went on, "We rolled over and over, hanging on so tight to each other that we must have looked like one big animal doing summersaults."

Hoover started laughing. I tried to laugh; however, it hurt too much, and no sound came out. Hoover was worried. "Can you hear me, Nicodemus?"

I nodded. It was a tiny nod, but at least I was able to move my head. That was encouraging. Hoover continued, meticulously scrutinizing my body for wounds as he finished the story. "That stupid rat was hanging on to me like I was the last piece of cheese left in the world. I had no idea what to do. Then out of the blue, his leg was right in my face. So I bit it. Why not? Shocked him big time. Guess what he did?"

Hoover looked at me expectantly waiting for a response, then remembered that I was struggling, and went on, his words coming out faster and faster as the story intensified. "The dude let go of me! Just like that! I flipped over onto my side and hit the floor really hard. That must have knocked the wind out of me. All I could do was lay there for a few minutes, trying to catch my breath."

Hoover paused. I could feel him combing the fur on my back with his paws.

"Ouch!" I flinched when he touched a sore spot, then managed to get out a weak, "Then what happened?"

"I heard the idiot groan and mutter something under his breath, then saw him hobbling over to his nest. Out of the corner of my eye, I saw ER 002 sauntering away, and I got worried that something bad had happened to you. I forced myself to stand up. As soon as I could move, I came right over to you and here I am."

"By the way, I'm looking you over to check out the damage," he told me, confirming what I already knew.

After walking around me twice, making an even closer examination the second time, he began talking as though he were a doctor having a serious conversation with one of his patients. "Hmmm, it appears that you have a few small bite marks on your left shoulder and the arch of your back, a bleeding toe on your front paw, and—" He hesitated. The pregnant pause was ominous.

I spoke first, breaking the tension. "Well, Doc, am I going to die?" I tried to inject a little humor into the situation, but neither one of us laughed.

Hoover started speaking so fast I could barely understand him. "And a big cut on your face around your right eye. This one doesn't look too good."

It was as though he hoped that saying the words faster would somehow lessen their impact. As an afterthought, he added, "Can you see anything out of that eye?"

"I don't know," I groaned as I tried to open my right eye. The pain I felt was like nothing I had ever experienced before. My eye was throbbing and burning so much it felt like someone was jabbing a red-hot poker in and out. Fortunately I could see just fine out of my left eye. That was a relief. At least one eye was okay. Good thing I had two of them.

I managed to put a paw over my left eye and tried to look around with my right eye. I could barely open it. I finally managed to lift my lid a tiny bit, and all I saw was blackness. Please let me see. Please let me see. I was begging an invisible helper to change my fate. I was scared of being blind in one eye, and it seemed like that might actually be the case.

"Hoover. Bad news, very bad news. I don't think I can see out of this eye." I remembered the no-tolerance policy for sick or injured rats at the pet store. "What's going to happen to me?"

Hoover knew exactly what I meant. He shuddered. Thanks to Sugar, all the rats at CarPet World understood all too well that sick and injured rats were transferred from the exotic rat bins to the feeder bins.

"Maybe they'll never know," he said optimistically, referring to our caretakers at CarPet World. "They probably won't notice if we can stop the bleeding and it doesn't get infected. It's not like they give us eye tests to check our vision. Look … I have an idea. I'll stay beside you and hide your eye whenever they're around. Your other cuts will heal fast. I know it will work out, Nicodemus! It has to!"

I knew better. Mr. Jaguar and Cat would notice. It was just a matter of when and what they would do with me once they discovered my wound.

"Maybe you're right," I lied. "But no one will want to buy me like this!" I added despairingly, trying hard to keep the panic I felt in my heart from creeping into my voice.

I was not one to give up easily, but this seemed like a hopeless situation. I had a headache. What a depressing end to my life story. As I contemplated my situation, another piece of the puzzle unexpectedly fell into place causing the pain in my head to intensify and my stomach to feel sick as well. I now realized what ER 002's motives were when he attacked me. Sure, he wanted to disfigure me so Willow would be *his* sweetheart and not mine, but that's not all. What he really longed for was to land me in the feeder bins. It all made sense. That's why he backed off so quickly and smugly at the end of the fight.

Killing me would have been better for me, not for him. His aim was to wound me just enough that I would survive, be humiliated when my girlfriend dumped me, and then be eaten by a hungry snake. Great future.

I looked at Hoover and sighed, then mustered the strength to share my realization with my friend. "You know what, buddy. I just figured it out. ER 002 never wanted to kill me. He only wanted two things, that sneaky devil, and he got them. He wanted to make me so ugly Willow did not like me anymore *and* he wanted to hurt me enough that Mr. Jaguar would move me to the feeder bins."

Hoover paused and stared at me, his tongue sticking out in midair, and then he continued licking my wounds. His response was reassuring. "Look, Nicodemus, you don't know that for sure. Try to stay calm. It's true that you were badly hurt by that fur ball, but I think you're panicking. Let's wait and see what happens. Things may seem a lot worse right now than they really are."

"Yeah, I guess you're right, Hoover. All we can do is take one day at a time and hope for the best," I groaned, speaking slowly now, the pain from my wounds sapping my strength.

"So for now, my friend, you need to sleep, and I do too. Let's go lay down." His voice sounded tired. The events of the night had taken a toll on Hoover as well.

Hoover helped me move back into the corner of the cage, practically dragging me on his back. I had no energy and could barely walk. We must have looked like two wounded Civil War soldiers staggering off the battlefield. I guess ER 002 wasn't so far off after all when he called me General Lee.

When we finally made it to our nest, Hoover covered me with some shredded paper that was part of our bedding material and then lay down beside me to keep me warm. I felt soothed and cared about.

Suddenly a fatigue like I had never known before enveloped me. I could not even lift one paw off the soft bedding or raise my head. Despite my best attempts to keep my one good eye open, I could not do it. My body felt as heavy as if there were ten elephants lying on top of me. I felt like I was sinking through the thin layer of bedding and molding into the floor. Sleep covered me like a blanket, and I slept.

Karin woke up feeling refreshed. The feeling was so unusual that it caught her attention. She realized that this was the first time she had felt like this in the morning since her father died. The heaviness of grief was beginning to lift. Dusty and Raspberry had boosted her spirits. Watching Claire and Sarah play with the young rats was like eating a steaming bowl of her own mother's chicken soup, definitely nourishing food for her soul.

The two girls gave Dusty and Raspberry lots of individual attention and enjoyed building complex mazes for them with their toys, giving them rides on their shoulders, and feeding them delicious tidbits of food. Even Doug seemed to be warming up to them, albeit slowly.

To her surprise, Karin found that she really enjoyed carrying the little fellows around on her shoulder and was beginning to see what Mr. Jaguar had meant when he said that rats made excellent pets. More than once she found herself wondering what it would be like to have a little rat of her own, but she dismissed the thought as quickly as it had come into her mind, convinced that two rats in one household was definitely enough.

Karin made a cup of coffee, added some half-and-half, and took one sip. Then she took another and paused for a moment to savor the delicious flavor. She smiled and drank a little more, watching a hummingbird zoom by the feeder just outside the kitchen window.

Still smiling, she walked over to the young rats' cage with the steaming coffee mug in her hand, eager to see their little black faces and to give them a rat block for breakfast. This morning, something felt different. When she reached the cage, she let out an involuntary gasp.

Raspberry was lying motionless on his side, the soft gray bedding on the floor of the cage cushioning his lifeless body. Karin was shocked. Hurriedly setting the coffee mug down on a nearby bookshelf, she spilled some coffee in her haste. Completely unaware of what had just happened, she focused on Raspberry and squinted into the cage, puzzled by what she saw.

It had only been ten days since Sarah transported Raspberry home from CarPet World. He seemed healthy and strong. In fact, Sarah took Raspberry out to play daily, and he seemed fine. Karin had held him a few times herself. She noticed an occasional sneeze, but she thought it normal. *Maybe I should have paid more attention to the sneezes*, she thought as she stood, staring at him, dumbfounded. Obviously something went very wrong.

As Karin gazed at the lifeless form of Raspberry, Dusty looked up at her with a quizzical expression as if to say, "What happened to my friend?" Neither of them could believe that he was dead.

She picked Raspberry up to make sure he was really gone. The feel of his cold, stiff body removed all shadow of doubt.

Her heart sank as she thought about how her younger daughter had already become attached to him. *How will I ever tell Sarah?*

She gently laid Raspberry down in the cage and latched the door. Dusty watched. Then she started walking away but thought better of it. She did an about-face and turned back.

"Dusty, you need to come with me," Karin spoke to him as though he could comprehend every word that she said. Little did she know that he actually did understand her.

Dusty walked over to her, and she picked him up, placing him on her shoulder, her favorite place to *hold* a rat. Moving as though slogging through mud, Karin slowly made her way downstairs to wake up the girls and deliver the bad news.

As she walked, she confided in Dusty. "I have no idea how to do this. How do you think I should say it, Dusty? Raspberry went to visit Papoo? Or Raspberry is with the angels? Or Raspberry's time has come?" Karin treated animals with great respect, considering them to be very important members of her family.

Dusty snuggled closer to her neck. The warmth of his little body was comforting. "There really is no easy way to talk about death, is there?" Dusty chattered his teeth.

"I don't think beating around the bush is a good idea. I think I should just come right out and tell her what happened, don't you?" She stroked Dusty's fur and found its softness soothing.

When she reached Sarah's room, Karin opened the window blinds and twisted the wand a few too many times in her distress. It made an odd clicking sound, so she stopped. The movement of a Black-capped Chickadee outside the window caught her attention. The motion of the blinds interrupted its search for the seeds that had fallen to the ground from the feeder above. She watched the bird fly into a nearby shrub, and then she sighed.

Sometimes being a mother is really hard. Karin sat on the edge of Sarah's bed, taking a moment to glance at her peaceful, sleeping face. The corners of the child's lips curled upward into a smile like she was dreaming about something that made her happy. Dusty settled down on her lap, waiting.

Great! I get to burst the bubble. Even though she was confident Sarah would survive the disappointing news, she wished she could wave a magic wand and make Raspberry come back to life, sparing her daughter the feelings of grief and loss.

Karin watched the chickadee fly away, wishing for a moment that she could follow, but instead she looked back at Sarah. She stroked her hair gently and said, "Sarah, it's time to wake up."

Sarah's eyes fluttered for a few moments and then opened, lazily focusing on her mom's face. Her gaze zeroed in on her mom's, and the smile disappeared. The transformation was so immediate it was as though a cartoonist had erased Sarah's smile lines and then penciled in the furrows of a frown that seemed as out of place on her young forehead as a fir tree in an apple orchard. Always very intuitive, Sarah immediately sensed that something was not right. "What's wrong, Mama?"

Karin sighed. "I have some really sad news."

She was stroking Dusty's fur again in an unconscious, rhythmic manner much like a young girl whose fingers massage a treasured baby blanket when she's feeling anxious.

Sarah's eyes widened. "What, Mama?" she asked in a worried tone. Last time her mom said those words was when her grandfather died.

Then Sarah noticed Dusty sitting peacefully in her mom's lap. "Why is Dusty here without Raspberry?" she asked, her voice sounding higher than normal.

Every morning, Karin brought the two rats downstairs to awaken their respective owners. Raspberry and Dusty, apparently happy to be alarm clocks, seemed to enjoy snuggling by the girls' necks and then climbing all over them until they woke up. They would run up and down the hills made by their legs and bodies with the dexterity of skiers coming down a difficult run.

"Raspberry died last night," Karin spoke the words as gently as she could.

A look of shock and disbelief spread across Sarah's face, draining it of color as quickly as bleach whitens a dark fabric, and then tears welled up in her eyes. "Why? What happened to him?"

"I don't know. He must have been sicker than we thought when we brought him home from CarPet World." Sarah remembered that Raspberry sneezed quite a bit at the pet store.

Mr. Jaguar noticed the sneezing and expressed concern about adopting the little rat, but Sarah, who had bonded very quickly with him, insisted that she wanted him anyway. Being new to the rat world, Karin supported her daughter's choice and said it would be okay to adopt him, not understanding that respiratory problems were very serious and sometimes deadly for rats.

Karin lifted Dusty from her lap, cupped him in her hands, and then placed him close to Sarah, who reached for him. She picked him up gently and held him near to her. "You poor thing, Dusty. Your best friend is gone," Sarah said in a shaky voice. "You must be so sad."

After she comforted Dusty by petting his fur for a while, Sarah looked up at Karin and asked, "Have you told Claire?"

"No," Karin replied. "I told you first since Raspberry was your rat. Do you want to tell her?"

Sarah, balancing Dusty on her shoulder, nodded, climbed out of bed, and walked to Claire's room at a snail's pace. She was in no hurry to tell her sister the awful news.

"Claire, wake up!" Sarah yelled, too upset to think about a more gentle strategy for awaking her sibling. This approach was not well received.

"Go away," Claire responded in an irritated voice as she pulled the covers over her head. "I want to sleep some more."

"No, Claire, it's an emergency. Raspberry died!" Sarah blurted out, her voice cracking. Claire pushed the covers off, waking up with a start.

Sarah handed Dusty to Claire and then bolted out of the room. She raced up the stairs and shouted, "I have to go see him."

Karin, Claire, and Dusty followed close behind her. When they reached the rat's home, they paused, moved by what they saw. Sarah was holding Raspberry's motionless, stiff body close to hers, lovingly stroking his fur. Standing slightly behind Sarah, respecting her grief, they bowed their heads. Tears were streaming down Sarah's young face. Claire, sensing the depth of Sarah's sadness, put her arm around her little sister's shoulders to comfort her. She was still holding Dusty and held him out toward Sarah. "You can share Dusty with me if you want to."

Sarah smiled, touched by Claire's kindness. "Thanks, Claire."

Sarah looked up at Karin and asked, "What do we do now, Mama?"

Karin knew it was one of those once-in-a-lifetime moments when the mothers who do everything correctly say exactly the right thing. Did she know what to say? No. Were profound words falling off of her tongue? No. Not knowing what else to say, she lamely replied, "Well, I think we should find a special place outside for his grave."

Why did I say that? Of all things I could have said, why that?

Sarah seemed to think it a fine response. "When will we bury him, Mama?" she asked.

Karin looked at her watch, relieved that her reply was good enough for her daughter, then said, "We have time to bury him now or we can wait until after school. Which would you prefer?"

Sarah looked out of the window and saw that the sun was shining. "I think I would like to bury him, now, Mama, while the sun is out."

She spoke like a true Seattle area native who is well aware of the transitory nature of the sun in the Pacific Northwest.

Sarah carefully placed Raspberry back in his home and then went downstairs to change from her pajamas into her clothes. Claire, still holding Dusty, followed quickly and did the same, thinking about how they could honor Raspberry. Maybe they could make a special gravestone.

"Sarah, let's write something about Raspberry on a really cool rock," she suggested while she put on her favorite necklace. "Then we can put it on top of the grave and remember him every time we walk by and see the stone."

"Okay. I like that idea. While you do that, I'll get some pretty flowers to put around him," said Sarah, picking out two socks from her sock drawer. In her signature style, she grabbed two socks that did not match, one pink and one green, and pulled them on her feet. Focusing on what she could actually do to honor Raspberry helped ease her sadness a little bit.

After a brief discussion, the human members of the group agreed that Dusty should definitely attend the service. The four of them made a small, somber funeral procession—Sarah, Claire, Karin, and Dusty.

The sun was filtering through the trees, softly lighting the front yard. Sarah went first, holding Raspberry, who was carefully wrapped in a soft blue washcloth. Claire followed, carrying a small flat rock she found near the side of the house and a thick-tipped black marker. Dusty rode on her shoulder. Karin came last, carrying the shovel in her hands. They chose a spot to the left of the driveway. While Karin dug a small hole, Sarah gathered flowers.

When everything was ready, Sarah gently lowered Raspberry into his grave, covered him with beautiful flowers, and then put dirt on top of the flowers. The sun was high enough in the sky by now that it illuminated the ground where Raspberry was buried.

They took turns spooning dirt over his motionless body. He was only about four inches long, not counting his tail. Claire placed the headstone on which she had written, *Raspberry, we love you. Rest in Peace*, on the grave, and then she said a prayer. Sarah gently placed a purple rhododendron flower on the top. The sun made the dewdrops on the petals glisten like diamonds.

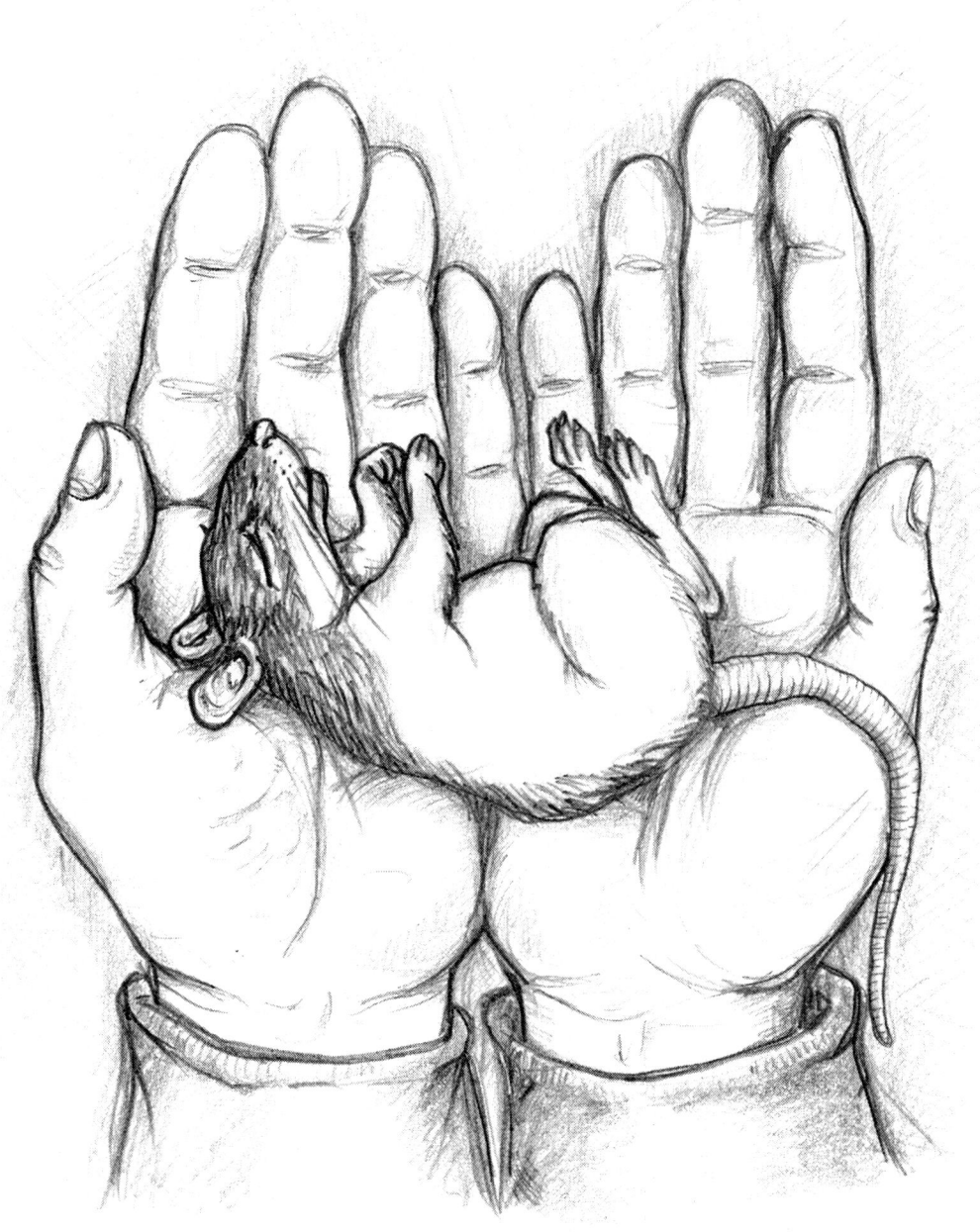
Sarah cradles Raspberry's motionless body.

After a few moments of silence, Karin looked at her watch again. "Uh-oh, girls. We have to leave for school right away!"

They raced inside to get ready, leaving behind a beautiful grave to honor the memory of Sarah's first rat.

It was not until she was sitting in the car on the way to school that Sarah realized the full implications of Raspberry's death. There would be no little rat buddy of her own to hold or carry on her shoulder. Even though Claire had offered to share Dusty with her, it was not the same as having a rat of her own, and Dusty was not Raspberry. Sarah felt a new batch of warm tears streaming down her face as another wave of sadness overcame her.

She spoke, her voice shaky and filled with emotion, "Mama, I really loved Raspberry and hope this is okay to ask, but can I get a new rat? It's not fair that my rattie died! All the bad things always happen to me." Sarah started sobbing.

"Yes, we can do that, sweetheart. We will go this week as soon as we have some free time. We can even go at night if we need to since CarPet World is open until 9:00 p.m.," Karin added, handing Sarah a tissue.

Sarah wiped her eyes and blew her nose. Then she opened the car door and pulled her backpack out of the car after her. Sarah stuck her head back into the car. "Bye, Mama. Bye, Claire. See you later. Love you." She was still sniffing but trying to compose herself before walking into the school building.

"Love you too, sweetheart. It's going to be okay," Karin reassured her.

Sarah closed the door, and her mother and sister watched her walk slowly into the school building, head down. Karin turned on the windshield wipers. It was starting to rain.

As is often the case in life, this apparent tragedy was not an ending but rather a beginning to an adventure and new chapter in the three girls' lives. Events were about to take place that they never imagined in their wildest dreams. Nor had the little, sad, sore rat at CarPet World named Nicodemus.

Chapter Six

The Calm before the Storm

"HEY, DID YOU HEAR THAT, NICODEMUS?" Hoover glanced in my direction, his dumbo ears spread wide to receive sounds, his body visibly tensing as he watched Joe and Fred leave the store.

I had heard it. About ten minutes before this, the two deliverymen had marched into the rodent pavilion, carrying a cage filled with baby rats. Hoover and I immediately moved to a good vantage point from which we could observe the action. Sitting as close as we could to the wall of our bin, ears plastered against the cold glass in order to hear every word they spoke, our heads must have looked like they were glued to the side panel.

"Well, if it isn't Sherlock Holmes and Dr. Watson. Trying to solve a mystery, boys?" ER 002's taunting voice distracted me, and I momentarily *unstuck* my head from the glass to glare at him as he sauntered past us.

"It's no mystery, boys," ER 002 went on. "In fact, it's elementary. They're bringing in new rats. Competition for us. Too bad you got injured, Nicodemus." He snickered with a noticeable lack of compassion in his voice.

I ignored him and went back to my post.

We listened very carefully to the whole conversation between Mr.

Jaguar, Joe, and Fred. You see, my position in the exotic rat bin was reasonably secure as long as no new rats moved in. These new arrivals could drastically alter the landscape.

I heard Mr. Jaguar exchange a few pleasantries with Joe, joke with Fred, and then thank them both for the new shipment of rats. However, after Mr. Jaguar's next statement, my ears perked up, and a shiver ran down my spine.

Speaking to them in a casual voice as though he were saying, "Nice day, isn't it?" he said, "Well, gentlemen, I guess I'll have to look for injured and sick rats when you leave to make room for these cuties."

We could see him holding the cage of agitated rat kittens at eye level, admiring them as he spoke. Mr. Jaguar, unaware that there were two rats in the exotic rat bin clinging to every word he said, did not notice the horrified look we exchanged after his comment.

Hoover and I needed no translation. We knew exactly what he meant when he said he needed "to make room" for the new rats. Mr. Jaguar intended to identify the rats in my bin with flaws or health issues and ship them down to the feeder bins to create space for the new ones.

It was like we were in high school, and some of us had to graduate to accommodate the needs of the new freshman class; however, this was no typical graduation. There would be no pomp and circumstance, no bright future and no exciting start to a new chapter of life for us. If we *graduated*, we faced a death sentence.

"Yeah, I heard it," I replied, moving away from the side of the bin and pausing to take a drink from the water bottle. My throat had suddenly become extremely dry. "I was hoping we would have a little more time."

It had been five days since the surprise attack by ER 002 and his sidekicks. All of my wounds were healing up just fine except one, my eye. It was still unbelievably sore. Every time I washed my face with my paws, I would sweep my front legs down over my ears and eyes, forgetting about the injury. A sharp, burning sensation in my right eye would interrupt my cleaning ritual, the intensity of the pain surprising me.

For the life of me, I could not figure out why my eye was not getting better. I was really worried. It was not the pain that worried me: I could withstand the pain. It was not even the fact that I could not see anything out of that eye that disturbed me, because I knew I could hide that.

What worried me was that my right eye seemed permanently stuck in a half-open position like a broken window shade that was jammed at half-mast, unable to go up or down. I could close it okay, but no matter how hard I tried, I could not fully open that eye. This was something so obvious that it would sooner or later attract the attention of one of the workers at CarPet World, exactly what I did not want to happen.

Every day, as though prompted by an invisible cue card, Hoover asked, "How's the old eye, Nicodemus?"

Every day, as if prompted by my own cue card, I gave the same answer, "No change, my friend."

By the fifth day, I sounded quite dejected.

However, Hoover was not. The eternal optimist, my constant companion was determined to boost my spirits. Whenever he sensed my discouragement, he surprised me with a seemingly endless stream of ideas to help my eye improve.

"I have an idea," Hoover said, deftly balancing his body so that he could scratch his back with his hind foot. "Let's try everything we can think of to help your eye see again. Come on. I've thought of some things to try. Are you ready?"

I nodded reluctantly. "Do you really think it is worth trying again, Hoover? Nothing seems to work."

"Of course, Nicodemus! Just wait until we try my newest ideas. This is what I was thinking. Maybe if just a tiny bit of light gets inside your eye, it will jump-start everything, and it will start working, kind of like a dead battery in a car getting new juice and running again. You know, the way it only takes a tiny spark to get a fire going?"

He sung the last few words to the tune of the familiar song while he spun around and did a little soft shoe. He stood on his hind legs and held his tail like a cane. He looked so funny that I laughed out loud.

Hoover excitedly tells Nicodemus (also known as Petey), "I have an idea."

Hoover sounded so hopeful that I could not disappoint him, so I halfheartedly agreed. "Right," I said while I settled into a comfortable position in the corner of the bin near the food dish.

I have to confess that I was skeptical of his idea, but at this point I was willing to try any approach no matter how far-fetched it sounded.

Hoover explained what he wanted me to do, demonstrating as he spoke, "First, cover your left eye with your paw and squint your right eye like this." He exaggerated the motion as he raised his left paw to cover his left eye. At the same time, he narrowed his right eye into a slit.

"Okay, let me try," I replied.

I covered my left eye and squinted my right eye as hard as I could, tolerating the stabbing pain this caused, but to no avail. Whenever I squinted, it felt like small shards of glass were piercing my eye, and it really hurt. "No luck, Hoover. It's still all black."

"Well, I didn't really think something that easy would work, but it was worth a shot. Let's try something different. How about turning your head upside down? Maybe your eye will only work if it is flipped over, you know, like an hourglass."

He demonstrated by attempting a headstand, but then he toppled over on his side. We both laughed. It felt good to laugh together. "Okay, your turn!" he said, feigning hurt feelings.

I looked at him with bemusement, but I decided to try it. I tucked my head under my chest. The top of my head rested on the floor, and I tried to see out of my right eye.

"Nope, doesn't work," I reported.

"All right, I have another thought. Maybe your eye will start working if you totally lose your balance and confuse your brain. Watch carefully so you can see exactly what I want you to do."

Hoover began spinning like a top and then staggered around in a daze that reminded me of how Templeton moved the night he sampled some of Annabelle's wine back at the rattery. Hoover sat down with a thump. When he had recovered his equilibrium, he met my astonished gaze and said, "Did you watch carefully?" I nodded, choking back a giggle. "Okay, this is what you do. Run around in a circle until you get really dizzy and then cover your left eye and try seeing out of your right eye."

"You have got to be kidding," I said, unable to hide the pessimism in my voice, knowing how queasy I would feel, but he was dead serious.

After I protested for a few minutes, I was willing to give his idea a try. I ran in circles until I was dizzy to the point that I fell over. We both started laughing so hard that tears filled our eyes. But no magic had been wrought by our spiraling antics. I still could not see out of my right eye.

"It's no use, Hoover. Every time I wake up, the first thing I do is cover my left eye and then try to see something with my right eye. Nothing but blackness. My eye simply does not work anymore. I've tried everything you can think of and everything I can think of. I've tried things in the dark, and I've tried things when it's light. Nothing has helped. Nothing has fixed it so I can see out of it again."

I exhaled noisily, a long drawn out exasperated sigh, as I reflected upon the depressing reality of my situation.

Hoover sighed, too. He looked so dejected that I wanted to cheer *him* up. We switched roles so that I was the encourager. "Let's not give up, my friend," I said with false hope in my voice. "I have a yogurt drop stashed away. How about we share it? Come on, buddy. We'll get through this somehow."

Hoover brightened at the thought of the yogurt drop. There is nothing like a nice treat to eat to help a rat feel better. As we sat there and munched on this delicious morsel, I continued to mull over my situation.

Even though I knew I sounded hopeful, the reality was that I was extremely worried. Actually, exceedingly panicked would be a better way to describe my feelings about my eye. And then, things went from bad to worse. Hoover was thoroughly enjoying his yogurt drop and was about to take another bite when he stopped and stared at me.

"Hoover, what's wrong?" I mumbled, my mouth stuffed with yogurt drop.

Hoover dropped his treat and pointed with his right paw, and said,

"Nicodemus, there is yucky stuff coming out of your eye. Looks kind of thick and greenish-yellow." I suddenly lost my appetite.

This was not a good sign. I felt an intense, ominous awareness that something was very wrong. I knew that the sight of *yucky stuff* would be a huge red flag for any of my caretakers. I had to keep this new development secret and hidden.

I was hyper vigilant, watching with my good eye for any sign of a red-shirted CarPet World employee. When in sight, I immediately turned my right side to the wall. When that was not possible, Hoover was my shield, gluing his body to mine as tightly as if we were joined at the shoulder with Velcro.

As strange as it must have looked to see two rats moving in sync like members of a high school drill team, this strategy worked. Hoover was able to successfully maneuver his body to block my right eye from view no matter where we were in the bin. Fortunately, none of the humans in the pet store had noticed anything unusual about me, except one. Moose.

A few nights after the fight, it was my turn to accompany Moose while he did his nightly cleaning. I thought my injury would remain undiscovered because I mounted to his shoulder without being found out.

Just as Moose finished polishing the last guinea pig bin, he dropped the spray bottle filled with the nontoxic cleaner used to clean the glass surfaces. When he bent down to pick it up, I slipped off his shoulder and landed on the floor with a thump. I instinctively froze. After a few seconds, I was about to make a beeline for a hiding place (just in case there were any predators around) when Moose crouched down on the floor beside me, his hand outstretched, and said, "Hey, ER 22, come here, dude. I'm really sorry, man. Are you okay?"

I stared at him for a moment, my mind racing. I immediately understood that I could make a run for it and hide in the dark recesses of CarPet World, but what would I accomplish by doing that? Well, I could watch for the chance to escape to the outside only to attract an owl or eagle with my light-colored fur. Or I could sneak around, subsisting on scraps and garbage, hoping to live long enough for my eye to heal before I returned to the rat pavilion. Neither seemed like a good option. I thought better of it and slowly walked over to Moose.

I glanced toward my bin. Hoover was watching me. The anxious, distraught expression on his face told me that he had seen the whole thing.

He was going bananas, trying to do anything he could to distract Moose. First he paced back and forth in the bin. Then he jumped up and down, spun around, and even performed a spectacular backflip. Moose noticed.

"Hey, what's with your friend?" Moose said to me. "That dude should be a break dancer," he added with genuine admiration in his voice.

He looked back at me, and despite Hoover's best efforts, Moose then noticed my eye. "Hey, buddy, what happened to your eye, man? It don't look too good. Jeez, I hope I didn't hurt you. Look, come back on my shoulder, dude." Moose picked me up gently and then slung me over his shoulder like one would fling a scarf around one's neck on a cold day.

I dug my toenails into the fabric of his soft hoodie just in case there were any other unexpected jolts. Moose headed toward my home. I assumed my turn to help clean the store was being cut short. He retrieved me from his neck, my toenails sticking in the cloth, making it more difficult to lift me up.

When he finally had me, he held me in both hands, looked at me in my good eye, and then spoke in a very fatherly voice. "Now, ER 22, I want you to take care of that eye. You're cool, dude, and I don't want nothing bad to happen to you. Deal?"

I nodded, and then he placed me back in the bin. I scurried over to Hoover.

"Wow, that was close!" I told my friend, who was still a bit winded from his acrobatic adventures. "I don't think he's going to say anything, Hoover."

"I tried to help," Hoover admitted. Despite the fact that he was still breathing hard, he did one more backflip for my benefit.

I laughed. "I know you did, man. I really appreciate it, my friend!"

Once again I was touched by his devotion to me.

Shortly after the incident with Moose, Hoover and I were Velcroed together again. We were sashaying our way over to the food dish when I heard the melodic, high-pitched laughter of a doe. I turned so quickly in the direction of the sound that Hoover had to make a giant leap to stay close to me.

"What in the world are you doing, Nicodemus?" Willow said and laughed from the bin next door, an amused expression crossing her beautiful face.

I smiled awkwardly. "Well, would you believe we're practicing the tango?"

She giggled and said, "You and Hoover are so funny!" Then her tone of voice changed, becoming more serious. "How are you feeling?" Willow was worried about me. I hate to admit it, but I liked it that she was concerned.

Although separated by glass, Willow and I enjoyed each other's company and had frequent conversations in the early morning long before any of the red-shirted employees or inquisitive shoppers arrived at CarPet World. We determined long ago that it was easier to hear each other's squeaks through the glass of our side-by-side bins if the store was quiet.

Of course, ER 002, Sketch, and X-Con interfered as often as possible by making loud, obnoxious sounds, but we were determined enough to communicate that we managed to find time to talk despite all of the obstacles in our way. Sugar frequently helped distract ER 002 and his cronies by engaging them in a game of tail tag. ER 002 was the tail tag champion of the exotic rat bin and he relentlessly defended his title, playing every challenger he could. Thus, he could not resist when Sugar enticed him to play.

Tail tag was a game the rats loved to play. The rat who was *it* had to touch the tail of another rat with his front paw, and then that rat became *it*. The winner was the rat who was *it* the least number of times during the game.

ER 002 was actually quite skilled at this game. After a particularly sweet victory for the big bully, Sugar confided in me that sometimes he let ER 002, known to be a sore loser, win by a wide margin just so he would continue to play. Sugar's strategy gave me and Willow more time to talk in peace.

Willow was bright and witty and could make me laugh even when I felt very discouraged about my situation. I was grateful that I still had one good eye with which I could see her beautiful fur, sparkling pink eyes, and cute dumbo ears.

We often spent the early mornings conversing until we were too tired to talk anymore and it was time for bed. Ironically the injury inflicted by ER 002 drew us closer together and deepened our feelings for each other—the exact opposite result from what ER 002 had intended. At least one aspect of ER 002's plan had been foiled.

News traveled so fast in the rodent pavilion that it was only a matter of minutes after the fight began when Willow heard that ER 002, Sketch, and X-Con had attacked Hoover and me. Willow wanted to talk to me right away, but I was too weak. It was not until the next day that I felt strong enough to engage in conversation.

It was then that she recounted her side of the story. On the night of the big fight with ER 002, the sound of Hoover's unnerving scream alerted all the does that something was very wrong in the bin next door.

"We had never heard a scream like that before, so we raced to the glass wall next to your bin to see what was wrong," Willow said and then paused. She washed her ears with her front paws then continued. "We could barely make out shadows moving in the dim light. But we could hear everything! It was so scary. There was nothing we could do to help. I thought of you and started to panic. It was awful."

I imagined the does lining up in morbid fascination. They all had ringside seats from which to watch and listen to the remainder of the fight.

Willow spoke again, "Oh, Nicodemus, I actually saw ER 002 attack you. You were in a dimly lit area and all I could see was your silhouettes. It was like watching a horror movie. I thought for sure he was going to kill you. I stopped breathing until you hurt the evil monster so badly that he slunk away."

Willow paused to wash the cream-colored fur on her back and then continued, "But the worst part is that I can't forgive myself. It's all my fault. It's all my fault!" She cried in a sorrowful voice, a big tear streaming down her delicate face. "Nicodemus, I am so, so sorry."

I stared at her, my head cocked to the side so that I could focus my good eye in her direction, a puzzled expression on my face, my whiskers twitching with confusion. "Willow, what are you talking about?" I asked. I touched the wall of the bin, wishing I could wipe away her tear with my paw, but the glass between us was an impenetrable barrier.

"Oh, Nicodemus, immediately after the fight, your sister, Peony, told me ER 002 attacked you because he wants me for himself. That means it's all my fault that you got hurt! I just feel sick. I love you so much, and your poor eye looks so bad." Her voice was filled with sadness.

She was standing sideways, leaning as hard as she could against the glass of her bin, her enchanting, cream colored fur pushed so hard against the pane that her fur parted, exposing the lighter even more bewitching ivory underfur. It was as though she thought she could magically travel from her bin to mine if she just pushed hard enough. She was so captivating that I just stared at her for a few moments, fixated on the fact that she said she loved me, before I replied.

"Willow, it was not your fault! ER 002 is a mean rat. That's all there is to it. He is unbelievably jealous that you and I ... ah ... like each other so much." I couldn't quite bring myself to say *love* yet. "And well, you know the rest of the story. It was *his* fault, not yours," I spoke emphatically.

The strength of my feelings was reflected in the movement of my tail, which swished back and forth as fast as a sword brandished by an angry pirate.

We went round and round about this for quite a while, Willow adamant that she was to blame and me countering her argument at every turn. Finally she seemed to feel a little better and reluctantly conceded that maybe I was right. Despite her protests to the contrary, I could tell that she was relieved.

Willow expresses her worries and fears.

After we resolved this issue, I decided it was time for me to talk to Willow about something that had been bothering me ever since the fight. To do so, I had to pose a rather awkward question.

"Uh, Willow," I began, my mouth suddenly very dry. I could feel my heart beating faster and my chest tightening. This was not a good time for me to be anxious, but how could I not be? I felt vulnerable.

"What is it, Nicodemus?" she responded, her beautiful rose-colored eyes looking at me intently. I was washing my back vigorously to hide my anxiety. Slow breaths. Take slow breaths, I reminded myself.

"Oh, nothing," I muttered, exhaling deeply, the air rushing out of my lungs, washing some of the fear out with it.

"Please tell me," she prodded, her soft voice melting my heart.

"Oh, well, all right," I started again. "You see, I don't quite know how to ask this, but—"

My rate of speech increased as I spoke, gaining momentum like a train moving faster and faster as it pulls out of the station. I spoke the last five words about twice as fast as the rest of the sentence.

"Well, do you still think I look ... um, attractive with only one normal eye and one droopy eye?" I blurted out, then washed my back again to hide my embarrassment that I even cared.

"Oh, Nicodemus, of course! Don't be silly. I wouldn't care if you had grown a third eye. You would still be the most handsome rat in the world to me! Besides, the way your eye is now, you look like you are constantly winking at me! I like that idea," she declared without hesitation, her whiskers twitching excitedly.

I felt she had overdone it a bit, but it was still reassuring to hear her speak these words. I was not convinced she was telling the truth, but I decided to believe what she said anyway since it made me feel better.

Suddenly feeling too vulnerable, I abruptly changed the subject, and we began to talk about other things. This was enough talk about feelings for one day for me.

During the late afternoons, the exotic rat bin was quiet. It is normal for rats to sleep soundly at this time of day. I usually enjoyed a very restful sleep, but on this occasion I was restless, so I stretched, stood up, and looked for a place to be by myself. I found it—the sleeping dome. It was empty as usual, so I crouched down to fit into the opening and walked inside.

I found myself in a comfortably large circular room with small holes in the ceiling. The magenta plastic cast an odd hue on the bedding and my fur, turning it the color of a hot dog fresh out of the package. This was not a particularly flattering shade of pink. Regardless of the fur tint, I had found a nice, quiet, secluded place. I pushed some bedding against the side of the dome and shoved it into a pile with my paws creating a nice soft resting place.

For the first time since the fight, I had some time to think. My thoughts were so mixed up that I felt like they had been thrown into a blender and spun around. I did not know what to make out of this sudden, unexpected change of circumstances in my life. It seemed like one of three things could happen.

In the best-case scenario, my eye would heal, I would be able to see out of it, and it would look normal again.

If my eye did not heal, I was confident that I could eventually come to terms with a funny-looking eye or even the loss of sight in one eye. These things were difficult to accept, but they would not kill me. I knew that I could also cope with the disappointment of having a disfigurement that would destroy my chances of winning Best of Show. It was a blow to my hopes of honoring my family with a major accomplishment, but maybe I could bring honor in a different way.

The third scenario had a much darker outcome. If I was transferred to a feeder bin and sold as snake food instead of as a pet, I would meet a premature death and that would be the end of me. This thought was the hardest for me to consider. Although I was definitely depressed about my circumstances, I was absolutely sure that I was not ready to die.

I knew that Sugar had come back and defied his death sentence, but none of the others had done that. I could try to fight like Sugar did, but the odds of surviving were very slim.

The uncertainty of my future was constantly on my mind, hovering over me like a big black cloud, however it was overshadowed by a more practical problem. I had to learn how to navigate with only one eye. Rats do not have very good eyesight to begin with, so we depend more on our acute, highly developed sense of smell.

In fact, our olfactory sense is so well developed that we smell in stereo. This amazing ability allows us to locate an object within seconds after we smell it. We also use our whiskers, which are called vibrissae, to sense objects in our vicinity. Sometimes we can determine what something is by touching it with only one whisker.

However, we do rely on using two eyes since our vision is binocular. Even though it would be hard, I was determined to learn to move as skillfully as I had with two eyes by using my one functioning eye in combination with my other senses.

While I was formulating a navigational strategy, a helpful memory from my childhood surfaced. When I was only a few weeks old, I woke up in the middle of the day and couldn't go back to sleep. The rest of my family was piled on top of one another like a rugby scrum, snoozing. Pops, his snores as regular as the ticking of a clock, was unusually loud today. I decided to get up.

After I stretched and scanned the environment for any signs of predators, I chose to investigate an uncharted area of our cage. I was barely big enough to climb up the bars to the wooden shelf directly above our nest.

It really was not that high, but I felt like I was on top of the world. Surveying the room from this new vantage point, I could see out the window, and I saw a man walking a tiny black dog with curly fur and a long tail that reminded me of a velveteen rat.

The man paused as the dog sniffed around the base of the tree. Up higher in the forked branches, a fat gray squirrel was climbing, a nut held tightly in his mouth. I was focused intently on the squirrel when I felt the odd sensation that someone was watching me. My guard hairs stood on end, anticipating danger.

When I turned away from the window and surveyed the room, my eyes stopped at a bookcase near our cage. The shelves were sparsely covered with a random selection of books punctuated by open spaces. It was in one of the open spaces that I saw a large white rat, her pink eyes glowing in the dim light.

I recognized her immediately. She was an older rat who was our breeder's pet. Although I had seen her many times, she was a stranger to me. Our eyes locked for a second, and then she began moving her head slowly back and forth in a sweeping motion like the pendulum on a clock.

Intrigued by this motion, I found myself moving my own tiny head in rhythm with hers. I realized that she actually had not seen me yet. She was scanning the area as though she knew I was there, but she could not find me.

My curiosity gave me the courage to clear my throat loudly and then say, "Excuse me."

She turned toward my voice, moving her head in that odd oscillating motion. Finally she located me, and the motion stopped.

"Yes, hello, who said that?" she asked in a soft, soothing voice.

"I did. My name is Nicodemus," I said quietly, feeling a little shy.

"Hello, Nicodemus. My name is Belle. How may I help you?" Her tone was warm and friendly. She seemed very nice, so I began to relax.

"Well ... I was wondering why you move your head from side to side like that," I stammered, not knowing what else to say. My voice sounded rather tentative and small.

She laughed. Then she squinted at me and explained, "Oh, my boy, you've probably never seen a rat do that before. The answer is simple. It helps me to see. My vision isn't what it used to be, not that it ever was very good. Rats with pink eyes have especially poor eyesight, you know."

"I didn't know that," I responded, feeling a bit tongue-tied. "Nice to meet you," I added. Then because I felt uncomfortable and self-conscious, I turned around, jumped off the ledge, and ran back to my family.

This is all that I remember about my conversation with Belle. At the time I did not give what she said a second thought, but suddenly her words captured my attention. "The answer is simple. It helps me to see."

Maybe her strategy would help me to see as well. I crawled out of the sleeping dome so that I could experiment and see if it helped.

I moved my head very slowly from side to side in a sweeping motion just like I had when I was imitating Belle.

I *scanned* the exotic rat bin. This movement worked well. It allowed me to observe the part of the bin that my hurt eye could not see. I was pleasantly surprised by how much better I could navigate this way. Belle was right. Scanning combined with relying more on my whiskers and guard hairs to give me a sense of my location and to warn me of obstacles in my path was quite effective.

The only problem with this technique was that it was noticeable. I did not want ER 002, Sketch, or X-Con to become aware of how much difficulty I was having or to know that I was blind in one eye.

ER 002 was sitting across the bin, his back toward me, eating rat food. I noted that he had not escaped unscathed after our confrontation. A jagged scar on his back marked the spot where I had bit him during those last fateful moments of our encounter, but that would soon disappear when his fur grew back again.

However, the most noticeable reminder of our fight was the two triangular pieces missing near the top of his left ear. They were so close together that it looked as though someone had clipped his ear with pinking shears, leaving the letter W permanently snipped out of it.

Once a piece of a rat's ear is missing, it does not grow back, so ER 002 was branded for life with this unusual mark. It also meant that he would never win Best of Show either. I found some comfort in this thought.

Some rats would have been proud of leaving an indelible battle scar on another, but I felt no sense of satisfaction. It was not my nature to feel proud of hurting others. All I felt was a deep sense of sadness that jealousy had led to unnecessary pain for both of us.

Cat came in to feed us our dinner. I had no appetite. Even the special treat of frozen banana slivers that she brought for us did not tempt me. I forced myself to eat a little, and then I curled up in the corner, hoping the sleep that had eluded me that afternoon would come.

I needed to escape from obsessing about the events of the past few days, but it was virtually impossible for me to turn off my thoughts while I was awake. I was in luck. Within a matter of minutes, I dozed.

Suddenly Hoover was standing right in front of me.

"Hey! Nicodemus! Did you hear me?" Hoover was looking at me very intently, his black eyes wild with terror. "I just heard Mr. Jaguar say they are going to move you to the feeder bins."

I focused my good eye in his direction and stared back at the rat, thunderstruck. I had heard him, but I was speechless. I tried to speak, but no sound came out. As the meaning of his words sunk into my consciousness, I felt that horrible sick feeling growing in my stomach.

"Snake food! Not that!" I shuddered.

I could feel the fur on my back standing on end as my tail twitched.

"Shhh!" whispered Hoover, speaking into my ear as he glanced furtively around the room. "I don't want ER 002 to hear me. I don't think he knows yet."

I scanned the room with my good eye. ER 002 was snoring, lying flat on his side, his body sprawled out next to Sketch and X-Con.

My next question was only one word, "When?" I winced after I asked the question, not really wanting to know the answer.

"Tomorrow!" he hissed. "They're moving you to Death Row tomorrow!"

"No. No, they can't do that. No. No. No." I was shouting again and again. Then without warning, something or someone started shaking me harder and harder.

I could hear a voice calling to me. It sounded far away.

"Nicodemus! Wake up! Can't you hear me?"

I opened my one good cranberry-colored eye. Hoover was standing over me, a very worried expression on his face.

"Nicodemus, you were squeaking really loudly, saying *no* over and over again. I think you were having another nightmare." His voice trailed off.

As I blinked hard several times, I looked around. I was confused. "Hoover, did you just tell me that Mr. Jaguar was going to move me to Death Row tomorrow?" I asked, holding my breath.

My heart was beating so fast that I thought I was sure to have a heart attack at any moment.

Hoover gazed incredulously at me. He looked as shocked as if I had turned into a water bottle right in front of his eyes. His expression was one of total bewilderment. "No, man, you must have been dreaming."

"You mean I'm not going to the feeder bins?" I could not contain the excitement and relief in my voice.

"Not that I know of," Hoover assured me as he licked his front paw and washed his face.

"Oh, that is the best news I have heard in weeks. You are right. I must have had another nightmare, but it was so real that it scared me to death." I sighed deeply, and my body relaxed as though an IV full of relief was flowing through my veins. My heart rate slowed, and I sighed again.

"Yeah, my friend, it was a dream. All I said to you was that Mr. Jaguar just brought us some yogurt drops for a treat. You didn't answer, so I figured you were fast asleep," Hoover explained, shaking his head as though he was trying to dislodge the last bit of confusion.

"I guess I was," I said groggily, caught between the vivid world of my dream and the mundane world at CarPet World.

My thoughts were processing at an unusually slow speed. A few minutes later, when I could retrieve Hoover's words from my molasses-like memory, I asked, "Did you say something about yogurt drops?"

Nothing worked as effectively as the thought of something delicious to eat to divert a rat's attention.

"I did," Hoover replied, washing his face with his front paws as he spoke, a dead giveaway that he had already helped himself.

"Are there any left?" I was not optimistic since yogurt drops disappeared like magic in the exotic rat bin.

"I saved one for you." Hoover scurried over to the corner and retrieved an ivory-colored delicacy. He carried it in his mouth with great pleasure like a dog retrieving a stick tossed by her human owner.

Hoover gently placed it at my feet with aplomb and finesse. "Here it is," he declared, beaming with pride.

We shared the yogurt drop, its sweet taste momentarily distracting me from my problems and my fears. As we were just finishing our snack, the sound of familiar voices floated in our direction.

"Over here, Fred and Joe!" yelled Mr. Jaguar, his big smile welcoming the deliverymen from the far side of the store. "Looks like you've got another fine shipment of rats!"

Suddenly Fred stopped walking. He was gazing at his finger with a look of horror on his face while at the same time he shouted at Joe with an increasingly panicked voice.

"Joe, that white one with the brown head just bit me! Quick, call 911! I'm going to get bubonic plague!"

"Good grief, Fred! You are not going to get bubonic plague. These are pet rats, not sewer rats. Besides, we're not living in the Dark Ages! Let me see that finger."

Fred held out his finger. He closed his eyes and turned away, not wanting to look at it.

"Jeez, Fred, it's just a little red. It's not even bleeding. I think you'll live," Joe replied, rolling his eyes as he spoke.

"Are you sure, Joe?" Fred just could not let this one go.

"Of course," Joe said with a combination of mounting exasperation and amusement. "Now shut up and help me with this cage. Jag is waiting for us."

Fred reluctantly picked up the cage and then stared at the tip of his left index finger to make sure that no blood was oozing out of the minuscule bite mark. Joe, not one to miss an opportunity to share his knowledge, especially when he had a captive audience, spoke in a professorial tone as he and Fred walked toward the rodent pavilion.

"You know, Fred, it really wasn't the rats that caused the spread of the plague. I was watching TV the other night, and someone was explaining that it was the fleas, not the rats themselves that carried the germs." Fred expounded, speaking as though he were a college professor addressing a lecture hall filled with students.

"Is that right?" Fred did not sound convinced or comforted.

"Yeah," continued Joe, looking over the top of his glasses. "The fleas rode around on the rats. Every once in a while, one jumped off and bit some unsuspecting person who became infected. See, you can't get bubonic plague from a rat bite after all. Does that make you feel better?" Joe asked as he pushed past a group of young men eyeing the latest model of the hottest sports car at CarPet World.

Mr. Jaguar, who was walking toward them and gesticulating with his right arm, interrupted them. "Let's take them in the back for now, and we'll move them into a display bin after I look them over. It's getting a little crowded out there in the exotic rat bins. Have to check for sick or injured rats and move the new ones in tomorrow," he muttered more to himself than to Fred and Joe.

"What's that, Jag?" asked Joe.

"Oh, nothing, just talking to myself," replied Mr. Jaguar as he pointed, indicating where they should place the new rats.

Fred and Joe carefully positioned the cage on a large square table and then looked at Mr. Jaguar to see if there were any further instructions.

"Thanks, guys. These look great," Mr. Jaguar said, the jaguar pendant swinging back and forth in agreement as he bent over to look more intently at the new arrivals. Then he mumbled, "See you later, Fred, Joe."

Fred and Joe waved good-bye and headed for their truck. Fred was still gazing at his finger while Joe walked slightly behind and stared at him, shaking his head.

I turned and stared into Hoover's horrified eyes, my heart rate rising again, and said, "This is no dream, my friend. It's the real thing."

Chapter Seven

A Bad Dream Come True

I WAS ABSENTMINDEDLY MUNCHING ON A particularly bland rodent block the next morning when I spotted Cat and Mr. Jaguar approaching from the other side of the rodent pavilion. What could possibly be in this food that tastes like baked sawdust?

When I noticed that Mr. Jaguar had a clipboard in his hand, my body immediately stiffened. The uneaten food in my paws fell into the bedding on the floor.

I scanned the bin with my one good eye until I found Hoover. He returned the gaze knowingly. I noticed that his guard hairs were standing out straight from his body, which made him look like a pincushion. He was stressed just like I was. Mr. Jaguar and Cat walked right up to our bin and stopped.

"Okay, guys, inspection time!" Mr. Jaguar announced as cheerfully as if he was saying, "Yogurt drops!"

Doesn't he get it? Does he have any idea what his words are doing to me? Apparently not.

Mr. Jaguar smiled as he handed the clipboard to Cat so that he could open our bin. I inhaled sharply.

This was definitely no hallucination or nightmare. Hoover and I exchanged meaningful glances. He scurried over to me and assumed his Siamese twin position, blocking my injured eye from Mr. Jaguar's view.

Mr. Jaguar turned to Cat. "I'll call out their names, and then you write down what I say about each one. Ready?"

She nodded, her cheerful sky-blue eyes scanning the residents of my bin. There were seven of us left—my brother Templeton, Sugar, Hoover, ER 002, Sketch, X-Con, and I.

Mr. Jaguar and Cat were just about to pick up Sugar for his inspection when they were interrupted by the sound of enthusiastic voices. They turned around to see a man and two boys staring into one of the exotic rat bins, apparently shopping for pet rats.

I heard one of the boys say, "Hey, Dad, I like this one. Look at her white paws and tummy."

He was pointing at Peony, my youngest sister. "She is an American Irish black rat. That means that she is mostly black but has white gloves on her paws, a white tail tip, and a large white oblong patch on her stomach."

My heart sunk when I heard the boy talking about her. As much as I wanted her to be happy living with a very special family, I had a strong bond with Peony and would miss her terribly.

The father replied as he patted the boy on the back, admiration in his cheery voice, "Well, son, it's obvious that you've done your research on the different types of rats. American Irish, eh? Pretty spiffy. I don't care if she's from France, Greece, Ireland, or any other country. She looks fine to me."

The dad was smiling at his son, but he was not particularly interested in Peony. I figured out right away that, unlike his son, he knew nothing about rats.

By this time Mr. Jaguar had walked over to the prospective rat owners. He smiled, cleared his throat, and then interjected, "Good morning, sir. Welcome to CarPet World. Name's Arnold Jaguar. Looks like your son is interested in one of our rats. Would you like me to take her out so that your son can hold her?"

"That would be great," the man said as enthusiastically as if Mr. Jaguar had said, "Would you like to take one of our brand-new sports cars for a spin?" Then he turned to his son and animatedly added, "Listen here, Jason. This nice man is going to let you hold that rat you like. Now put out your hands so he can give her to you, okay?"

Picking up the doe the boy wanted was more of a challenge than he expected because, unbeknownst to Mr. Jaguar, the girls liked to play a game with him. Since life at CarPet World was not exactly full of exciting moments, all of the rats sought entertainment wherever they could find it. One of the ways we livened things up was to thwart Mr. Jaguar's efforts to show any of us to a prospective buyer. This small thing made our rather boring, routine existence a bit more interesting.

I heard my sister Rose squeak, "Okay, girls, five, six, seven, eight. Start dancing!"

The girls began to dance around the cage, eluding Mr. Jaguar's grasp as long as possible. I could hear the females creating quite a ruckus, but Mr. Jaguar was triumphant at last. "Got her!" he said with great satisfaction.

Jason held out his hands, and Mr. Jaguar transferred my sister to him. Cradling Peony with the expertise of an experienced rat owner, Jeremy smiled like the Cheshire cat. "Dad, she is perfect. I want her."

"Well, then let's get her," his father said as authoritatively as an auctioneer proclaiming, "Sold!" to the highest bidder.

When he turned to his other son, he asked, "Which one do you like, Josh?"

"That one." The younger boy was pointing to a different rat in the bin, but I could not see which one it was.

"Sure, kid. I'll get her for you," Mr. Jaguar assured him as he reached into the bin. "This one is a beauty."

"Oh, she's so cute!" the little boy exclaimed, holding her close to his body and stroking her fur.

My heart, already sinking at the prospect of Peony leaving, plummeted to a new low. What else could possibly go wrong? The rat the boy had selected was Willow.

I could hear her squeaks and could see her velvety beige fur shimmering in the glow of the lights of CarPet World. Unbeknownst to the boy, Willow was talking to the other does in the bin, telling them that she was excited but scared to go to a new home.

Most people are unaware that rats communicate with one another with extremely high-pitched sounds that are inaudible to humans. We often carry on extensive conversations right next to humans who are completely oblivious to the fact that they are missing out on the latest rat news.

"I want her," Josh said decidedly, referring to Willow. "I think she likes me. Look, Dad. She's sitting on my shoulder."

The boy was standing just outside of my bin, so I could see Willow quite clearly. He was right. She was perched atop his shoulder, appearing regal, her head held high with the demeanor of a bald eagle roosting majestically at the top of a tree. She seemed to like this little boy, and that gave me a good feeling that counterbalanced the rather selfish disappointment that was mounting in my heart.

I focused on her so intently that I felt like an artist sketching her image in my mind with a permanent marker. I knew that in a few moments, we would say a final good-bye. Willow's luxurious creamy fur was shining in the light, her dark brown points framing the lighter fur. She looked beautiful.

Before she saw me, I saw a mixture of apprehension and anticipation on her face. Those were pretty normal feelings under the circumstances. I understood that she was both afraid of leaving CarPet World and excited at the prospect of a new life with a human family, something we all wanted.

Then our eyes met—her two passionate pretty pink eyes and my one adoring dark ruby eye. All three simultaneously filled with tears of sadness.

"Nicodemus. I think—" she said, choking up.

That was all she could say. The rest of the words stuck in her throat with the tenacity of an old piece of chewing gum attached to the underside of a table, abandoned by some school kid long ago.

"I know, Willow. That boy is going to take you home. It's what we all dream about, my love. It's going to be okay. Plus it looks like you get to go home with my sister, Peony. I think that will make it easier.

Peony is a real sweetheart." I tried to sound encouraging, and then I added, "Besides, she will never let you forget me!"

I laughed to break the tension.

"Oh, Nicodemus, don't be silly. Of course I will never forget you! That's why I am so sad. I can't stand the thought of living without you in my life. I guess I secretly hoped we would go to the same home. I knew it was a silly fantasy, but I really wanted to believe it would come true."

She sighed a deep, sad sigh and then paused for a few seconds to wash her creamy fur. I listened, holding back tears. She continued, "Plus I'm scared to leave you. I don't know if you are going to be okay. Your eye, you know. I'm really worried—"

Her melodious voice trailed off, leaving the worst scenario unspoken. I was touched by Willow's kindness. It was bittersweet. It felt good to know she cared, but it felt awful to be separated from her.

"I'll be fine," I spoke bravely, trying to portray confidence I did not feel. "This old eye will heal up, and I'll be as good as new. But I will miss you terribly, Willow. I love you so much." Yikes! I actually said *love*. I sighed and then continued, "I mean, we knew it would come to this sooner or later. Do you remember that day when we talked about it?"

She nodded.

I went on, "We even said how we knew it was not a good idea to fall in love with a rat from the same pet store because it so rarely works out. It's really hard, but we will both be okay, don't you think?"

I tried to sound strong and reassuring, but the shakiness of my voice exposed my true feelings.

"Everything you say is true, Nicodemus, but I still feel like my heart is breaking. I don't want to leave you, and I can't imagine life without you. And ... you said you loved me." Her voice was quavering but she was smiling.

There was a pause, and I waited. I thought she would say more, but then I realized that she stopped because she was crying. I heard a loud sniff. Willow's eyes suddenly widened with anguish as the boy began to walk away from my bin toward his father.

"I love you too, and I will remember you always," she squeaked, her voice cracking with sorrow, as the distance between us widened.

Willow was sitting in the boys hands now and he was petting her, totally unaware of her sadness. I noticed Willow wiping the tears from her face with her front paws.

"This is a great rat, Dad. I really like her." The boy was grinning. "Look how cute she looks when she washes her face."

"Okay, Josh, we'll take her home too," the boys' father stated with an air of finality. Then he did an about-face, looked at Mr. Jaguar, and declared, "Mr. Jaguar, we'll adopt these two rats."

At that moment Peony peeked at me from under Jason's hooded shirt and spoke, "Good-bye, my brother. Thank you for helping me whenever I was scared. Willow and I are good friends, and we will take care of each other."

Peony's words were comforting. I told her that I would miss her, but I wanted her to be happy. The thought that Willow and Peony were going to a good home together was my only consolation.

On a more selfish note, I longed to go to a good home too, but I feared that my fate would not be as fortunate.

My eye hurt.

As the father and sons began walking toward the small animal supplies, I could hear the older man say to Mr. Jaguar, "We need a nice cage and some food. Do you have water bottles too?"

"Yes, sir, right this way." Mr. Jaguar's booming voice trailed off as they went over to the cage section. I watched Peony and Willow until they disappeared behind the row of guinea pig bins.

"Need a tissue, lover boy?" ER 002 and his two partners were staring at me, a bemused expression on their faces. ER 002 continued, his voice dripping with sarcasm, "Too bad you lost your good looks and your girlfriend in the same week!"

"Oh, shut up!" I snapped, immediately regretting what I said.

ER 002 knew he had gotten to me once again and was delighted. I lost my cool. That was exactly what he wanted. He laughed.

I walked away, ignoring the rest of their teasing and snickering.

A few minutes later, Mr. Jaguar came back to resume the

inspection. "Okay, here's the first one." Mr. Jaguar's voice snapped me back to the immediate problem I had to face. He was examining ER 002, who was scowling at him, irritated by the process.

"What a handsome rat! Uh-oh. Looks like a scar on your back. Hmmm." Mr. Jaguar parted the fur with his fingers to make a closer examination. "Looks like its healing up just fine. Your fur will cover it soon. Now what is this?"

He was holding ER 002 so that he was facing him and was scrutinizing his left ear. "What in the world happened to your ear? Cat, make a note that he has a zigzag cut in his left ear. Wonder how he got that. Doesn't look bad though. Gives him some character!"

ER 002 puffed out his chest, reveling in this last comment. He shot a triumphant glance in my direction; however, his moment of glory was cut short by Mr. Jaguar's next remark.

Holding ER 002 at eye level and staring at him, he continued, "Hey, buddy, have you been fighting? You need to stop that. It doesn't help your good looks."

He paused, inspecting ER 002 for a long time, examining him from all angles like an art critic examining a fine sculpture. I watched Mr. Jaguar stop and think carefully about the fate of my nemesis. ER 002's expression had changed. He looked anxious, immediately understanding the meaning of Mr. Jaguar's momentary hesitation. He shot a glance at Sketch and X-Con, who were watching Mr. Jaguar's every move with intense interest, their heads and eyes moving together as if they were performing a carefully choreographed duet.

Mr. Jaguar pronounced his verdict as he put him back into our bin. "I'll leave you in this bin for a few more weeks and see how you look then. You're good to go for now."

ER 002 glared at me, squeaking as he strode by. "Too bad for you, Cyclops. I'm going to be in here awhile longer. I doubt that you will though. You'll make a really tasty meal for a snake. I've heard some snakes actually prefer injured rats. Kind of a special treat!" He sneered and laughed at his own joke as he sauntered over to his friends.

"Okay, next."

Mr. Jaguar, completely oblivious to the drama taking place in the rat bin, reached toward Hoover, who responded by walking over to Mr. Jaguar's hand and licking it.

"Wow, you are a big fellow! Nice temperament too. Definitely want to keep you in the exotic rat bin." He cupped Hoover in his large hand, scratched the back of his head right behind his dumbo ears for a few seconds, placed him back in the bin, and then turned to the next rat he saw.

"Let's take a look at this guy," he continued as he picked up my brother Templeton. "Very nice looking rat. Definitely a keeper. Did you get that, Cat? He is ER 23. Mint condition."

Mr. Jaguar lifted Sugar out of the cage. "Hey, my boomerang man! Still can't believe you're back here. What a handsome devil you are too! That snake sure missed out on a good meal."

Mr. Jaguar laughed so loud several customers glanced in our direction to see what the commotion was all about. Sugar, not finding that last comment particularly funny, nipped Mr. Jaguar on the pinky.

"Ouch! Okay, dude, sorry. I shouldn't have said that! If I didn't know better, I'd think you understood what I said."

When he turned to Cat, he commented, "ER 89 looks just fine. I'm putting him back in the bin."

Sketch and X-Con, ER 002's henchmen, passed the test with no problem. I was last. My heart was racing as Mr. Jaguar lifted me out of the bin. He examined me very carefully, spending a long time—too long of a time—squinting at my eye.

"Cat, make a note that ER 22 has a bad eye. Looks like it got scratched somehow. I need to decide what to do with him. We should definitely give him some antibiotics." He continued talking but more to himself than to Cat. "He's so smart and such a handsome brute that I'd like to give him a chance to heal up. Doesn't look good, though. It's too bad. He's one of my favorites."

Mr. Jaguar was frowning and shaking his head as he spoke. I did not view this as a particularly encouraging sign. However, he was giving me a chance, and that gave me some hope.

Hoover was licking his right rear paw and then started cleaning a particularly dirty spot on his back. He winked at me. "You made it so far, bud! Round one is over."

"I definitely feel relieved," I replied, feeling a little calmer. "But he did make a note that I have an injured eye."

I tried to clean my eye with my paws. It was hurting more than ever, and that worried me. Besides, ever since the night of the fight, the world had gone dark in that eye. I had hoped that the vision would return, but it seemed less and less likely with each passing day.

Shortly after the inspection, I was practicing my scanning technique when my good eye focused on ER 002 crouched over in the corner, huddled with his two cronies. As he glanced furtively in my direction, he whispered something to his buddies.

He met my glance and shouted, "Hey, Blondie, I saw Mr. Jaguar make a note about that eye. Too bad. Might win you a transfer to the feeder bin."

He laughed his most sinister laugh and slunk away, swishing his tail, Sketch and X-Con following closely behind him. I ignored him and spent the rest of the night with Hoover, Templeton, and Sugar. We talked, ate a few snacks, played tail tag, and exchanged pleasantries with the girls in the next bin. Light was just starting to stream into the window at CarPet World when we both fell asleep.

Two days later, Mr. Jaguar strolled over to our bin followed by a little girl, her brother, and their mother. I heard him say, "These are our best exotic rats right here."

"I'm picking out the rat, not you!" the girl yelled at her little brother, rudely interrupting Mr. Jaguar midsentence. Her curly brown hair bounced as she spoke, adding emphasis to each word she uttered. I immediately had a bad feeling about her. She must have been about ten years old.

"Are not! I am!" said the boy. He was smaller and had very light hair, a color we rats called champagne. He punched his sister in the arm. In the next moment, she was running to her mother, "Mommy, David hit me!" The mother turned around in a split second, her conversation with Mr. Jaguar stopping as abruptly as if someone had just hit a pause button on a remote.

"Behave yourselves, both of you. If there is any more fighting, we leave the store with no rats!"

Something about her reminded me of Pops. I had not thought about him for a long time. Good ole Pops. What would he say if he saw me now? How disappointed he would be if he knew about my eye and even more disappointed if I ended up—I couldn't even think about that possibility. He had been so optimistic about my future. I sighed a deep, sad sigh.

I glanced up as Mr. Jaguar lifted the lid off my bin and reached in. "This one?" he asked as he picked up ER 002.

"Yeah! He's awesome," said the boy, reaching out to hold ER 002, who was reveling in the attention.

"Good luck with him," I muttered to myself.

"He's dark gray with a lightning mark on his face. He looks like Harry Potter. What a cool rat. He even has a jagged ear! And look. Here's another scar on his back. Sweet! I can tell he likes me. Can we get him, Mommy?" The boy fired off one thought after another.

His sister, Erin, was eyeing ER 002 with disgust. I started warming up to her, questioning my first impression. "I don't want a rat with a white mark on his head, Mommy," she whined. I saw ER 002 glare at her. It was an almost imperceptible change in expression that only another rat would notice. I smiled.

"May I please see that one?" she asked Mr. Jaguar, pointing to Sketch, the agouti bareback rat. "Oh, Mama, he's so nice! I like his brown face. Look at him snuggle under my hair. Please, please!"

"Gross. He's a girlie rat," said the boy called David. Sketch winced at his comment. ER 002 laughed. "Look at mine. He's tough and strong ... just like me!"

Erin rolled her eyes and made a face. The mother looked at Mr. Jaguar as if to say, "Help. What should I do?"

Mr. Jaguar, sensing the impending crisis in the family and, as always, hoping to make a sale, tactfully said, "Well, you know rats are very social creatures and really prefer having a cage mate to living alone. They love humans, but they do best when they have one of their own kind to keep them company. You know what I mean?"

David, stroking ER 002 behind the ears, seized the opportunity to say, "See, Mom, we should get both of them! Please! Please!"

I could see the writing on the wall.

"Okay then," the mother said, choosing to take the path of least resistance. "We'll take both of them!"

The kids jumped up and down.

"Oh, Mommy, thank you so much. I'm calling mine Ratzilla," said David, holding ER 002 out in front of him so he could look into his eyes.

I could see ER 002 puffing out his chest once again, pleased with such a ferocious name. Then he abruptly turned his head, and like an owl stalking its prey, he peered into the exotic rat bin until his beady coal-black eyes locked on mine. The big smile on his face looked oddly out of place below his hate-filled eyes. I knew why he was gloating. He was being adopted, and I was not.

"Eat your heart out, Captain Hook." His high-pitched squeak was filled with malice. "Oh, wait a minute. I think I have that wrong. Captain Hook was missing a hand, not an eye."

He roared with laughter just as Mr. Jaguar stuffed him into a CarPet World To-Go box. It looked like a Chinese food container, but it had the CarPet World logo on one side, the words *Live Animals* in big letters on the other, and a few air holes scattered here and there.

ER 002 managed to stick his head out of the top, stared at me, and then began speaking. "Oh, and one more thing," he added. "Don't think this is the last you'll see of me, Romeo. I'm not finished with you yet!"

What did he mean when he said this wasn't the last I would see of him? At that moment I really did not care. All I knew was that I was overjoyed that ER 002 was moving out.

The two children began talking to Mr. Jaguar again.

"I'm calling mine Hank," said Erin, cuddling Sketch against her body. Sketch squirmed, not sure that being cuddled fit his tough-rat image.

"Why Hank?" asked Mr. Jaguar as he reached out to put Ratzilla and Hank into their To-Go boxes.

ER 002's parting comment, "Don't think this is the last you'll see of me, Romeo. I'm not finished with you yet!"

"After Hank the Cow Dog, of course," she stated with an incredulous look as she handed Hank to Mr. Jaguar. "You don't know who Hank the Cow Dog is? There's a whole bunch of books about him. They are my favorites. I have read all of the books, haven't you?"

She went on without waiting for his response. "And sometimes Mommy plays CDs of the stories when we are riding in the car. I really like Hank, but Drover, his dog friend, is really funny too. Have you ever read about Hank and Drover? In fact, that other rat over there has a short tail just like Drover does," she said, pointing to X-Con.

Interrupting herself, she stopped talking to Mr. Jaguar, turned toward her mother, and spoke in an urgent, very high-pitched voice, "Mommy, we have to get that rat over there too. Hank and Drover must be together."

The mother hesitated and then, unable to say no to her children, asked if they could hold *Drover* as well.

"Sure," said Mr. Jaguar, who was always more than willing to do anything that would help find homes for his animals. "Here he is. Who wants to hold him?"

"I do!" both children said at once, and they began fighting to get the rat. Mr. Jaguar did not want to be caught in the middle of a family dispute, so he handed X-Con to the mom.

"Well, he is pretty cute. Why not? We'll take all three," she said with a smile. The mom actually seemed pleased with her decision.

The little girl looked at Mr. Jaguar, and because she was not one to let things go, asked again, "Have you ever read *Hank the Cow Dog*?"

"Matter of fact, I have. Read it to my kids, but that was a long time ago," Mr. Jaguar responded as he took X-Con from the mom and put him in the CarPet World To-Go box with the other two rats. He then handed the small box with the CarPet World logo printed on its side back to her as the little girl continued talking to him.

"Well, I named my rat after Hank because he seems really smart just like Hank," she stated as though she was commenting on the obvious.

"Cool," acknowledged Mr. Jaguar as he motioned for them to

follow him over to the cages. "Do you want to start out with separate cages or put them all together right away?"

"Well, what—" The mother's voice faded as they moved out of my listening range.

I stared after them in amazement. ER 002, aka Ratzilla, my nemesis, was going to live with a family with his two cronies, Sketch and X-Con, now known as Hank and Drover. Something about the three of them leaving together made me feel uneasy. So did ER 002's parting comment about finding me again in the future. I hoped that little boy and little girl would have a better relationship with them than I did.

Hoover sauntered over to me with a big smile on his face. "Isn't that great? ER 002 is gone! Ratzilla! What a perfect name for him. That little human is going to keep him really busy."

"Yeah, I hope you're right," I said. Then I grabbed some rat food and munched it without really tasting it.

My eye was throbbing.

"I'm feeling anxious, Hoover. This eye doesn't seem to be getting much better, and it really hurts."

Hoover, pretending he was Mr. Jaguar, came over and inspected my eye. He lowered his voice, imitating the big man, "Hmm, well, ER 22, that eye looks a little sticky, but we'll keep you in with the exotic rats a little longer. I think it will be just fine in a few days!"

I laughed. Hoover always made me feel better.

Our conversation was interrupted when the real Mr. Jaguar returned from the cage area. Cat was walking by his side, her braid swinging back and forth as usual. "I've inspected all the new rats, and they are ready to go," she informed him.

"Okay then," said Mr. Jaguar. "Let's put them in the exotic rat bin with the others. How many are there?"

"There are six boys and four girls," Cat said, peering into Willow's bin and then glancing into ours. "Do you think we should move ER 22 out before we put the new ones in?"

I froze. My stomach flip-flopped when I heard those words. How could Cat, my good friend, even suggest this?

Wait a minute. I had only been on antibiotics for two days. This was not fair! I felt sick as I listened to them talk. It was obvious that they had already discussed my fate.

"Yeah, good idea. Why don't you do that while I get the new rats from the back?" Mr. Jaguar replied while he walked toward the door to the back room.

I glanced at Hoover with my one good eye, and I saw a panicked look on his face. His ran over to me, whiskers twitching so rapidly they looked like a propeller on a plane, and then Velcroed himself to my side.

"Right," acknowledged Cat as she turned to focus on me. "How are you doing, little guy? We've got to move you to a new home."

My heart sank. That could only mean one thing. After she gently moved Hoover aside, she picked me up and looked at my eye. Then she stroked my fur while she closed the lid on the exotic rat bin.

I stared at Hoover, suddenly feeling dizzy and light-headed. My stomach hurt. He was staring back at me, his face looking whiter than usual. The timing of the move was so unexpected that there was not even a chance for us to say good-bye. We were shocked, sad, and scared.

Before I knew it, I was carefully placed into a bin full of about fifteen other rats, none of whom looked particularly happy or healthy.

The move was not very far since the feeder bins were located just below the exotic rat bins. I was still within squeaking distance of Hoover, but it would be somewhat of a challenge to get each other's attention.

"We're giving you a new name now," Cat said in a cheery voice so as not to alarm me as she wrote something on a clipboard hanging next to my new home. "It is FR 22."

The pain in my stomach felt much worse now, and my head began to throb. All the air hissed out of my lungs as the reality of what was happening to me sank in.

FR meant one thing and one thing only in the rat world—feeder rat. I was now an inmate on Death Row.

Nicodemus (also known as Petey) is lowered into the feeder bin.

Chapter Eight

The United Federation of Feeder Rats

"HEY, NICODEMUS! NICODEMUS!" SQUEAKED a scruffy voice.

I whirled around with a start, scanning with my one good eye to see who could possibly have called to me. How could any of the feeder rats know my given name?

There actually is a rather interesting story about my name. Evidently Mama and Pops had quite a heated discussion concerning the names for their newborn children.

Mama's name was Iris. Because she placed a high premium on maintaining traditions, Mama wanted to name us after flowers or plants in keeping with a longtime family practice.

Pops had a very different idea. Pop's name was Whiskers. Always somewhat embarrassed by what he considered to be a rather commonplace rat name, he wanted something better for his children and became quite passionate about naming us after famous literary rats. Because he had listened to many children's books read aloud in the breeders' home and had read a number of them himself, Pops had compiled quite a list of potential names.

However, since both of my parents were rather strong-willed rats, neither was willing to give in to the other on this issue. Threatened with the prospect of having a litter of nameless babies as the only possible resolution of this impasse, they finally compromised. Thus, Mama named all the girls after flowers, and Pops named all the boys after literary figures.

How ironic that my namesake is Nicodemus, the rat with the eye patch from *The Rats of NIMH*. Little did Pops know that I, too, would be a one-eyed rat. What an odd coincidence.

"Nicodemus! Nicodemus!" The strangely familiar scruffy voice called me again. "Is that really you ... you?"

There was only one rat I had ever known who had the annoying habit of repeating the last word he said when he finished speaking.

"Harry, you old son of a gun! What are you doing here?" I exclaimed, looking as startled as if I had just seen a ghost.

Harry and I grew up together, but he was the last rat I ever expected to see at CarPet World, let alone in the feeder bin. Although he was from a different litter and was a little older than I was, our families used to play together. Harry was the king of hide-and-squeak, but I always outshined him at tail tag.

I remember the day he left the breeder's home. It was the first time I was old enough to be aware of what was happening when a group of rats left. He waved good-bye to me as Mrs. Hamsterford ushered him and his siblings out. I remember feeling really sad when Pops said I would never see him again.

"Oh, it's where they brought my whole family when we arrived here at CarPet World. Don't think we were handsome enough to go in the exotic rat bin ... bin," he said and laughed, his beady black eyes sparkling.

Harry, a black hooded rat, had always been one to tease and joke around. "But what about you? I heard that all of your family was up in the beauty bins ... bins." Must be what the feeder rats call the exotic rat bins.

"Well, it's a long story, Harry, but the bottom line—" my explanation was interrupted by his exclamation.

"Hey, Nicodemus, what in the Sam Hill did you do to your eye ...

eye?" Harry's black face was about one half of an inch away from mine as he leaned forward for a closer look.

"Calm down, Harry," I stated emphatically. I backed away a little because I started to feel bothered by this intrusive fellow. "I was just getting to that. Be patient, and you will hear the whole story."

Harry smiled and put his front paw on my shoulder.

"No problem, Nicodemus ... Nicodemus. I'm just excited to see you ... you."

The hint of irritation in my voice quickly evaporated as I realized how truly happy Harry was to be reunited with me.

I explained the series of events that led to my eye being scratched in the fight with ER 002. I embellished a bit as I described the actual fight scene, and I told him about the various techniques Hoover and I had tried to make it better.

"That stinks ... stinks!" Harry commented, speaking with a mixture of outrage and compassion in his tone. "But I don't get how you ended up here ... here."

"Well, we had an inspection yesterday." I paused, momentarily distracted, as I glanced around the feeder bin, checking out my new home.

The feeder bin was bare in comparison to the exotic rat bin. There were about fifteen or twenty rats lying in a heap on the other side of the bin, cushioned by a thin layer of shredded wood shavings. The sleeping dome looked like an old hunk of Swiss cheese. It was so chewed and dilapidated.

My voice shook a bit as I continued, betraying my apprehensiveness about being here. "Mr. Jaguar took one look at my bad eye and shipped me out of the exotic rat bin and into this one, making room for some *more desirable* young rats."

"Oh, so he sent you down to us because you weren't so perfect anymore ... anymore?" he teased in his cynical way as he twisted his head so that he could wash his back.

"Well, you could say that," I said and then hesitated.

This was awkward. I tried to refocus the conversation. "What's life like here, my friend? Do you have any good buddies?" I queried, deliberately changing the subject.

An unexpected reunion between old friends.

I learned a long time ago that sarcastic humor often contained a significant amount of truth, and I did not want to encourage discussion of a potentially sensitive issue at this time.

I could not blame Harry for being bitter. I quickly learned that living on Death Row had that effect on rats. Most of the rats here were either depressed or angry. Only a few seemed at peace. I found out later that those were the ones with a strong faith. I hoped to fall into the latter category since I had always believed in God.

Pops used to say, "Kids, you've had a good life so far, but it won't always be that way. Hard times come to all of us. But never forget that God will be with you no matter how tough things get and will walk with you through even the roughest situations."

There was no doubt about it. Moving into the feeder bin was the most difficult challenge of my life so far, exactly the kind of situation he was talking about. It was hard to hold on to my faith and believe there even was a god under these circumstances, but I did.

Finding meaning in this suffering was going to be a challenge for me, but the alternative of becoming angry or bitter was, well, to be blunt about it, not what I wanted for my last days.

From the moment I arrived at the feeder bin, Harry stuck by my side like glue, reminding me of Hoover Velcroing himself to me to hide my bad eye. Despite his irritating pattern of incessant speech, he was a good companion. Harry told me everything about life as a feeder rat. He explained to me that there were four very difficult challenges the feeder rats had to face.

The first hard thing was when a human came and *adopted* one of us. Harry was particularly sensitive to this issue. All of his brothers and sisters had already been adopted. Every feeder rat knew that *adopted* was the code word for "being fed to a snake." Needless to say, there was a very different feeling down here in the feeder bins when a rat was adopted than there was when a rat was adopted from the *beauty bins*.

I was struck by the contrast. It was like night and day. Up there we were thrilled when people came to look at us, vying for the attention of the human peering into the bin. Sure, we played hard to get with Mr.

Jaguar, but that was just for our amusement. We really did want to become pets. Consequently, when a human came to CarPet World and chose one of us to take home, we felt joyful and happy for our friend or sibling, knowing that he or she would now have the opportunity to live with a nice family. We even felt a little envious.

Here, it was the opposite. When a human approached the feeder bin, all the feeder rats tried to hide, piling on top of one another, hoping the humans would not see us, holding our breath, waiting for a death sentence. It was so depressing when one of us left because we knew that the chances of surviving in a battle with a snake were very slim. There had only been one—Sugar.

After the rat was gone, there was the guilt—the guilt for feeling relieved, relieved that the snake owner had chosen that rat and not me. It was awful.

The second hard thing was the crowded conditions. There must have been fifteen of us in that jam-packed bin, all fighting for our lean rations and all sleeping on top of one another. Even the water ran out too fast. The little metal ball in the water bottle would often rattle around loudly, the bottle empty before every rat had had a chance to drink.

The third hard thing was the food. We were given lower-quality rat food than the exotics since our longevity and health were not of primary concern. Fortunately we were hungry enough that anything tasted good. Just like water tastes like the best drink in the world when one is really thirsty, bland food tastes as good as cheddar cheese if a rat is hungry enough. I was almost starving all the time, so those rat blocks that I used to complain about because they tasted like a mixture of cardboard and wood chips seemed as good as one of my coveted, prized yogurt drops.

The fourth hard thing was the sickness. Many of the rats in the feeder bins were sneezing or injured. Rats are highly susceptible to respiratory viruses that spread quickly from one rat to another through direct contact or the air, especially when conditions are crowded. There are two viruses that are particularly harmful to rats—Sendai, causing sneezing and stuffiness, and SDA, infecting our salivary glands. In addition, there is a bacterium we dread called myco, short for *mycoplasma pulmonis*. I learned about myco when I was a baby. It causes a chronic respiratory condition that makes us sluggish and weak, and it also shortens our life spans. Mama told us about it.

"Children," Mama spoke to us in her soft, gentle voice. We were gathered around her, more interested in finding a spot to nurse than to listen to words of wisdom. She knew that, but continued hoping we could nurse and listen at the same time.

"There is an awful disease that most of us have. Unfortunately, mothers pass it to their babies a few days after birth." Her voice began to shake a little. "I know that I have it because I had a rough bout a few months ago. Our breeder gave me some medicine, and I am fine now. But because of that, I am sure you all have it as well. I am so sorry."

Templeton stopped nursing and stuck up his head. "Mama, does that mean we are going to die?"

Sensitivity was not Templeton's strong suit.

Mama smiled and then licked Templeton's fur. She laughed a little to cover the emotion her son's question evoked. I loved it when she laughed because her laugh sounded like the tinkling of bells.

"We are all going to die, Templeton. We simply try to delay that day as long as possible. Many of the rats in our family live very long lives. Remember Grandma Rose? She lived for more than three years."

"But what about this disease, Mama?" chimed in Rose, almost on cue when Mama mentioned her namesake. Mama licked the milk from Rose's face before replying.

"Well, all rats seem to have it, but not all of us show symptoms of it. Many of us only have problems from it when we are very old rats. Some of us have symptoms on and off yet still live fairly long lives. Others carry the disease but are lucky enough to never have any health issues from it at all." Mama moved forward a little, pulling those of us who had latched on with her as she moved toward the food dish.

"Are *you* going to be okay, Mama?" Peony's tiny voice sounded very worried. "I mean, you aren't going to die now, are you?"

"Oh, don't worry about me, sweetheart," Mama said, riffling through the food in the dish, looking for a particularly tasty morsel.

She took a bite of a sunflower seed and then continued, "Peony, I am a strong rat, and I feel fine. Fortunately humans have medicines that help us when we are sick, so even if the disease is not cured, we can feel really good and live a long time." She gave Peony a few reassuring licks, and Peony went back to nursing.

I was thinking about that conversation with my mother as I listened to the perpetual sneezing in the feeder bin. Her words came back to me, "As you can see, the most common maladies from which we rats suffer are ones that affect our respiratory tract, so sneezing is a common symptom. If a lung infection develops and is not treated, we can become very sick and die."

The crowded conditions, perpetual hunger, and low quality of food created a perfect breeding ground for grumpy, irritable rats. It was quite simple. The crankier we became, the more we fought, biting one another out of sheer frustration.

Because puncture wounds from teeth often do not bleed very much, it could be days before a caregiver noticed our injuries. Even if our injuries were noticed, we were not given antibiotics. There was no point. We were snake food.

Consequently some of the feeder rats had wounds that became severely infected, and a few had hard, raised yellowish bumps on their bodies from untreated abscesses. I had personal experience with the harsh reality of minimal medical care. After I moved to the feeder bin, I was no longer given medicine for my eye.

CarPet World was a good pet store, but it was also a business. The bottom line was that Mr. van Goat simply did not make room in his budget for the care of sick or injured feeder rats.

From a business perspective, this made sense. From a rat's perspective, this was unacceptable.

It was hard for me to imagine that the living conditions in the feeder bins could have been worse before I arrived, but Harry assured me that circumstances had actually improved significantly over the past few months. "Nicodemus, we had to do something. We were all so depressed and hopeless that life was unbearable. It was actually FR 89 who started the union ... union." Harry began the historical account in his unique style of speaking.

I stared at him with an awkward, lopsided gaze, my good eye widening, my bad eye staying stuck at half-mast as I realized that I knew FR 89. "You mean Sugar?" I asked incredulously.

"Yeah, Sugar. He is quite famous and is a hero in the feeder bins. We call him The-Rat-That-Came-Back. He is the only rat we know of who left the feeder bins and came back alive ... alive."

Harry spoke quietly in a tone reflecting a mixture of awe and reverence for Sugar's accomplishment. He paused and gazed upward with a dazed look in his black eyes. If he had been wearing a hat, he would have taken it off and placed it over his chest in a gesture of utmost respect.

"Yeah," I agreed emphatically as I recalled Sugar's account of his encounter with Jimmy, the snake. "Sugar is our hero, don't you think?" I continued without waiting for his response. "Tell me what he did."

Harry cleared his throat and then began to speak. "Well, he gathered us together one day and said, 'Fellow rats, we are going to organize! The conditions in this bin are appalling, and we need to do something about them. So we are going to unite to protect our rights and let the management know when we are being treated unfairly.'

"He must have noticed the blank look on some of our faces, so he spoke again, clarifying his last statement ... statement." Harry paused for a moment and then continued, quoting Sugar so effectively that I felt like I was actually present at that historic organizational meeting.

"'The management, by the way, is Mr. Jaguar, Cat, and the other caretakers.' Then he paused and moved his arm in a sweeping motion as though he were including all of us. 'We are the oppressed. So we are going to come together and form a union. It will have a powerful name, the United Federation of Feeder Rats; otherwise known as the UFFR.'

"We looked at one another, not quite sure what this meant. A twittering sound could be heard as we speculated among ourselves

Sugar rallies the members of the United Federation of Feeder Rats.

how this might change our lives. Sugar held up his paw, and we immediately became silent again, not wanting to miss one single word ... word.

"'There will be amazing benefits to each of you when you become a member of the UFFR! Your life will never be the same!' Sugar explained with great enthusiasm.

"The excitement in his voice spread throughout the room like a wildfire. 'When you first join, you will receive a red union card that looks like this.' Sugar turned to his left and picked up something from the floor that turned out to be a small piece of irregularly shaped red cardboard with edges that were ragged, obviously chewed by a rat.

"Sugar paraded back and forth in front of us, holding the red scrap in his mouth. He looked exactly like a cat who has just captured a bird, or worse. Our heads moved to the right and then to the left as he moved in front of us. Sugar stopped moving, looked down and then carefully placed the union card on top of the bedding as gently as if he were lowering a soap bubble onto a surface without breaking it.

"Raising his head and facing us again, he continued. 'Once you join the UFFR, you keep your membership current by paying your union dues, two bites of food each night.'

"'Excuse me, Sugar,' shouted a rat in a loud voice that interrupted Sugar's presentation.

"I turned to see Big Tommy, a dumbo fawn buck known for his bossiness, standing up, his guard hairs bristling and his tail twitching. 'How in the world do you expect us to pay dues? We have nothing! I think that is ridiculous!' A flurry of yeahs followed his comments ... comments." Harry paused again for a minute, took a drink of water, and then continued on once more.

"'Hold on, Big Tommy.' Sugar's voice was calm. 'Let me explain how it will work. Each rat needs to save two bites of food each night and put them over here in the corner.'

"Sugar gestured toward the far corner of the bin. It looked like he had already cleared out a space. 'This will accomplish two things. First you will have a special feast every Wednesday, the night before bin-cleaning day, when we bring out the food we have squirreled away after the store closes and eat it. But there is a second reason. We want more food, so we need to make it look like we don't have enough. Paying the dues will help our cause because it will look as though we are going through our food faster. My hope is that they will feed us more food more often.'

"Sugar ended with a satisfied grin on his face, obviously pleased with his plans. Big Tommy's guard hairs were relaxing. He seemed mollified, so he sat down to pay attention once again.

"We listened very carefully, hanging on to every word that Sugar spoke. As we really started to understand his ideas, a glimmer of hope slowly spread from rat to rat ... rat."

Harry paused, a faraway look in his eyes as he relived what happened that day. After he twisted his neck to wash the fur just above his left hip, my friend continued with the story. "You know, Nicodemus, the way the hope spread was like magic. It reminded me of the way water dripping from a leaky water bottle slowly spreads from the spot where it lands until all of our bedding is soaked ... soaked."

I stared at Harry for a moment, taking in all that he said. It was definitely an interesting image that he used to illustrate his point.

"Then," Harry went on, "Sugar explained that he was the president of the union and he wanted me to be the shop steward. I couldn't believe it. Sugar was actually asking me to do something to help him ... him. I was so pleased at being offered a position that sounded so important that I accepted without hesitation. Then I thought about it for a second and asked, 'Uh, Sugar, what exactly is a shop steward ... steward?'

"'It is a very important position, Harry,' Sugar explained to me, an uncharacteristically serious expression on his face. 'You will be the most important rat in the union ... other than myself, of course.'

"He laughed uncomfortably, placed his right paw on my back, cleared his throat, and then turned to address the uplifted faces of mesmerized feeder rats.

"'If any of you rats are upset about something in the feeder bin, you are to go to Harry here and tell him what is wrong.' Sugar patted me on the back so hard that I almost lost my balance. 'This is called filing a grievance. It is Harry's job to present the grievance to me. Then I will present it to the management. Any questions so far?' A large black hooded rat in the back raised his paw. Sugar acknowledged him, 'What's up, Papa Joe?'

"Standing on his hind legs, his front paws outstretched for emphasis, Papa Joe stated gruffly, 'I am upset about the food we eat. I think we should have better food.'

"'Yeah!' The congregation of feeder rats nodded their heads in agreement with what Papa Joe had said.

"'Perfect example of a grievance, Papa Joe,' Sugar affirmed, looking intently in Papa Joe's direction. 'What you need to do now is talk to Harry about it after this meeting since Harry is the shop steward. His job is to listen to the grievances. Then he will talk to me about it and I will make sure we get some action.'

"Papa Joe nodded, glanced in my direction, and then sat down, a look of satisfaction on his face.

"Sugar scanned the faces of the other rats in the bin and then asked, 'Any other questions?'

"An agouti rat named King Pin cleared his throat as his paw shot into the air. Sugar recognized him, 'Yeah, King Pin?'

King Pin's voice was low, gravelly, and strong. 'This is all well and good, Sugar, but how exactly do you propose to *present* our grievances to the management? I mean, you speak our language, and the humans speak English. They aren't going to have any idea what you're talking about.'

"Another chorus of yeahs arose from the newly formed union's potential members.

"'Good point, King Pin,' Sugar replied. He stared at the bedding on the floor so long that I thought he must have been watching a bug walk across the bottom of the bin. 'I have thought about that problem as well, and frankly I haven't figured out what to do about that yet. I give you my word that I will get back to you on that at the next union meeting.'

"King Pin seemed satisfied with the answer, so he settled back down to listen to the issues other rats raised. The meeting went on like this for a long time ...time.

"After the meeting ended, Papa Joe came over and talked to me. I thought it a little silly since I had already heard about the food issue at the meeting, but I did my job and listened to what he had to say. I repeated his concerns to Sugar. Since I had accepted the position of shop steward, I was going to be the best I could be ... be.

"Sugar said, 'I'll talk to the management about it.' That was good enough for me, so I passed the message on to Papa Joe. He nodded his head and seemed satisfied ... satisfied.

"A few days later, Sugar strode over to me, an intent look on his face, and stated matter-of-factly, 'Harry, we need to have a rally. Help me get all the union members assembled for a meeting.'

"I had no clue what it meant to have a rally, but I did what I was told. 'Right ... right,' I said and went off to round up the troops.

"All the feeder rats came to the corner of the bin where we held our meetings. They filed in behind me and positioned themselves in rows as if in church.

"Once assembled, we gazed expectantly at Sugar, waiting to hear what he had to say. The big white rat stood in front, and silence fell over the rat assembly, the kind of silence where you could hear a pin drop. Except for an occasional cough, no one made a sound.

"A few moments later, Sugar announced in a tremulous voice, 'Rats of the United Federation of Feeder Rats, we are going on strike!'"

"We looked at one another to see if anyone had any idea what this meant, but all of us had blank stares on our faces once again. You see, we had never been on strike before.

"Our whispers began to crescendo to a loud murmur as we tried to figure out what this meant ... meant.

"Sugar held up his paw for silence and then continued, his voice quieter now, 'I tried to communicate with the management about our first grievance, you know, the one brought up by Papa Joe about the quality of the food. I was unsuccessful. Humans don't understand rat talk. *So we need to strike!*'

"He shouted these last five words so loudly that all of us flattened our ears. It was as though his words had blown them over. Not knowing what else to do, we stared at him and waited.

"Sugar toned it down a little, but he continued to speak passionately. 'This means that during the hours that CarPet World is open, we lay around and look absolutely miserable, so miserable that not even a snake owner would want to buy us. We do this until the conditions improve. This is called collective bargaining.'

"We looked at each other again, somewhat mystified by this new idea. Another louder murmur ensued until Papa Joe, our self-appointed advocate, raised his right paw.

"When Sugar nodded in his direction, he spoke in his gruff voice, putting words to what we were all thinking, 'Uh, Sugar, I am confused. It seems to me that it would be a *good* thing if a snake owner did not want to buy us. If we were able to appear so undesirable that we just stayed here, wouldn't that be better than getting higher-quality food?'"

"A chorus of yeahs from the union members followed Papa Joe's question ... question."

Harry stopped talking for a moment to take a drink of water, then went on with the story. "Sugar nodded, indicating that he understood Papa Joe's point. He spoke confidently, a reassuring tone to his voice, 'I know what you mean, Papa Joe. It would seem that appearing so undesirable that even a snake owner would not want us would work to our advantage, but just the contrary is true. If we look miserable for too long, I believe the management will replace us. Dispose of us. You know what I mean? Do you understand what *chew-thin-ice* means?

"Papa Joe stared blankly, 'I have heard Mr. Jaguar talk about it. He says he will take a rat away to *chew-thin-ice it*. Then, the rat never comes back. I never got what he meant. How could chewing some ice hurt a rat?'

"Sugar was revving up again. His speech became more rapid and raucous. He was passionate about this and his emotion electrified the room. "Papa Joe", he paused to catch his breath, "*Chew-thin-ice* means kill!

"There was a collective gasp and twittering as the feeder rats inhaled this reality. Sugar raised his hand and it was quiet again. Papa Joe looked at Sugar and nodded. He understood.

"Then Sugar spoke again, 'At least when we are taken home as snake food, there is an outside chance we can fight back and escape. We really do not know how many of our buddies have actually done that, do we? So I think it is the lesser of two evils.'

"Papa Joe nodded his head again, acknowledging Sugar's point. The union members exchanged glances, and once more a loud murmur arose.

"We quieted when another rat, Big Tommy, shot his paw into the air. 'What happens if some rats do not want to strike?' he asked loudly, his voice hoarse from a throat infection.

"Another chorus of yeahs, this time a little louder, followed his question. Many of our heads were bobbing up and down, indicating that we were wondering the same thing.

"'Ah, another good question, Big Tommy,' Sugar said with more patience than I would have had ... had. 'If a rat decides he does not want to strike and refuses to act lethargic like the rest of us, well, that rat will be called a scab and will lose the respect of the other rats in the UFFR. He could ruin it for the members because the management might not think there is a problem that needs to be addressed.

"Sugar hesitated while he was washing his tail and then went on, 'Or worse yet, the management might decide to keep the scabs and make those of us who look weak and starved *chew-thin-ice*. This is why it is so important that we stay unified.'

"There was a low rumbling sound as we discussed this information amongst ourselves. We were beginning to understand how the UFFR operated and to see that it really could help us ... us."

Harry stopped to wash his face, giving me a short intermission from the recounting of the story. I appreciated the break because it gave me time to digest what he told me so far.

"Harry," I began after I washed my face as well. "I had no idea there was such a thing as the United Federation of Feeder Rats. Up in the exotic rats bin, we didn't have a union."

"No, probably don't need one ... one," Harry replied between bites of a partially eaten rat block that he had found on the floor.

"Unions are needed the most when conditions get bad. I've heard that the rats in the beauty bins are treated like royalty ... royalty."

"I guess you're right, Harry. I see what you mean." I thought back to my days as an exotic rat. It seemed like such a long time ago now, but in reality, it had only been a very short time since I had been forced out. There was no doubt that the conditions in the exotic rat bin were significantly better than the ones down here.

When I realized that my comment had sidetracked Harry, I brought our discussion back to the history of the UFFR. By now I was truly interested to know what happened next.

"So, Harry, what happened next? Did you guys actually strike?"

"Well, Nicodemus ... Nicodemus," Harry replied after a big yawn. "It turns out that we did strike. We sprawled on the floor of the bin, barely lifting our heads when a human approached. Our acting must have been convincing since it was not long before Cat noticed that we looked sick ... sick."

"Yeah, Cat is a really nice human. I'm not surprised she was the one who cared," I commented, remembering all the corn wheels she had given us.

"Yeah," Harry agreed. "We heard her tell Mr. Jaguar that he needed to feed us more and give us some vitamins, whatever they are, or risk all of us dying. He agreed, and since then, we've had a lot better food and more of it. The UFFR is now working on figuring out a way to improve our crowded living conditions ... conditions."

Harry stopped talking abruptly and stared at me, his eyes wide as though he was seeing me for the first time.

"Oh, my gosh, Nicodemus, that reminds me ... me!" Harry exclaimed, his whiskers twitching agitatedly as he spoke.

"What reminds you, Harry?" I asked, mystified by this sudden change in his demeanor.

"Well, talking about the UFFR reminds me, of course. I almost forgot to tell you the most important thing of all. You need to join the union! I *am* the shop steward after all, and I forgot to sign you up! I can't believe it ... it." Harry shook his head, clearly disappointed in himself.

He sighed and then went on, "Every rat that moves into the feeder bins is required to be a member, so we need to get you registered! Since Sugar is now in the exotic rat bins, a huge blow to the union leadership by the way, Papa Joe has become the new president. Let's go talk to him about registering you right now and getting you a union card … card."

I followed Harry. He was moving as fast as he could as he snaked his way through the crowd of feeder rats in our bin in search of Papa Joe.

That night, I joined the UFFR. I was skeptical about the union's effectiveness, but even if it accomplished nothing else, the UFFR seemed to be a morale booster for the feeder rats. Belonging to a group that was united behind a common cause gave us hope. Focusing on making our living conditions better now and for the next generation of feeder rats lifted our despair a little by adding some meaning to our suffering.

The daily union meetings gave us something to look forward to. In addition, the activities of the United Federation of Feeder Rats distracted us enough that some days we actually forgot about the fact that our days were numbered and that the reality for every single one of us was that we were living on Death Row.

Chapter Nine

Going Home

ALTHOUGH HARRY COULD BE UNBELIEVABLY annoying, I was grateful to have a companion and friend with me in the feeder bin. We passed the time by reminiscing about our childhood, trading stories about the good ole days in the rattery.

At the same time, I really missed Hoover. He and I had a strong friendship, the kind of relationship that develops from the intertwining of a series of shared, highly emotional experiences, good and bad. It was as though we were veterans who had fought in the same squadron in the war, forever linked by traumatic bonding. I felt intensely sad whenever I thought about how our paths had abruptly diverged.

All of the rats, whether in the exotic rat bins or the feeder bins, felt frustrated by the fact that we had no control over our fates. The humans, or the management as Sugar called them, managed our lives for us. Dwelling on this aspect of our existence was definitely not helpful, so I tried to distract myself. One of my favorite ways to do this was by looking around the pet store.

As I stared out of the feeder bin and scanned the vast array of cars in the center of CarPet World with my one good eye, I found myself daydreaming about Hoover's future. I could see it as clearly as if I were a fortune-teller gazing into a crystal ball.

Hoover would be adopted. One day a child who was excited to

have a pet rat to take home would come into the pet store, pick up Hoover, fall in love with his dumbo ears and silly grin, and decide to take my buddy home. Watching from the feeder bin, I would smile, wave good-bye, and wish him a great future.

Well, I would like to think I could do that, but I was not that noble. Yes, I would be genuinely happy for him, and I would wave good-bye; however, I knew that I was self-focused enough that despite my best efforts to the contrary, I would be envious.

Still gazing into the imaginary crystal ball, I saw Hoover's image blur and then fade away into the swirling fog inside the ball to be replaced by a blurry image of my odd-looking face with the half-open eye, the details sharpening as I stared.

I was sitting in my bin at CarPet World when a young man came in and bought me, took me home, and then tossed me in a cage with a huge snake. The snake, sensing the heat from my body, prepared to strike.

As I watched, horrified, the image in the crystal ball gradually disappeared into the swirling fog. I sat up as straight as a board and then stared into space.

Suddenly the reality of my situation came crashing down upon me. My life was soon to be over, my light snuffed out by a cold, scaly reptile. The more I thought about what was going to happen to me, the worse I felt.

All my hopes and dreams had been dashed by one swipe of ER 002's paw. No Best of Show ribbon. No mate. I would not even have kittens that would carry on my family's lines.

The despair I felt was so intense I did not think I could survive it. I wanted to stare death in the face and laugh at it, but instead I slowly walked over to the corner of the bin, curled up into a ball, and began to cry. Tears streamed down my face for a long time, forming a tiny pool of salty water in the coarse bedding of the feeder bin.

Totally exhausted, I finally fell asleep.

"Are you three back again already?" Mr. Jaguar's booming voice woke me out of my restless sleep. I looked to see to whom he was speaking. It was the woman with the fawn velveteen hair who had been in a few days ago. Her two daughters were with her.

They did not interest me, so I closed my eye, intending to go back to sleep, but their conversation caught my attention. My ears rotated to better catch the sounds.

"He died?" Mr. Jaguar exclaimed, shocked by the news, the jaguar hanging around his neck sparkling as if it were blinking its eyes in disbelief.

By this time I was wide awake. Fritz was dead. He was only a little older than I was.

"My mom found him lying in his cage this morning," said Sarah in a very sad voice, avoiding Mr. Jaguar's gaze by looking at the floor, feeling uncharacteristically shy. "We buried him today. We had his funeral before school."

I saw a tear running down her cheek. She was really feeling sad that the little guy died. Wow. I wondered what it would be like to have a human care enough about me to cry when I died. I sighed, painfully aware that I would never know.

"I'm real sorry, kid," Mr. Jaguar said, his voice sounding empathetic as he shook his head. "What a shame. We try to keep all our rats here at CarPet World healthy and strong, but every once in a while, something like that happens. Why don't you pick out another one? What kind do you want?"

Mr. Jaguar's lackadaisical attitude bothered me. Were we really that easy to replace? She might as well have said she broke a food dish and needed to buy a new one or complained that the water bottle she bought did not work and wanted to replace it. I am sure Mr. Jaguar would have grabbed another one off the shelf, calmly saying, "Here take this one instead," as he handed it to her and sent her on her way.

I felt angry and cynical. Was I becoming bitter?

"A black hooded boy just like Raspberry," Sarah stated, her brownish eyes scanning the rat bins, looking for a rat that looked like Fritz. She paused and then moved toward the object of her gaze. Instead of walking to the exotic rat bin, she made a beeline for the feeder bin where I was sulking.

After she peered inside, she asked, "Could I please see that one?"

She was pointing to Harry. He glanced at me with disbelief, his mouth gaping open, a confused expression spreading across his black face.

"Okay, little lady. I'll show him to you, but our best rats are up here in the exotic rat bin. How about one of these instead?"

I felt a sharp twinge of despair mixed with fury when I realized that Mr. Jaguar was pointing to my old home. There really was a class system at CarPet World.

"No, I definitely want to see this one first," she said, gesturing toward Harry one more time. Harry turned toward me, his eyes filled with fear, and whispered, "Hey, Nicodemus, do you think she has a snake ... snake? Maybe that's what happened to Fritz ... Fritz."

"No, I don't think she knows you're a feeder rat or even knows what a feeder rat is. I just can't see her being the type to have a pet snake," I replied in a hushed voice. I started vigorously washing my fur to distract myself from my anxiety about what was going to happen next.

Mr. Jaguar opened the top of the feeder bin, and the members of the UFFR began scurrying around, confused by the unexpected disturbance. He picked up Harry and handed him to Sarah.

I made my way over to the closest side of the feeder bin and pressed my face against the glass so I could see what would happen next. Harry craned his neck so he was able to look in my direction, and we exchanged a meaningful glance. I gave him a wink with my good eye, the universal code shared by all intelligent species to signal that you wish them good luck.

He squeaked to me, "Nicodemus, are you okay ... okay?"

I nodded affirmative and squeaked back, "Hey, my friend, I hope you go home with this family. They seem really nice."

"But what about you ... you?" he queried as he tried to maintain his balance after the girl placed him on her shoulder. I laughed as he slid down her sleeve and then scrambled back up. He was about as stable as a rat running across a high telephone wire for the first time.

"Don't worry about me, Harry. I'll be fine," I lied, trying to hide my true feelings with a reassuring smile. I knew I was not a very good liar, so I quickly changed the subject. "Be sure to be on your best behavior, and whatever you do, don't mark her."

"Right ... right," Harry said thoughtfully and nodded, appreciating the reminder.

Male rats often feel the need to mark any new desirable, uncharted territory with a few strategically placed drops of urine. Through observation we have also learned that this behavior does not endear us to humans, so a little self-control greatly increases the likelihood of adoption.

I was so focused on Harry that I was startled to feel my guard hairs stiffen, an involuntary response rats have when we sense another animal staring at us. This protective response serves us well when we live in the wild and have to be aware of the presence of predators before we can actually see them. I slowly turned my head and scanned my environment. My one good dark ruby eye found the source of my uneasiness. The two green eyes of the velveteen adult human were staring at me.

Without breaking her gaze, she spoke in a confident voice, her words so totally unexpected that I thought I was dreaming again, "Mr. Jaguar, could I please hold that cute little beige one? I think he has something wrong with his eye."

I looked behind me to see where she was pointing, but there was no other rat in my vicinity. She was actually pointing at me! Could this really be happening?

Having a human come into the store and ask to hold me was something I had hoped and prayed for when I was in the exotic rat bin, but I dreaded it now. I had hoped and prayed for the exact opposite since I had moved in with the feeder rats. But this human was no snake owner. My heartbeat quickened, betraying my excitement. I had a fish on the line. A real, live human was interested in me.

"Let me see," said Mr. Jaguar, staring at me through the glass with about as much enthusiasm as a rat show judge evaluating a low-scoring, scruffy rat with wrinkly ears and a short, blocky tail.

"Looks like he does. Sometimes these guys get pretty rough and

Karin and Nicodemus (soon to be known as Petey) find each other.

accidentally scratch one another in the eye. You probably don't want him. I don't recommend adopting a rat with a problem. Never goes well. How about looking at one of these exotic rats in the upper bin?" Mr. Jaguar turned and again pointed toward my old homestead, the exotic rat bin.

He was not willing to let that idea go. Oddly enough, the jaguar around his neck did not move with him but continued to face my direction as if it did not agree with its owner.

So much for my chance to go to a new home. I sighed.

"No, there's something about that little beige guy that I like," she insisted firmly.

Her persistence was surprising. Most customers followed Mr. Jaguar's lead. The velveteen's friendly, penetrating green eyes reconnected with my hopeful dark ruby eye.

Suddenly I felt a warm feeling in my heart like the sun was shining inside by chest. It reminded me of the first time I tasted cheese. There was something about this human that I instinctively liked.

Her next words were shocking. "Please take him out so I can hold him."

Mr. Jaguar nodded, shaking his head in disbelief as he acquiesced, the jaguar hanging around his neck swinging back and forth like a pendulum on a grandfather clock. I could have sworn that it winked at me.

"I'll get him out for you. Come over here little fellow," he said to me as his big hand reached down into the bin and ladled me up with the ease of a bulldozer scooping a very light load.

He paused for a moment and held me up so he could look at me more closely. He stared at me for a few seconds, and then a smile spread across his face as he recognized me, "Hey, ER 22. How are you doing, old buddy? Hmm. Seems like that eye hasn't gotten any better. Guess what? Someone who doesn't care that one of your lamps is out wants to meet you."

He chuckled. Mr. Jaguar really was a good guy. It was hard for me to stay mad at him for long.

With the finesse of a waiter presenting a very fancy dessert, Mr.

Jaguar placed me in the smaller hand of the woman with the welcoming green eyes. It felt warm and just the right size for me. I sat there, motionless, too nervous to move.

As she held me close to her body, she immediately started petting the fur on my back and then scratching behind my left ear. This felt surprisingly good, so good that I found myself settling in, feeling safer than I expected. I tried not to enjoy this experience too much. I knew that the chances of my going home with her were about as big as Mr. Jaguar showing up with a full head of hair tomorrow. At the same time, I could not help but feel a little glimmer of hope because of the way she was treating me.

Simultaneously, I heard the other rats in the feeder bin running around. Whenever a rat was taken out of the bin, the rest of us would jockey for a new position in the sleep corner, our name for the little section of the floor where we piled on top of one another.

We had to make a nest with our bodies because the lean ration of litter on the floor of the cage was simply not enough for a nest or to keep us warm. Unlike in the exotic rat bins, the well-chewed sleeping dome was well utilized but not big enough for so many of us.

Despite several strikes, the UFFR had not found a way to convince the management to increase our litter supply or to communicate that we needed improved sleeping conditions.

The sound of a loud, commanding voice abruptly interrupted my thoughts and captured Mr. Jaguar's attention. I knew that voice. It signaled that Joe and Fred were here with a delivery.

"Hey, Jag, where are you?"

The voice came from behind a blue four-runner that obscured its owner.

"Right this way, Joe," yelled Mr. Jaguar, who also recognized the voice before its owner came into view. "What do you guys have for me today?"

"Well, we've got a load of new rats. Look at all these critters—black and gray fuzzy ones," Joe replied, looking over his glasses at the rat kittens with as much pride as if he had fathered them himself.

"Must be velveteens," Mr. Jaguar concluded with the confidence of someone who has been around rats for years. He peered through the white bars of the cage Joe was holding. "Yup. Haven't had any rats like these in a donkey's age!"

"Joe, help!"

The sound of rapid walking punctuated by intermittent shrieks signaled Fred's arrival. When he came into view, it was apparent that the large fuzzy occupant of the cage he was stiffly carrying caused his panic.

I could not help but laugh when I saw Fred's long, tattooed arms extending straight out from his body so that the cage was as far away from him as possible.

"Jag, am I glad to see you! Look what Joe gives me to carry in ... the tarantula! And what does he take? The rats!"

To my surprise, Fred started laughing. His laughter was so contagious that Joe and Mr. Jaguar could not help but join in.

"Here," Fred barked the word as he rapidly handed the cage to Mr. Jaguar. "You take this thing. I about had a heart attack when that big, hairy sucker started moving around in there. I'm sure it was thinking about eating my fingers for lunch. Never did like spiders. Had bad dreams about them when I was a kid."

"Jeez, Fred! Would you grow up? You're not a kid anymore, and we've got work to do!" said Joe, irritation seeping back into his voice. He had been helping Mr. Jaguar get the new rats settled in the back room and was frustrated by Fred's interruption.

"Yeah, well, when you talked me into taking this job doing deliveries for CarPet World, I thought we'd be working for the car division, not the pet division! I pictured myself dropping off new six-speed sports cars, and I'm delivering tarantulas instead! I still haven't told my mother the honest truth about my job. She thinks I'm selling Porsches."

He broke into a deep, contagious laugh again, and I found myself laughing too. It was the first time I had laughed in a long time.

"Well, I did too," said Joe, his good humor returning as he waved good-bye to Mr. Jaguar. "But we got lucky!" Joe gave Fred a hearty pat on the back as he spoke.

"Yeah, right," said Fred, his voice dripping with sarcasm. "Let's see. Which would I rather deliver—a new pickup truck or a new tarantula?"

"Oh, stop your complaining. You're lucky to have a job," retorted Joe, their familiar bickering growing fainter and fainter as they walked away.

During all this time, the velveteen was stroking my fur and talking to me. I liked her voice. The little girl with satin agouti hair called Sarah came over holding Harry so close to her body I did not think anything could separate them.

She declared, "I want this one, Mama. He really likes me. I can tell. I'm going to name him Huckleberry."

Harry, his black eyes sparkling like water glistening in the sun on a summer day, looked like he was about to burst at the seams with excitement.

"Okay, Sweetheart. Let's get him. Maybe we can call him Huckle for short!" replied Karin, studying Harry for a moment. Then in a gesture communicating her approval, she scratched the smooth black fur just behind his ears.

All this time, I was resting on her shoulder, watching what was happening with baited breath. I felt like I was one of the top-ten vocalists on a reality show, waiting to hear if I was going to come back the next week or if I was going home.

Yes, we did watch TV quite a bit at CarPet World. There were monitors all over the store that constantly ran videos about the virtues of owning a pet or the advantages of a particular type of automobile.

After the store closed, the employees immediately switched off the videos and turned on the TV. Sometimes we saw movies, sometimes sitcoms, and occasionally an animal show. Once in a while, the last human to go home would forget to turn the TV off, and it was as though we had our own private movie theater.

The entertainment definitely made the time pass quickly. So I did know what a reality show was and had seen the intensity of anticipation and the agony of disappointment on the human faces. I could really relate to them now. My anticipation was almost unbearable.

The velveteen reached up, lifted me from her shoulder, and then cupped me in her hand so that she could show me to Sarah. "What do you think of this guy?" she asked.

I inhaled sharply.

"Well," Sarah stared at me and then shook her head. "He seems nice, but I want this rat," Sarah replied, holding Harry close to her jacket as if she wanted to ensure no one could take him away.

Harry glanced in my direction, a smug look on his face, his whiskers twittering with amusement. I smirked back at him, sharing in the fun, but I was still anxiously awaiting Karin's decision. I was still holding my breath.

"No, not for you. I was thinking about getting him for me," Karin disclosed in a quiet voice as though she was revealing a secret.

In actuality, this was the first time she had verbalized her desire to have her own pet rat.

"Oh, that would be so fun if you had a rat too," said Claire, the girl with the velveteen agouti hair who had been looking around at the other animals in the small animal section of CarPet World. She had come back just in time to overhear Sarah's comment. I exhaled with relief.

"Mama, are you really going to get a rat? Then we will have three! I like that idea." Claire gazed intently at me, a worried look darkening her face like a shadow darkening a doorway.

"He's really cute, Mama, but is his eye okay?" Claire continued as she turned her head to the side, examining me very carefully.

"I hope so because I really like him. I have had so much fun playing with your rat and Sarah's that I have decided that I would like to have a rat for myself," Karin replied as if she needed to justify the adoption to herself. The girls needed no explanation. She was rehearsing for the moment when she would be explaining her decision to Doug who was not as big of a rat enthusiast as Karin and his two daughters.

She placed me back up on her shoulder again, and I snuggled in, placing my side against her neck. I liked sitting up here. Although many things made me anxious, heights did not. I thoroughly enjoyed viewing the world from a higher elevation than our bin or the ground.

"Are you going to get him, Mama?" Claire asked again as she gazed up at me with her warm brown eyes.

"If Mr. Jaguar says his eye will be okay, I will."

My heart leapt for joy. I think it actually did a somersault in my chest. I could not believe what I was hearing. Was it possible that I would escape my death sentence?

Just then Mr. Jaguar came back, smiling as usual, and asked, "How are you ladies doing?"

The velveteen responded first, "Great, thank you, Mr. Jaguar. I really like this beige rat, but I want your opinion on something. Do you think this little guy's eye is okay?"

"Well," said Mr. Jaguar, picking me up and looking me over, a frown forming between his deep brown eyes as they scanned me up and down like an X-ray machine.

He shook his head. The gold jaguar pendant mimicked his motion, swinging back and forth like a pendulum. I held by breath once more and waited. He continued, his voice uncharacteristically pessimistic. "Hmm, I think it was too damaged for him to ever be able to see out of it again. The thing I'm worried about is that it looks infected. The infection will need to be treated, and that could be expensive." Mr. Jaguar paused a moment, hand on his chin as if he was deep in thought. Then he went on, his voice brighter. "On the other hand, if he lives in a cage with other rats, his cage mates might chew out that eye. They do that kind of thing in the wild, you know," Mr. Jaguar spoke matter-of-factly like one so used to the idiosyncrasies of animal behavior that nothing fazed him.

Karin shuddered and then just stared at the tall, bald man. She was as speechless as a rabbit.

Noticing Karin's look of horror, Mr. Jaguar explained further, attempting to reassure her, "No, it's not a bad thing. It's nature's way. The rats try to take care of each other by getting rid of infection in the only way they can. They can't go to the doctor, you know."

He threw his head back and laughed.

Not knowing what to do with this new piece of information, Karin replied as if she had not heard what Mr. Jaguar said, "I want to adopt both of these rats, the black and white one for Sarah and this beige one for me. I had not planned to adopt two rats, but I love this little guy too much to leave him behind!"

My heart, already beating so fast I was afraid I would die of a heart attack before we even left CarPet World, skipped another beat. This human was saying that about me! This was beyond belief and too good to be true.

I had to bite myself on the tail to make sure that I was awake and that this was really happening. As you know, my dreams are so vivid that sometimes I confuse dreams with reality, so I had to check.

"Ouch!" I squeaked out loud, feeling a twinge of pain that was very real. I was definitely awake!

Something told me to glance up at the exotic rat bins. Hoover was looking right at me, a huge grin on his white face, his broad dumbo ears twitching happily. He winked one of his shiny black eyes while he squeaked good-bye. I extended my paw in a gesture of fond farewell and waved, wishing so much that he was coming with me.

For a moment I felt guilty like I was abandoning ship, leaving my buddy behind to go down with the boat. Then I remembered that Hoover was not a feeder. He had a good chance of going to a nice home too.

Like a slide show on a timer, my feelings kept flipping from one to the next too quickly for me to process any of them. I felt so many things—shock and relief that I was going to be adopted by a human rather than fed to snakes, helplessness and guilt that I could not take my friends from the feeder bin with me and save them from their awful fates.

I was excited to be leaving with Harry while at the same time intensely sad to be leaving Hoover, knowing that the chances of seeing my best friend ever again were about zero.

When Willow was adopted and we were separated, it was really painful, but I had always known that the chances of a boy and girl rat going to the same home were very slim. With Hoover, it was different. I think I had secretly expected that some fun-loving human family would notice how well we got along and want to adopt us together because of that.

My head was spinning. Life had pitched me a curveball, but I somehow managed to hit a home run anyway.

Mr. Jaguar was speaking again. "I'll even give him to you for half price because of his eye," he added in a warm voice as he and the velveteen walked toward the cash register. "Here, hand him to me, and I'll put him in a CarPet World To-Go box for you."

Karin reached under her hair, extricated me from the back of her neck where I was resting comfortably, and handed me to Mr. Jaguar.

I was half price. That was a bitter pill to swallow.

Just before I was lowered into a small container lined with a thick layer of paper shavings, I squeaked a guilt-laden good-bye to the other rats in the feeder bins.

This time I could not shake the feeling that I was abandoning ship. "Don't give up hope, guys. If a miracle can happen to me, it can happen to you too!"

They responded with a loud cheer, celebrating the fact that two more members of the UFFR would never meet death at the mouth of a snake. I had such respect and admiration for those guys. Even though they were still on Death Row and could face death at any moment, they were happy for Harry and me.

How different they were from my nemesis and his sidekicks. I thought about ER 002 and how he would have responded, most likely slinking off to the corner with Sketch and X-Con, glaring at us, his beady black eyes filled with jealousy and hate. I imagined him looking back over his shoulder, saying something like, "Nice work, Lance Armstrong. You sure fooled those stupid humans."

When Big Tommy's strong, husky voice rose above all the others, I forgot about ER 002. He spoke directly to me and Harry, "Nicodemus and Harry, remember that even though you have left CarPet World and can no longer pay your union dues, you will have lifetime membership in the UFFR. Mark my words." He paused and then spoke in a hushed voice as if he knew something we did not, "There may come a dark day in the future when you are in deep trouble. We will be there to help. You never know when you might need the union again."

"We will remember, Big Tommy. Thank you," Harry and I said in unison, Harry adding a second *you* at the end as always.

The humans continued their conversation, completely unaware of the significant communication that had just taken place among the rats. Karin, cradling my To-Go box in her arm, was talking to Mr. Jaguar.

"We actually don't need to buy a cage since he'll be in with the other boys. Besides, my friend gave me a small cage she is no longer using just in case we need it."

"Sounds good then," Mr. Jaguar replied. "We have some great cages though if you ever change your mind. Just got some new models in last week with three levels and a built-in wheel," he added, always hoping to make a sale.

"I'll remember that," Karin replied.

I could hear the cash register whirring and clicking and assumed she was paying for me and Harry.

"Thank you for all your help, Mr. Jaguar. I am so excited," Karin added.

I could barely see her face as I tried to peek out of one of the air holes in my box. She looked really happy.

"No problem, ladies. So sorry about that first little guy you took home. Let's hope these two new rats will work out without a glitch. They are sure lucky to go home with you ladies! I actually didn't think anyone would want that little guy with the hurt eye. But to be perfectly frank, he is actually one of my favorite rats." Mr. Jaguar laughed his warm laugh.

I knew what he meant when he said we were lucky. Karin, Claire, and Sarah had no idea how much of an understatement that was.

I joggled around in my To-Go box as we made the journey out of CarPet World toward our new home. Since the walls of this carrier were literally paper thin, I could easily overhear the velveteen talking to the girls.

"Petey. I am going to name my rat Petey after that man with cerebral palsy—you know, Claire, in that book we just read! Petey was an amazing man despite his disability, and I have a feeling this little rat will be amazing too, even though he has a problem with his eye."

Karin spoke with confidence that I was going to be all right. I liked that. After I turned around three times in my tiny box, I settled down. I smiled.

Harry's To-Go box was next to mine since Sarah was riding shotgun.

"Harry, can you hear me?" I squeaked.

"Yes ... yes," came the reply.

"Is this real? Are we actually going to a human home?" I asked, still skeptical, still doubting my ability to accurately perceive reality.

"Yeah, man. It's real ... real. This is it ... it," Harry answered, his voice extra squeaky with excitement. "This is as good as winning a Best of Show ribbon at a rat show ... show!"

"Yeah, it sure is. What do you think of my new name?" I had been repeating it over and over in my head.

"Oh, you mean Petey ... Petey?" Well, it's a lot better than ER 22, FR 22, or any of those nicknames ER 002 gave you ... you." He laughed. "I was kind of used to Nicodemus, but I like Petey ... Petey," Harry added as an afterthought.

Even though I was ecstatic at the prospect of leaving the feeder bins behind forever, I felt sad about leaving. CarPet World was no rat haven; however, it was familiar and comfortable, and, most importantly, I had made many good relationships there.

Without warning, my heart started beating faster, and my breathing became more difficult. A tidal wave of anxiety caught me by surprise. This is so stupid. I am going to a wonderful new home. Why is fear gripping me?

"Harry?" I squeaked again.

"What's up, Nicodemus? I mean Petey ... Petey."

"Are you scared?" I asked in a strained voice, trying to hide my anxiety without much success.

"Of what ... what?" Harry answered, sounding puzzled.

I laughed. His response somehow helped me feel better. I hunkered down for the rest of the ride to my new home and then muttered, "Oh, nothing."

Chapter Ten

A Harsh Reality

"OH, PETEY, PLEASE DON'T DIE!" KARIN PLEADED, the crack in her anxious voice betraying the desperation she felt.

I could barely see her face from my cozy hiding place way back in the corner of my tissue box house. It had only been four days since we left CarPet World, but so much had happened that my mind had not processed any of it. For my own sanity, I tried to reconstruct the sequence of events, beginning with our departure from the pet store.

The ride home was uneventful, after I calmed down. The white To-Go box I was in was so small there was barely room for me to turn around. I could easily have been mistaken for a take out order of Chinese food. Unable to see or do anything in the tiny box, I closed my eye and slept.

I awakened when the car stopped moving. After she parked the car in the garage, Karin climbed out of her seat, extricated me from the box, and then placed me under her jacket so I could ride on her shoulder. This was my first experience with close human companionship. Even though I had lived in proximity to humans all of my life, was handled frequently at the breeder's home, and had ridden occasionally on Moose's shoulder at CarPet World, this was the first time a human had treated me with so much kindness and warmth. From the moment our eyes locked, there was a special inexplicable connection between me and Karin.

I noticed movement to my right and glanced over to see, Harry, aka Huckle, burrowing under Sarah's satin agouti hair. We communicated with each other in high-pitched squeaks.

"Hey, Petey, how are you doing ... doing?" squeaked Harry. I can't believe we made it out of Death Row alive ... alive."

"What a miracle, eh, Harry?" I replied while snuggling under the velveteen's jacket. "By the way, should I start calling you Huckle? How do you like your new name?"

"Well, funny you should ask. My dad was a big fan of Mark Twain and used to read *Tom Sawyer* and *Huckleberry Finn* to us. Huck Finn was always getting into all kinds of trouble, you know. I can relate to him and admired him so I am actually enjoying the name. Huckle sure beats being called FR 76 ... 76." He laughed, winked at me, then added, "and you? How's the name Petey ... Petey?"

"I like it. I'm ready for a change," I replied, trying to remember why the velveteen had chosen that name for me. Something about a book, but I could not quite recall what she told her daughters.

Claire was walking a little ahead of her mom and sister. She swiveled her head around as she kept walking and spoke. "Hurry, Mama," called Claire excitedly. "I want to introduce Dusty to Huckle and Petey."

Sarah spoke to Huckle, her voice bubbling with excitement, "Look, Huckle, this is going to be your new home," she said as she wrapped her two small hands around him and held him out in front of her so he could see where they were going. He looked like a figurehead on a Viking ship as he forged ahead of her toward our destination. The expression on his face was so comical that I chuckled out loud.

"Let's try introducing Huckle and Dusty first. We'll see how they get along before we put Petey in with them," Karin suggested, as she took off her shoes and jacket. "Petey, you just stay here on my shoulder for now."

"Hey Huckle," I squeaked, practicing using Harry's new name. "Do you remember Dusty, the other rat who lives here?"

"Yeah, Nicodemus, I mean Petey, I do, don't you-you? He was called Snake Eyes back at the pet store and hung out with ER 002, Sketch, and X-Con. I remember him very well since he started out in the feeder bin, then for some unknown reason was moved into the exotic rat bin right after I arrived at CarPet World. Seems to me that he had a reputation for taking an instant liking or disliking to any new rat he met. He seemed to think I was okay ... okay."

Huckle twisted his head around to look at me in owl-like fashion, his body, still pointed toward the rat bin. Sarah was trying to position him to face Dusty.

"Well, with my luck, I can guess what his reaction to me will be—instant dislike," I said grimly as I reflected upon the experience with ER 002 and his henchmen. "Guess I'll find out soon enough."

Before he had a chance to respond, Huckle was whisked away with Sarah and Claire. By the time the velveteen arrived with me, Huckle was in the container with Dusty aka Snake Eyes.

Dusty's home resembled the glass-paneled bins at CarPet World. The two rats were checking each other out in the way that rats do when meeting for the first time. Their initial interaction was unremarkable. Huckle's whiskers were twitching rapidly as he sniffed every corner of the glass box. Dusty was watching him like a hawk.

Huckle looked up suddenly as though an invisible puppeteer had moved his head. When he caught sight of me, he held up his right paw like a policeman stopping a line of traffic. He signaled with the urgency of one friend admonishing another of imminent danger, as if warning me to not take another step lest I fall off a cliff.

"Petey, you don't want to come in here ... here," he warned, his speech rapid, his black eyes darting over toward the other rat in the bin. "I think you are on Snake Eyes', um ... Dusty's hit list ... list ... list," he squeaked in his low voice, repeating the last word three times instead of his usual two due to his level of distress.

He paused to take a deep breath, and then resumed his rapid-fire message. "Look, Dusty and I exchanged greetings and that was fine, but when I told him that you were here, too, he snickered, muttering something about untimely death. He told me that he and ER 002 were really good buddies. They used to be in the same bin before he was moved to the other exotic rat bin. They hated you even before that incident with Willow ... Willow." He spoke so fast that I barely understood him, but I heard enough to know I was in danger.

"Great. Now what do I do?" I asked, more to myself than to Huckle, feeling more anxious by the minute. Untimely death. Yikes!

An involuntary shudder ran up and down my spine.

Huckle continued, his voice getting higher as his stress level mounted. His squeaks were so high-pitched I thought he might shatter glass when he next spoke. "I tried to get him to give you another chance, you know, turn over a new leaf and all that, but he won't do it. He told me he'll be waiting for you and it won't be pretty ... pretty."

"Well, Huck, I feel like a bull about to be released into the bullfighting ring to face the human with the red cape," I said and sighed.

Until this moment, I thought my new life was going to be stress free and that I would live happily ever after with my human family. Unfortunately, my nemesis' influence was following me. Why did ER 002 and Dusty hate me even before the incident with Willow? They did not even know me.

As an afterthought, I asked, "Did he say what I did that got me on their bad side to begin with?"

"Well, not really. He mumbled something about you being a brownnoser. Said they used to call you Mr. Clean because you were too nice ... nice."

Unbelievable! Another nickname to add to the list. Huckle, obviously feeling uncomfortable with the conversation, began vigorously washing his back.

Good idea. I washed my back as well, licking my fur with fervor as though it had never been washed before. I thought a moment and then responded with resolve, "Okay. I'll talk to him when I get in there and see if we can work this out."

My voice cracked a little, revealing how shaky I felt about this plan. I was angry. Being bullied by a rat who did not even known me was wrong.

This apparent no-win situation with Dusty reminded me of

something. My thoughts suddenly drifted away from the present and I flashed back on my days as a kitten.

When I was a very young rat at my breeder's rattery, there was free time out of our cages every night. The boy and girl kittens could run around together since we were too young to be interested in mating. Sometimes, we would stop and talk to rats from the other families that lived close by, and other times, we would look for food.

On one such occasion, we were scurrying around with Mama while Pops enjoyed a few rare moments of peace and quiet as he napped in our nest. Mama and I were exploring an unusually interesting collection of garbage in the trash can when Peony came dashing up to us, tears streaming down her cheeks.

"Mama, ... she's ... so... mean. She's ... so ... mean," she cried, the words sputtering out of her mouth with the pounding rhythm of a bass drum as she paused, gasping for breath after each word. "Why is she so mean to me?"

Mama gently placed her paw on Peony's back and began to stroke her ruffled fur, "What's wrong, Peony? Who is being mean to you?" she inquired in her protective mama-bear-voice, her brow furrowed in concern.

Peony took a deep breath and pointed one small, trembling paw toward a cage where a young agouti hooded rat with a very short tail was glaring in our direction, her black eyes flashing with hatred. "She is! Gertrude!"

I glared back at Gertrude, my guard hairs stiffening like an army of soldiers who had been at ease and were suddenly commanded to snap to attention. The thought of someone being mean to my sister aroused every protective instinct there was in my tiny body.

"What did she say to you?" I wanted to know immediately, my dark ruby eyes shifting from Peony to Gertrude and then back to Peony.

"She said that she never wants me to talk to her or come near her again ... ever. And she said I was ugly!" Peony blurted out sobbing so hard that she had to stop for a minute to compose herself. After she washed her face with her front paws, she continued in a shaky voice, "I know I made her mad one day because I ate a treat that she wanted. I didn't know it was that important to her. I apologized that very day and she was pretty nice after that. But just now she got really mad at me."

Peony snuggled next to Mama finding comfort in the warmth of her body.

"Why?" Mama asked in a bewildered tone as she continued to stroke Peony's soft black fur, "Was she still mad about the treat?"

"I don't know," Peony tried to explain. "Everything seemed okay until we started talking about the humans. I was saying how much I liked our breeders and how I hoped I would live in a nice home someday and then, out of the blue, Gertrude says, 'Don't be stupid, Peony. Humans only breed rats so they can sell us for snake food. That one human you always kiss up to doesn't care about you at all. She just wants you to be a nice rat so that the pet stores will keep buying rats from her. I'll bet you will make a tasty morsel for a snake someday'. And then she laughed, an awful evil laugh."

Peony paused for a moment and this time vigorously washed her ears with her front paws, turning her head from side to side so she could reach the backs of her ears. As I moved in a little closer so I could catch every word, my guard hairs brushed against the side of the trash can. I was definitely unaccustomed to the extra space I needed to clear objects when my fur was sticking out so far.

Peony finished washing, then resumed her story, "I felt my fur bristle when she laughed like that. I looked just like you do now, Nicodemus! Then, my heart began to pump a little faster and I shouted, 'Gertrude, you are wrong! She really likes me. She doesn't want to sell me for snake food. You don't know what you are talking about.'

"Gertrude laughed again, then began pacing back and forth in front of me, her stubby tail swishing and her whiskers spinning furiously. All of a sudden, she stopped and wheeled around, glaring at me with so much hatred in her eyes that I jumped back.

"I couldn't believe what she said next! 'You're a liar Peony and I hate liars. You told me that you would give me the next treat that your human friend gave you since you ate mine *by mistake*. That's a joke! But, guess what? You never did. You're a liar and as ugly as a long, scaly snake. I want nothing to do with you. I was stupid to ever be your friend!'

"Her words made me feel sick. Part of me wanted to do anything possible to make up with her. But, another part of me wanted to bite her as hard as I could. I was shaking so hard that I had to sit down. All I could say was, 'I just forgot, Gertrude, really. I didn't mean to.' And that's when she said she never wanted to talk to me again as long as she lived."

Peony broke into sobs once more and pressed her small body even closer to Mama's.

Still stroking Peony's fur, Mama motioned to me to come over and lay down beside them. Whenever Mama wanted to tell us something really important, she would give us the signal to gather close to her and sit in a semi-circle, so I nestled in with my sibling to hear what she had to say. It was one of those priceless moments when I learned something about relationships with other rats that I never forgot.

"Little Peony, I am so sorry you are sad," Mama said, then paused to lick Peony's fur, a sign of nurturance and caring. "I wish I could protect you from this kind of hurt, but I can't. The reality is that not every rat is going to like you."

Peony just stared at Mama, an expression of disbelief and distress upon her face. I stared, too, my mouth open in surprise.

"But why, Mama? I'm a really nice rat. I mean, well, I make mistakes sometimes, but I'm good most of the time!" Peony protested.

Mama looked at her with tenderness and compassion.

"I know that, Peony and so do you. But, that does not change the fact that not every rat is going to like you. So, you are going to have to remember what you know to be true about yourself no matter how another rat treats you."

"But, why doesn't Gertrude think I'm a nice rat and want to be my friend?" asked Peony, truly perplexed by this situation.

Mama paused contemplatively, then sat up and licked the soft white patch of fur on her own tummy. After thinking for a moment, she went on, "I believe she does, Peony. But, some rats hold grudges and never forget it if you hurt them. It doesn't matter if what you did was an accident or on purpose."

Peony looked even more confused.

"But, why Mama?" You and Pops always taught us to forgive others, remembering that we make mistakes, too. You know, how you always say we have no business casting the first hazelnut?"

"I know, Sweetheart," Mama replied while settling back down again next to us. "Not all rats think that way. Some have been really hurt in their lives and are scared to get close to another rat. If they decide to take a chance and try to make friends and then that rat lets them down, they hold onto what happened. It's almost like they are looking for an excuse to build a big, thick wall around themselves that keeps other rats away and keeps them safe from being hurt again."

"But, don't these rats feel really lonely, Mama?" Peony queried, still struggling to understand why a rat would act this way.

Mama responded, "Yes, very lonely. You see, Peony, some rats would rather be lonely than deal with the inevitable hurt that comes with relationships."

Mama was trying hard to explain a very grown-up concept in a way that would make sense to her very young daughter.

Peony was still, so still it was as if a magic fairy had cast a spell on her so that she could not move. Not only was she motionless, but she was unusually quiet, saying nothing. The clinking of a water bottle and the squeak of a wheel sounded oddly loud in the silence. I waited for what seemed like forever.

Peony was silent for an extraordinarily long time. I was about to poke her to see if she were still alive when she finally said, "I think I understand."

I wasn't convinced that she understood at all and my suspicions were confirmed when, after a few moments, she added, "But, I still want her to like me."

Mama sighed and changed position.

"Peony, as I said before, not every rat will like you. It's just the way it is. I want you to be strong enough to accept that and still feel good about yourself. You know, the skunks learn this lesson at a very young age. They are rejected by so many creatures who don't know them at all simply because of their scent. That smell they make when feeling scared is so awful that most animals, including humans, stay far away from them. It's good for scaring off their predators, but we all stay away. How do you think the skunks feel about being rejected before anyone really gets to know them or gives them a chance?"

Peony thought for a moment and then said, "I think they must feel awful."

Mama nodded agreement.

"Like poop," I added.

Peony laughed.

Mama looked at me and frowned disapprovingly, "That's enough, Nicodemus." Then she went on, "You see, the skunks have had to learn how to feel good about themselves whether other animals like them or not. Now, Peony, your situation is somewhat different, but a little bit the same. It is important that you learn that you don't need every rat to like you to feel good about yourself."

"Oh," my sister said thoughtfully, trying to grasp what Mama was saying, but not quite able to absorb so many new ideas all at once. Peony began licking her front paws, then washed her face for the second time.

I could tell that something was bothering her. "Mama, there's something still worrying me."

"What is it, Peony?" Mama asked, her tone gentle and inviting.

"Well.... what if she says bad things about me to my friends?" Peony looked down and made patterns in the bedding with her tail while waiting for Mama's answer.

Mama sighed again, the kind of deep sigh adults make when they realize their children are growing up, the innocence of childhood fading away like a helium balloon rising higher and higher in the sky.

Recognizing that Peony was becoming aware of the darker side of rat nature, Mama responded to Peony without sugarcoating the truth, 'Well ... she probably will. Hopefully, your friends will make their own decisions based on knowing you and not based on what she says. But...you simply can't control that, can you?"

Mama sighed deeply one more time and shook her head. "Let's go home, kids. It has been a rough night."

We started walking toward our nest, Mama just a little ahead of us. Peony was sniffling, lost in thought. I gave one last piercing glance at Gertrude, my guard hairs still stiff. It did cross my mind that it would give me great satisfaction to bite the obnoxious rat on her nose, but I thought better of it and stayed with Peony.

Later that day, I was the only one of my siblings who was awake. I could hear Mama and Pops talking. Straining to overhear what they were saying about Gertrude, I noticed a loud voice calling a rat named Petey.

"Petey!! Hey Petey ... Petey!" I did not know a rat named Petey, yet the name seemed oddly familiar. The voice was pulling me back to the present, yet my thoughts and feelings were still back in my kittenhood.

Huckle's voice slowly penetrated my memory in the same way that a beam of sunlight finally pierces through a layer of thick fog. I felt really disoriented, as though I were caught in some weird time warp that left me suspended somewhere between the vivid memories of my youth and the challenging here-and-now experience of adulthood.

I opened my eye way too late. The velveteen was lowering me into the bin where Huckle, his eyes wide with fear, and Dusty, his teeth barred, were awaiting my arrival.

The velveteen turned to Dusty, her voice cheerful, totally oblivious of the drama that was unfolding. "This is Petey. Be nice to him since he has a hurt eye."

She lowered me into Dusty's territory and released me onto the soft bedding.

All three humans were peering into the glass cage, watching expectantly to see what would happen next. It was as if they had dropped three musicians onto a stage and were waiting to see if they could magically play music together. In stark contrast, I still felt like the bull that had just been forced into the Spanish bullring knowing he would soon have to face a merciless toreador.

I immediately stiffened. There was no mistaking it, Dusty was telling me to get out. But, I couldn't. I was trapped.

He growled.

The unmistakable menacing guttural sound was warning me to expect an aggressive move.

The human observers, unable to hear this rat sound, could have heard a sound similar to bruxing and noticed a quickening of the movements of his whiskers if they had been very observant. But they seemed unaware, talking and laughing as if everything was going along just fine.

A quick scan of the glass bin told me that there was no place to hide and no way to escape. Evidently Huckle was no Henry Kissinger. His attempts to negotiate a peaceful settlement to this situation had failed miserably.

Guard hairs sticking straight out like oars on a Roman galleon, Dusty began moving toward me in a sideways manner that rats reserve for attack mode. His fur was puffed out so much that he looked twice his size and his back was arched so high that I could have walked under him without crouching down.

Huckle tried to intervene, but was no match for Dusty. At first, he ran in front of Dusty to distract him. When that did not work, he bumped him with his side. Dusty was so pumped up that he shoved Huckle, smashing him into the wall of the bin with enough force to knock the wind out of him, leaving him dizzy and dazed. This gave Dusty just enough time to come after me.

With only seconds to weigh my alternatives, I concluded that I had only two options: to fight back or to roll over in submission. Based on my experience with ER 002's ethics, I knew that this fight would end up being brutal and bloody, not only highly unpleasant for me, but devastating for the two little girls watching us.

Rolling over was the only viable option. Although I would outwardly look weak and cowardly, it was the more sensible thing to do. Maybe Dusty would lose interest if I immediately surrendered.

Dusty attacks Petey.

Dusty danced sideways toward me in his aggressive arched position. Then he slammed into me with his right side and pinned me against the glass wall of the bin. He backed up, positioned his body differently now so he could defend himself if necessary, and waited to see my response, his squinty reptile-like black eyes flashing, eager for a fight.

So this was why he was called Snake Eyes.

I turned my head slightly and met his gaze, my dark ruby eye strong and courageous. Then I rolled over.

He stared at me, dumbfounded, and then he growled through his teeth, "You stinking coward!" and lunged in my direction.

Pops taught us to never attack another rat who had assumed a submissive posture. Dusty, on the other hand, appeared to have been raised with a different moral code. He was going for the jugular—*my* jugular!

Sarah screamed, "Dusty! Stop it!"

Claire gave the order, "Mama, take Petey out right now! They're going to hurt him!"

Sarah was crying.

"Help him, Mama ... please," she pleaded.

Karin immediately pulled the lid off the bin so quickly that she accidentally banged it into the tall, purple glass vase on the nearby table. The vase tumbled to the floor. We heard a loud thud when it hit the ground followed by the tinkling of broken glass as it shattered.

Dusty, startled by the commotion, suspended his attack and dove for cover. He crashed into Huckle as he made a beeline for the box in the corner.

Huckle shook himself then stared at the box, stunned and disoriented. I froze, suddenly confused about where I was. I felt like I was back at CarPet World fighting ER 002 all over again.

Ignoring the demolished vase, Karin seized the opportunity to scoop me up in her hand and lift me to safety.

As I was hoisted out of the cage, I heard Dusty's ominous voice in the background as he hissed, "Stay away from here, Petey, if you know what's good for you." I was surprised to hear him use my new name.

The velveteen hugged me close, and I found myself nuzzling up to her for comfort like I used to with Mama when I was a baby. I was tired of all the fighting, and my eye was hurting again.

As she stroked my fur, she spoke in a voice filled with concern, "Claire's right, Petey. I'm afraid that you need to be in a cage all by yourself."

I glanced back toward the bin and saw that Huckle was engaged in an animated, agitated conversation with Dusty.

Although rats are very social creatures, the idea of having my own cage sounded very appealing at that moment. As we walked across the room, I noticed a rather small cage with sides made of white bars that fit into a green plastic tray. There was a wire ledge that formed a second level about halfway between the floor and the ceiling that was big enough for me to sleep on or walk across. Karin lifted the opening at the top of the cage and then gently placed me on to the ledge. It was my new home.

Instinctively I jumped to the floor and began inspecting my surroundings. First I climbed up one side of the cage, walked across the ledge, and climbed back down the other side. The bars were easy for me to grasp, and it was actually kind of fun. A food dish containing assorted treats was on the floor close to a water bottle that was attached to the bars of the cage. I frowned. A sudden twinge of anxiety hit me as I remembered my childhood fear of water bottles. I shivered involuntarily for the second time that day, and then I immediately distracted myself by exploring the rest of my home.

On the floor was some soft gray bedding that framed the little cardboard house in the center in the same way that a grass lawn surrounds the homes that humans inhabit. My house was actually made of a tissue box that had been cut in two and then put back together in such a way that there was an opening on each side. It was the perfect size for my body and tail. Could the human who designed tissue boxes have known they would make ideal rat houses?

I jumped on top of the house and then tentatively ventured inside to study the interior features. I liked it, so decided to convert it into my den. With a few modifications, it would be exactly right for me, so I

Petey rests in his tissue box house.

quickly went about chewing the front door until it was the perfect size. There was a piece of tissue on the floor of the house that felt soft, but I did not want to sleep on it, so I grabbed it in my mouth and dragged it out of the house, placing it to the side of the opening. I would decide what to do with it later.

Without warning, I yawned. It was a huge yawn that betrayed how tired I was. Why was I so exhausted? At that very moment, as if in answer to my question, a ray of sunlight shone into my cage, bounced off the silver of the water bottle, and glinted right into my eye. I squinted in response to the brightness. The sun is out! That means it's daytime. No wonder I was tired.

My encounter with Dusty had taken place during the afternoon, but the afternoon was the middle of the night for me. I yawned again, my mouth opening so wide I was sure I could have fit a whole hazelnut in it with no problem. I walked over to the food dish and found a piece of soft, ripe banana. It was delicious. The sun was still shining on the water bottle. I decided to take a drink. The cool water was refreshing. I climbed into the tissue box house, turned around about three times, and then settled down to sleep.

My right eye, still stuck at half-mast, was throbbing. I closed my left eye, and try though I might, I could not fall asleep.

My unsettled mind kept replaying the confusing and unexpected events of the day, trying to make sense of all that had happened. It was a long time before my thoughts finally stopped racing.

The last thing I thought about before I drifted off to sleep was Mama's advice to Peony, "Not everyone will like you ... and you need to be strong enough to accept that and still feel good about yourself." Was I that strong yet?

While living at CarPet World, I was confronted with ER 002's hatred. Now at my new home there was Dusty, who clearly did not like me. "Not everyone will like you." Mama was right. The truth was a bitter pill to swallow. Was I strong enough now to accept it and still feel okay being me? I thought long and hard about this until I came to a conclusion. Yes, I was.

Chapter Eleven

Dr. Beed

I SENSED THAT A RAT WAS STARING AT ME. Although no other creature was visible, the intensity of the stare pierced my consciousness.

I rotated my head slowly and warily so that I could see behind me. ER 002's all-too-familiar black beady eyes were glaring at me, full of hatred. His guard hairs were sticking straight out, making his fur so stiff that he looked like a gray-blue bottlebrush with a long, skinny tail.

He lunged at me, and we were fighting again; however, this time we were in the backroom at CarPet World. Somehow we had escaped from the exotic rat bins and were tumbling over and over on the ice-cold, steely gray cement floor.

I broke free and made a run for it. As I frantically scampered around the many cardboard boxes and bags of supplies in the overstuffed storage room and scanned for a place to hide, I inadvertently ran down a long, thin corridor that was bordered by a brick wall. I was trapped. It was a dead end.

I panicked as my fear mounted. My breathing came in short, fast gasps that sounded unbearably loud as they echoed throughout the empty corridor.

ER 002 arrived just after I did, realized my predicament, and began cackling with glee as he grasped the significance of his advantage.

Using the flat, muscular side of his arched body to force me farther into the corner, he pinned me to the reddish brown wall and then turned his head to look at me, his blaze shining in the light.

My nemesis stared at me for a good minute, his eyes burning so hot with fury that they had taken on an eerie scarlet hue. The brilliantly white, jagged blaze on his forehead contrasting with his slate blue fur enhanced his evil expression. Even the W-shaped cut in his ear, the only lasting scar he bore from our last conflict, added to his nefarious demeanor.

Without further hesitation, ER 002 took about five steps backward and then lunged at me with the flair of a knight brandishing a sword, knowing he was about to fatally impale his victim.

"Prepare to die, Nick Fury!" he hissed.

It was another sarcastic reference to my eye problem. He flashed a warning when he bared his hideous yellow teeth in my face, but it was too late for me to defend myself.

An instant later I felt searing pain as those ugly, sharp yellow teeth sunk into my scruff. Within seconds I became aware of a thin stream of blood oozing out of my neck, running down the side of my body and covering my front legs and paws.

My vision started to blur, and I could feel my body weakening from the rapid loss of blood. With horror, I realized that his teeth were still there, tearing my flesh as he shook his head, the aroma of his hot, stinking breath filling my nostrils.

With my last bit of energy, I twisted my head and bit him as hard as I could in the side just below his head. His teeth suddenly jerked out of my neck like a cork popping out of a bottle. Then his body went limp. As he slumped on the chilly gray floor, he released his grip on me.

I was still alive, but the pain I felt with every breath was so intense that I thought I was suffocating. Despite my agony, my senses were still alert enough to detect danger. Could things get any worse? Another rat was approaching.

Unable to move, I feared that this would be the end of me. I was sure the encroaching rat was Sketch or X-Con coming to finish off what ER 002 had begun.

I closed my eye and prepared to die.

However, instead of attacking, this other rat began licking my wounds. Then the voice whispered, "Are you still alive, Nicodemus? Please don't die! I love you. Open your eye and look at me." It was Willow. The last thing I saw before my eye closed again was her beautiful creamy fur shining in the light. I wanted to see her face once more before I died, so I used my last bit of strength to force my eyelid upward.

I opened my eye, expecting to see Willow's beautiful carnation-pink eyes smiling at me, but instead I was greeted by the expressionless, dull light gray cardboard that lined the inside of my tissue box house.

Wait a minute! I was in my new home, not at CarPet World. There was no sign of Willow or ER 002. I was alone. I must have had yet another nightmare. Why did I have such vivid dreams? But there really was something oozing onto my neck. How could this be?

It was then that I realized that the gummy stuff I felt was coming from my injured eye. I must have rubbed it during my sleep because my front paws were all wet and sticky. When I cleaned them, the thick liquid smelled bad and tasted awful.

This was not blood. It was a gooey substance that was greenish yellow like a lima bean. Once my paws were clean, I tried to wash my eye, but that only intensified the throbbing. The pain was so overwhelming that it made me feel sick. I had no idea what to do.

I felt disoriented and confused. The dream was very unsettling to me. It was the last thing I needed. ER 002's image was so vivid that I had a hard time believing that he was not close by. Ever since I left CarPet World, I had been haunted by the final words he uttered to me, "Don't think this is the last you'll see of me, Romeo. I'm not finished with you yet!"

My tendency to obsess about things made it virtually impossible for me to put him out of my mind.

Willow's image was even more vivid. Her presence seemed so real that I foolishly looked around for her, thinking maybe she really was here. My heart jumped when I thought I saw her, so I ran over to the other side of the cage only to find out that what I really saw was a piece of tissue from my nest. Although I was alone, I felt embarrassed and began to wonder if the pain in my eye might be affecting my brain.

Vigorously washing my lower back fur helped bury my feelings. Even though I tried to be philosophical about the forced separation from Willow, I really missed her and selfishly wished she were here to comfort me.

I sighed.

Not knowing what else to do, I closed my eye, hoping to fall asleep again. Unfortunately I was in too much pain and too upset to nap, so I just lay in my den, absorbed in my thoughts waiting for morning when the humans began to stir and move around the house.

"Hey, you mousie! Time for breakfast," called the velveteen.

You mousie? Hmmm. Was that her term of endearment for me? I was not quite sure how I felt about that. Despite definite similarities in our appearance, rats are not large mice. In fact, rats take great pride in being a completely different species from mice.

Nevertheless, given that I had been endowed with a whole string of undesirable nicknames, terms of endearment seemed relatively hard to come by, so I decided to make the best of it.

By this time, I was feeling slightly more energetic, so I slowly climbed out of my den. Moving like a very old rat, I hobbled over to Karin. She picked me up, gave me a big hug, and then held me straight out in front of her so she could look at my face. Then she exclaimed in a high, stressed voice, "Oh, my gosh! That eye doesn't look very good, Petey. I think I'll see if I can take you to the veterinarian right away!"

After she gently placed me back in the cage, she reached for her cell phone and began pushing on it with her fingers. I did not know exactly who or what the veterinarian was, but I hoped it was not another pet store. I remembered Cat saying something about the rabbits being veterinarians. I think it had something to do with them eating plants rather than other animals.

Maybe the velveteen was going to return me to CarPet World like the snake owner returned Sugar. I doubted Mr. Jaguar would take me back in this condition. I imagined him saying, "Sorry, lady, but we have no use for a rat like this. I just don't think he is going to make it. What a shame. He was such a great rat! I'd be happy to show you some new rats if you ever need another one."

Wanting to ask someone about the veterinarian, I looked around for Huckle, but I could not see him anywhere. I remembered that his cage was around the corner in the next room, fortunately still within squeaking distance when the house was quiet. Right now there was too much commotion for me to attempt to transmit a message to my friend.

My cage was perched on a table at the top of the stairs. From this vantage point, I could watch all the comings and goings of the human family as well as their two cats. I was not fond of cats. In fact, snakes and cats were in the same category in my mind. Because I knew full well that a cat would not hesitate to eat me for dinner, I watched the house cats very closely, even though I knew that the bars of my cage protected me.

They were definitely not veterinarians like the rabbits. The orange one, who was called Purrcey, was the feistier of the two and had already given me several piercing glances while simultaneously smacking his lips. That was a pretty clear message.

The black-and-white one, Poppyseed, was extremely irritating because he emitted a constant, high-pitched meow, the equivalent of scraping toenails on the side of a glass bin. On the other hand, Poppyseed seemed gentle and less of a threat. However, I did not trust either of them and remained on guard unless they were outside.

Later that day the velveteen walked over to my cage and announced that it was time to go to the appointment with the vet. She was smiling and sounded happy about it, so I relaxed. Carefully lifting my cage, she took me out to the car. After a rather long drive, we arrived at a small brown house with a sign in front that said *Every Pet Veterinary Clinic* in big letters. I believed the name to be a good omen. We went inside and were greeted by a very friendly girl with short reddish hair. I stared at her for a few moments. Her hair intrigued me because I had never seen a rat with fur that color.

"Hello, my name is Ivy. You must be Karin, and that cute little

Ivy and Amber, the cat, at Dr. Beed's veterinary clinic.

rat must be Petey." Ivy was glancing in my direction, her voice warm and welcoming.

"Yes, I am Karin, and this is Petey. We are here to see the doctor about Petey's eye," she replied, her voice a little higher than usual, betraying her anxiety.

"Please have a seat. Dr. Beed will be with you in just a few minutes after she finishes with the patient before you. I have some paperwork for you to fill out about Petey," explained Ivy.

Ivy handed a clipboard with some white papers on it and a pen to Karin, and then gestured toward the seats in the small waiting room. I scanned the room. A large white, elderly cat was dozing on a well-worn pillow fastened to the seat of one of the padded chairs. Her ancient eyes, heavy with sleep, barely opened into two narrow slits. She dusted me with a glance of mild disinterest, blinked hard, gave me a rather dismissive look, and then went back to sleep.

Who is this cat?

"She belongs to Dr. Beed," Ivy explained as if she had read my mind. Then she added, "She is twenty-five years old."

I was duly impressed since the oldest rat I ever knew was four years old at the time that he died.

The velveteen settled into a comfortable chair in the waiting room, took me out of my cage, held me, and rubbed my head behind my ears. I was feeling exposed and anxious, so I made a run up her sleeve to hide under her hair.

She whispered to me, "Petey, it's okay. We're here to get some help for your eye."

Even though she meant to be encouraging, I did not feel reassured. I don't think she realized how unsettling it was for me to be so unprotected with a cat sitting across the room.

In a few moments, a man came into the waiting room. He was lovingly carrying an enormous brown rabbit. At first I thought this might be the veterinarian, still confused about whether a vet was a human or a rabbit. I soon realized the rabbit was a patient when I heard Ivy talking to the man about medicine and how to take care of the bunny. After the man and bunny left, Ivy returned and ushered us into another room.

I relaxed a bit, appreciating the distance from the cat. I scanned. This room was small with a long, flat, silver table in the middle and a sink off to the side.

"Dr. Beed will be with you in a moment," she said while she carefully placed a clean blue towel on the table, smoothing the edges so it was laid out flat. At the sound of the phone, she excused herself and walked away.

I took this opportunity to climb down the velveteen's arm onto her lap so that I could look around. The room was small with a window on one wall. A few rays of sunlight filtered through the glass and lit up the shiny metal faucet of the small sink.

Next to the sink were several bottles. One was labeled hand cleaner, and another was labeled Betadine. The table was flanked on one side by a scale and on the other side by a chair. A ferret was staring down at me from a picture on the wall, and there was a framed drawing of two rats eating sunflower seeds to the left of the table. After I surveyed the room, I began to breathe a little easier because there was a good feeling to the place.

I looked up when a small woman entered the room. She extended her hand to the velveteen as she smoothed the blue towel on the table with her free hand as she introduced herself to us, "Hello, I am Dr. Beed." So this is a veterinarian.

Dr. Beed was a slight woman with brown curly hair, a velveteen agouti in rat terminology, and big glasses that were a little unnerving because they reminded me of Mrs. Hamsterford. However, the resemblance stopped there.

Dr. Beed's voice was quiet yet strong. She glanced at the paper on the clipboard she was holding in her other hand, peered at the velveteen, and then focused on me, her eyes moving like a spotlight that highlights one performer on stage then another.

Her voice was magical. She spoke to me as though I were the most important animal in the world. "So you must be Petey." It was more a statement than a question.

I nodded.

She nodded back.

When she turned to the velveteen, she asked, "What is wrong with Petey?"

The velveteen explained what she knew about my eye trouble. Unfortunately she could not tell her the whole story since she knew nothing about what happened at CarPet World.

She then gently handed me to the vet. Dr. Beed studied me. Her mouth was expressionless at the moment, but she had the kindest eyes I have ever seen. Her hands touched me with a soothing combination of strength and gentleness. If only I could tell her everything. I wanted her to know about my fight with ER 002, but more than that, I wanted to tell her about the plight of the feeder rats and the desperate efforts of the UFFR to confront the injustices at CarPet World. My intuition told me that she could help.

Dr. Beed evaluated my condition with her touch, her hands moving very tenderly, checking my legs, tail, and abdomen. Then she stroked my fur as she placed me on the scale. I saw her open a folder and write something on a paper that was inside.

The last thing she did was grasp me firmly with both hands, then hold me in front of her, so she could position my face close to hers in order to examine my eye. I felt scared and safe at the same time. During my examination Dr. Beed said nothing. When she finished she gently handed me back to the velveteen and delivered her verdict in a kind voice, "Petey is in excellent health except for his right eye. Petey's eye is definitely blind. He will never be able to see out of it again. If you look closely, you can see that it looks dull and unfocused."

She moved her head in my direction, and the velveteen looked down at my eye, nodded, and then said, "Yes, now that you mention it, I see exactly what you mean."

Dr. Beed's words stung. I felt as though she had just poured a glass of ice-cold water on my back. I shivered. Of course, I should not have been surprised, but I guess I had been clinging to a ray of hope that she could fix my eye and that I would be able to see out of it again. There was an aura of finality about Dr. Beed's words that penetrated any remaining denial I might have had.

Dr. Beed resumed speaking, "My biggest concern is that Petey's

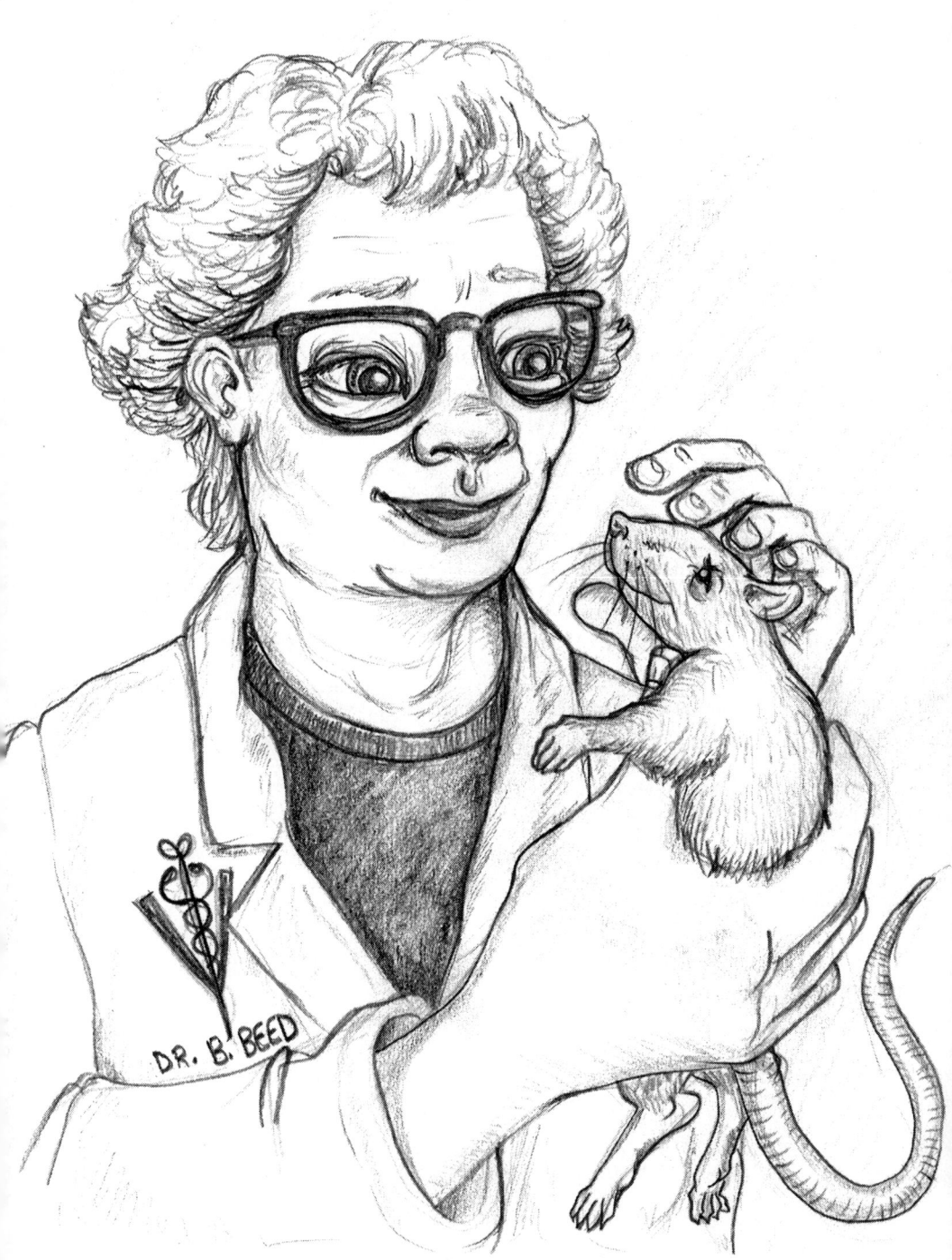

Dr. Beed examines Petey.

eye is infected. I'll prescribe some antibiotics for him to treat the infection, and we will hope it will respond to the treatment."

She left the room. I remembered taking antibiotics at CarPet World for two days before I was moved to the feeder bin. They tasted awful like a mixture of vinegar and lemon. Dr. Beed returned with what looked like a small narrow tube in her hand.

She inserted a thin dropper into the tube, sucked up some medicine into the syringe, forced it between my teeth, and then squirted something into my mouth. It tasted like bananas with a rather bitter aftertaste.

I tried to spit it out, but I only succeeded in getting some of the sticky stuff all over my face. I immediately washed my mouth and whiskers with my paws so that any remaining gummy liquid would be gone as soon as possible.

Before I could recover from the first round, she had inserted the syringe into my mouth again and squirted more of the banana like stuff into it. This time I was not fast enough to spit it out and swallowed all of it.

"Petey needs this medicine twice a day for two weeks. Let's see if it helps his eye," Dr. Beed explained as she handed the vial and the syringe to the velveteen.

She was smiling. Her smile was transitory, but when it was there, it lit up the room like the sun shining through the window on a bright, summer day. I was reminded of the afternoon Pops and I were searching for hazelnuts and had our rat-to-rat talk. She picked me up and stroked my fur. Then she held me so that we were face-to-face again and looked me straight in my one good eye.

"Petey, I don't think you like that medicine, but it might help your eye. I want you to take it," she said, speaking slowly and carefully.

Unlike most humans, Dr. Beed knew how to communicate with me so that I understood what she said. I was not particularly happy about her pronouncement, but she convinced me to take the medicine. She had such an effect on me that if she had said, "Petey, I want you to stand on your head and spin around ten times," I would have done it.

After she gently stroked my fur one more time, she transferred me to the velveteen. Once back in my cage, I crawled into my tissue box den and began washing my fur. If only the news about my eye had been more optimistic. I thought of Hoover and wished he were here with me to cheer me up.

I was momentarily distracted when we went out into the waiting room area to pay for the services. As I peered out of the door to my house, I noticed the large white cat had opened one eye and was watching us. I stared back at her, one-eyed rat to one-eyed cat, wondering how a cat could live so long.

She meowed, and to my amazement, I understood what she said. "Dr. Beed is good. She will take care of you."

I smiled back at her.

"Thanks," I said, confused about why a cat would care about the life of a rat.

Our communication ended when the velveteen picked up the cage and took me out the door, down the stairs, and back to our car.

I was sitting on the front seat next to her, my cage secured with a seat belt. After we were rolling for a few minutes, she commented, "Well, Petey, let's give the medicine a try and hope that it works."

As if she knew my thoughts, she added in a quiet voice, "I'm sorry about your eye."

I sighed.

She muttered something about awful traffic and then clicked on the radio. The motion of the car combined with the droning of the newscasters lulled me to sleep.

The remainder of that day and the next were uneventful. My new home was wonderful, but it was not the drama-filled life to which I had become accustomed at CarPet World. It was taking me a little while to adapt to the changes in daily routine and to the relative calm.

Because I did not feel well, I remained closeted in my den except when the velveteen held me or gave me my medicine. I ate a little but much less than my usual amount. Nothing tasted good. Even a corn wheel could not rouse my interest.

When the house was particularly quiet after the humans had

gone to bed at night, Huckle and I could hear each other's squeaks. Our conversations stayed fairly superficial since Dusty was privy to all that we said. Nonetheless, it brightened my nights to converse with a friend.

Two days later dawn was just about to break, so I said good night to Huckle and washed my fur, preparing for sleep. It was early. The rising sun was just beginning to turn the sky a faint pink color. The darkness was slipping away.

The first beam of morning sunlight came in the window, and I winced. I knew something was wrong when this little bit of light bothered my good eye. I was in horrible pain. Not only did my eye hurt, but my head was throbbing.

I felt confused, not knowing what was wrong. I tried to communicate with Huckle, but it was already too noisy in the house for him to hear my squeaks.

"Hey, you mousie!" It was the velveteen's voice.

Normally I would poke my head out of the tissue box, stretch, yawn, climb out, jump up to the second floor, and then wait for her to open the top and take me out. However, today her familiar greeting did not elicit my usual response.

I did not budge.

She persisted, "Petey, how is your eye today?"

By this time the sun was shining into the room so brightly that I retreated to the darkest place I could find.

"Can you come out so I can see?" she coaxed.

I desperately wanted to go out to see her, but I could barely move. She detached the upper portion of my cage, exposing the floor and my box. Then she removed the top covering of my den so she could see me.

I recoiled from the light.

"Oh, my goodness, Petey!" she exclaimed. "Your poor eye looks like it is bleeding. I'd better not pick you up right now, but I'll see if I can get some help."

I was as alarmed as she was. A bleeding eye could only mean a serious problem. Then I heard the velveteen talking to someone about my eye. By this time Claire and Sarah had come into the room and wanted to know what was wrong.

"Petey's eye is bleeding," the velveteen explained. Her voice was unusually tense. "It doesn't seem to be getting any better, so I am trying to find him some help. Unfortunately it is Sunday, so only emergency vets are open. They do not seem to have vets on call that are familiar with rats. One place said I could bring him in, but it would cost over three hundred dollars. And they could not guarantee there would be an exotic animal vet who could treat rats."

As she spoke, her tone rose higher and higher, betraying her mounting level of frustration with the situation.

"Is Petey going to be okay?" asked Sarah, her voice quavering. I could tell that she was worried about me and was trying to peer at me in my box. I could see her brownish green eyes filled with concern.

Still hiding from the brightness in the room, I stayed where I was, even though I really wanted to greet Sarah and reassure her, but I couldn't do it.

It made me feel a little better knowing these humans really cared about me.

"I don't know, Sarah," answered the velveteen in a worried voice. "I left a message at Dr. Beed's office, asking them to see Petey first thing tomorrow morning. I sure hope that they can. I really feel attached to the little guy."

I could hear her footsteps as she walked across the room, and then I recognized the familiar noise of dishes clanking. My cage was so close to the kitchen that I had learned to recognize the different sounds—the river-like noise made by the water running in the sink, the shrill whistle of boiling water in the tea kettle, the staccato beeps of the microwave, the quiet thud as the door to the refrigerator or the freezer closed, the musical ringtone of the telephone, and the roar of the water swirling around the dishes in the dishwasher. I liked the sounds. They made my life interesting.

That afternoon and evening, the velveteen kept a close watch on me, talking to me frequently. She explained that she did not want to pick me up out of fear of making my eye worse. I was quite listless, so I stayed in my box, unable to groom myself, eating and drinking almost nothing.

Was this the end? I had survived the fight with ER 002 and narrowly escaped Death Row at CarPet World. Was I going to die?

Wait a minute! There is no way I am going to die because of a wound inflicted by ER 002! Adrenaline pumped through my system.

I was determined to make it until I could see Dr. Beed again. I was confident that she could help me. I gritted my teeth and tried to rest, but I was unable to get comfortable, feeling fitful and restless.

The pain was almost intolerable. It came in bursts, starting out as a fairly mild ache and then would crescendo to a sharp, stabbing sensation that felt as though someone was poking a hot needle into my injured eye.

My thoughts began swirling around in a disorganized fashion. I learned later that this was a symptom of delirium caused by the pain. Sometimes I thought I was a very young rat again, sometimes I thought I was at CarPet World, and other times I knew exactly where I was in my tissue box house.

At one point my thoughts floated back to a warm summer day when Mama, Peony, and I were just settling down for our afternoon rest. I remembered asking Mama a question I had been meaning to ask her for a long time, but I had not found a good opportunity until that day.

"Hey, Mama," I said lazily. "I was wondering. Did it hurt when you had us? I mean, giving birth and all?"

"What made you think of that, Nicodemus?" she queried while she gave me a big smile. "You ask good questions, my son, but at the times I least expect them."

"I don't know, Mama," I said, licking my left front paw to remove a small piece of bedding that had wedged itself between my toes. "I was just curious."

I noticed that Peony was wide-awake now, listening very intently to our conversation.

"Well, to answer your question, yes, it really hurt. Giving birth was more painful than anything I have ever experienced, but it was worth it because now I have all my wonderful children," Mama answered with a deep sigh followed by a tiny shudder, suggesting she really did not want to revisit the memory of the pain.

"But, Mama," Peony chimed in as she moved a little closer to us, her black eyes widening, "How did you get through it? I'm scared because someday I will be a mama too."

"Well, I remembered something your grandmother told me when I was about your age. 'Iris,' she said, 'when you have babies, focus your eyes on something you can see. Focus your mind on a place where you love to be. Focus your ears on a sound that is comforting. Feel something soothing with your paw. Imagine a wonderful taste in your mouth, and think of someone who loves you. Then breathe deeply and slowly, and the pain will be bearable.'"

"So what did you do, Mama?" I asked, marveling at the fact that my mother was willing to endure this kind of pain in order to birth us.

"Well, I focused my eyes on some pretty, dried flowers that were part of our nest. I focused my mind on my favorite spot in the rattery that was behind the pillow on the couch as I listened to the pretty sound of the rain tapping on the roof. I touched a soft piece of nest material that was close by, imagined the wonderful taste of a piece of cheddar cheese, and thought about your father, who loves me and was anxiously waiting for you to be born. With my mind distracted by these wonderful things, I began taking many slow and deep breaths. Every time I felt more pain, I went back and did the same thing again." Mama smiled at us while she spoke and stroked our fur tenderly with her paws.

"So Grandma's advice worked?" inquired Peony with a hopeful voice and expression on her face.

"Yes, it did! You know, I think it will work for any kind of intense pain, not just birth pain," Mama asserted, not knowing at the time that these words would help save the life of her fawn son with the dark ruby eyes.

As the memory faded and my mind struggled to return to the present, I realized that it was the words "any kind of intense pain" that triggered the memory.

I was determined to endure the pain in my eye and survive until morning, so I decided to try my grandmother's method of managing pain. I began by looking around for something that calmed me when I concentrated on it. I saw a picture of beautiful flowers on the wall and decided to focus my eye on the cluster of soft pink roses.

For my special place, I decided to imagine I was back in the exotic rat bin at CarPet World with my best friend, Hoover, and my girlfriend, Willow.

The sound I chose to listen to was the rhythmic ticking of the big grandfather clock that stood in the corner of room close to my cage.

I had a soft piece of fleece in my tissue box house, so I put my paw around it as I thought about my favorite food, banana yogurt.

Now all I had to do was think of someone who loved me. To my surprise, the first creature I thought of was the velveteen, a human and not a rat! I had not known her for very long; however, I knew she loved me a lot, and I wanted to live long enough to spend some time with her.

Lastly I breathed slowly and deeply in and out, in and out. Although the pain did not go away, it became bearable. I was able to drink a little water and eat a few morsels of food so that I could stay strong. That little bit of nourishment restored my mind and gave me just enough energy to think clearly.

There was no way I would give ER 002 the satisfaction of knowing that he had inflicted a wound on me that ultimately caused my death. The combination of my grandma's pain management technique, my determination, and a few prayers worked like a charm. Although the odds were against me, I made it through the night.

Chapter Twelve

Surgery

"HEY, YOU MOUSIE!" I HEARD THE VELVE-teen's voice cheerily calling me as she peered into my cage. Her words, usually clear as a bell, sounded muffled and distant as if she were talking in another room, yet she was less than six inches away.

"Are you okay?" she added when I did not respond, the urgency in her tone piercing the fog in my brain.

The darkness of my tissue box den surrounded me like a soft, cuddly blanket that felt safe and soothing. Weak from lack of food or water and unable to move very well without feeling dizzy, I mustered up enough energy to poke the tip of my nose out of the door. A shaft of bright morning light greeted me, and I shrank back from it as quickly as if I had seen a snake. She removed the top of the cage and then lifted the lid of my box so she could have a better look at me.

"Oh, Petey, I'm so glad that you are alive. I hardly slept last night because I was so worried about you. I really want to hold you, but I don't think I should pick you up until after your surgery," she explained tentatively.

Stroking my fur with her finger seemed to be the alternative she chose. Being petted by a human, especially the one I knew best, felt wonderful and made me feel secure, but I was confused.

Surgery? I did not know what surgery was. It sounded a little like *sugary*, so I hoped it was something to eat. She stared at me intently and scratched her head with her other hand as if she was trying to remember something important, her finger still tracing figure eights on my back.

"Oh, my goodness, I haven't told you about your surgery yet, have I?" she asked, a shocked tone in her voice.

"I spoke with Dr. Beed this morning. After I told her that your eye seemed much worse, she said that the only way she could make your eye better was to operate on it. So back we go to the vet to get your eye all fixed up. She said we should arrive in the early afternoon, and she will work us in as soon as we get there." Her voice sounded cheery but not genuine, like a candy sweetened with an artificial sweetener. I wasn't fooled. I knew she was anxious.

The velveteen carefully replaced the lid of my box, surrounding me in comfortable semidarkness once more. I could hear the familiar snapping sounds as she reattached the wire top of the cage to the plastic bottom.

I had just started to wash my right front paw when she lifted my cage as gently as if she were carrying a carton of eggs. She lowered it gingerly onto the seat of the car and strapped it in with the seat belt. I was grateful for her gentleness since even the slightest bump or shake of the cage was difficult for me. I felt like a storm was ravaging my body. My eye was throbbing in seemingly endless waves of pain that ebbed and flowed like the surf pounding against a rocky shore. I was in agony. The pain from ER 002's bite was a piece of cake compared to this.

I was not sure what surgery was, but I was willing to do almost anything to stop this unbearable discomfort. When we arrived at Every Pet, Karin unbuckled my seat belt and then carefully lifted my cage off of the seat. She walked very slowly as she carried me inside.

The old white cat was sitting in the waiting room in her usual place on a cushion atop the threadbare, dilapidated chair. She lazily opened a sleepy eye, looked at me for a split second as if she had been waiting for me to arrive, nodded, and then went back to sleep.

Ivy, on the other hand, greeted us with a welcoming smile, her eyes warm and friendly. "Petey, how nice to see you again. You are going to be just fine! Dr. Beed is the best."

Her voice was comforting. I breathed a little easier.

Ivy exchanged pleasantries with the velveteen for a few moments as she checked me in and then ushered us into the exam room. With my cage placed atop the shiny metal exam table, Karin made the familiar clicking sound, inviting me to come out. Because I was much less cooperative than usual, the velveteen had to work at extricating me from my den.

She tapped her fingers on the bedding in front of the box, a sign for me to approach her hand. Normally I would walk right over to her. Immobilized by pain and fear, I sat still.

She tapped her fingers again and called my name. Her persistence paid off. She was finally able to draw me out, lift me up, and cup me in her hand. As she held me close to her body just like she had at CarPet World on the day we met, she sat down in a small green chair in the corner of the room across from the exam table.

I shuddered. She gently stroked my fur, and we waited.

The sunlight, trickling in through the small window, highlighted the picture of the two rats. As we waited, my whiskers began moving very quickly, and my nose twitched, behaviors that betrayed my anxiety to anyone who understood rat behavior.

My sensitive nose inhaled the myriad of smells. I distracted myself by trying to identify the scents of all the different animals that had been here before me, each leaving a distinct odor behind.

I detected one rabbit, two ferrets, a King Charles Cavalier Spaniel, two guinea pigs, and four rats. Although I detected many odors, I did not smell fear, and that helped me to relax a little. There was no smell of death. That was a relief.

A sudden noise caught my attention, and my gaze shifted to the right as Dr. Beed came into the room, her eyes twinkling behind her big glasses.

"Petey, nice to see you again. We are all ready and waiting for you," she commented as she deftly scooped me out of the velveteen's hands and transported me to the exam table.

I stiffened, and with a sudden unexpected burst of nervous energy,

I attempted to run off the table. I did not mean to, but I was frightened and a little crazed by the pain in my eye.

With the dexterity of a master, she caught me and then firmly immobilized my body with one hand as she stabilized my head with the other so she could study my eye. I did not resist.

She examined the eye for a long time, occasionally saying a thoughtful, "Hmmm."

Finally she pronounced her verdict, "Your eye looks very infected, Petey, and the medicine does not seem to be helping. I wish I could save it, but I think the best thing to do is to enucleate, a long word that means remove your eye. I am afraid that if I don't, the infection will spread, and you will die."

She looked at the velveteen as if to say, "Do you agree?"

The velveteen nodded. "I trust your judgment, Dr. Beed. Do what you think is best. I have grown really attached to Petey in a very short time, so I want you to do whatever you need to do to keep him alive."

What? Wasn't anyone going to ask me what I thought? Enucleate! What a scary word. Wasn't that what they called those big bombs that exploded in mushroom clouds? Pops read a book to us about them, and we learned that many animals were killed or became very sick after those bombs were detonated. Was she going to use a bomb to fix my eye? That could not be right. I wanted to trust her, but I felt worried and confused.

But wait a minute. If she *nuked* my eye, I would be a one-eyed rat. This prospect was as exciting to me as suddenly being turned into a banana slug by some dark magic. To be perfectly frank, I hated the idea. On the other hand, I knew I could not live like this any longer. If surgery could stop my suffering, I would do it, but the thought of losing my eye was more than I could handle at the moment.

Dr. Beed was speaking again, introducing the velveteen to another woman who had come into the exam room. "This is Jenny, my vet tech, who will be assisting with the surgery."

Jenny was tall with short brown hair, the color we rats call mink. That persistent beam of sunlight coming through the small window chose that moment to shine right into Jenny's warm brown eyes. She squinted at me and then picked me up. Her hands were kind and soothing as she massaged my tense shoulders. I felt my body relax a little more.

"Hello, Petey." Jenny's voice soothed me like that of a Zen master.

I felt contentment, the kind of contentment a rat feels when he or she is eating a big hunk of cheese on a moonlit night during a warm summer. But I was not eating a big hunk of cheese, and I was not outside on a warm, moonlit night. I was about to undergo a procedure to remove my eye. I sighed.

Jenny's gentle voice penetrated my thoughts. "I will be getting you ready for your surgery. You seem calmer now, but you were pretty tense when you first got here, so I'll massage your back again. After that, I'll give you some medicine to help you relax even more. I give excellent care to all my patients."

Jenny turned to look at Karin and then nodded. The velveteen took this as her cue to leave. She stroked my fur as she told me that she would be praying that the surgery goes well and promised to come back to get me when I was finished. I moved my head in the scanning motion that helped me focus and watched her walk around the corner until she was gone.

With swift experienced hands, Jenny held my head steady and inserted a syringe in my mouth. She squirted in some liquid that tasted like bitter cherries. This must be the calming medicine. It wasn't long before I felt mellower and less stressed. The next thing I knew, Jenny was transporting me into the back room for the surgery.

The back room was divided into three parts. We quickly passed the first section. It had a small desk covered with stacks of papers. Next to the desk was a fenced area where two large and energetic bunnies were hopping around.

As we walked through the second section, I saw about eight cages stacked against the wall. There was a basset hound asleep in one and a black cat with intense yellow eyes, wide-awake, warily watching us in another. The rest were empty. Off to the side was a small metal sink with a wall screen for viewing X-rays to the right of it. Many white supply cabinets with silver handles shaped like ferrets lined the walls.

When we reached the third section, Jenny paused, "Petey, this is the operating room."

Dr. Beed, with Jenny's assistance, operates on Petey's eye.

I immediately noticed a rectangular table with bright lights surrounding it. There were silver tools lying on a smaller table to the left that glistened in the lights. Just to the right of the large table was a singular tall white cabinet with ferret handles that I assumed contained needed supplies. A rust-colored tank shaped like a sausage sat close to the table and cast an interesting shadow on the floor. A thin tube snaked its way up from the tank to the top of the table.

Jenny put me down on the table, held me in place with gentle pressure from her hand, and then said, "This is the operating table, Petey. We are almost ready to begin your surgery."

I did not mean to, but I inhaled sharply. Panicky thoughts suddenly surged through my mind. Instinct began to take over, and I frantically scanned the room, looking for a place to hide. I found it underneath the tall white cabinet that was supported by short feet only about an inch tall. This was just enough room for me to scurry beneath it. I knew that once I was under there, it would be impossible for anyone to get me out.

My brain told me to struggle free and hide, but my body did not cooperate. As much as I wanted to follow this last-minute escape plan, I stayed motionless. I was in too much pain to move. Then I heard Dr. Beed's quiet voice, and it instantly settled me.

She was not even speaking to me, but there was something about her presence that assured me that everything was going to be okay. At that moment I decided she was magic.

"Are you ready, Jenny?" she asked. She glanced over her shoulder toward me as she scrubbed her hands at the small sink in the other section of the room.

"Ready, Dr. Beed," Jenny answered while she delicately transferred me to the middle of the operating table and Dr. Beed finished her preparations.

Jenny was massaging my back. Something that looked like a tiny, clear plastic walnut was carefully placed over my nose. I felt very woozy. The lights in the operating room grew dimmer and dimmer. The objects in the room faded into a nebulous haze, and my eyelid felt so heavy that I could not will myself to keep it open. That was the last thing I remembered.

Next thing I knew, I was back in my cage. I opened my eye and scanned the area, relieved that I could see. For a few moments, I felt confused and disoriented, not sure where I was. Then the discomfort I felt in the right side of my face reminded me that I was in the back room at Dr. Beed's office and had been *nuked*.

My right eye felt achy and itchy, but that horrible, excruciating pain had vanished like a puff of smoke fading into the atmosphere, never to be seen again. I reached up with my front paw to touch my eye and jerked my paw away in shock when all I felt was a rather bumpy ridge of skin with stiff prickly things poking out of it but no eye.

It was gone!

I felt foolish for feeling surprised, but to be perfectly honest, I think I had secretly hoped against hope that Dr. Beed would be able to save my eye. Timidly I reached back up one more time and felt my face where my eye used to be. Yes, it was definitely gone. I sighed a heavy sigh of resignation.

"What are *you* in for?" asked a soft, high voice. I turned around slowly, still feeling a little queasy and unsteady, and I saw the rather large, fluffy black cat with brilliant yellow eyes peering at me from one of the small cages.

Cats, as you know, are not my favorite animals. We rats have historically been in an adversarial relationship with felines. To put it bluntly, we are natural enemies and hate each other. Thus, I was surprised when this one appeared to be speaking to me in a relatively friendly voice.

"Are you talking to me?" I asked after I cleared my throat.

My voice was rather squeaky and hoarse. I assumed it was because this was the first time I had spoken since the surgery.

"To whom do you think I am speaking? Of course, I am addressing you. No one else is here," she replied indignantly, speaking in a very proper tone that hinted of a slight British accent.

She paused. "Except for him," she added as she turned her electric golden eyes toward the sleeping basset hound puppy.

Lavinia, the cat, and Petey have an unexpected conversation after the surgery.

The dog was zonked, lying on his side, one big ear flopped over his eyes and the other stretched out on the floor. At intermittent intervals he emitted a loud, snoring sound that reminded me of George, Isabelle's husband, back at the rattery.

"Oh," I said, unable to think of a more erudite response. Something about the way she spoke caused me to feel as though I needed to have a PhD like those psychologists in the rats of NIMH.

"You have not answered my question," she stated in a rather irritated manner, and then she abruptly turned her head to lick her long, raccoon-like black tail.

I tried to remember what the question was. But my mind was fuzzy, and my thoughts were as scattered as leaves on a windy autumn afternoon.

"Oh, I'm very sorry, but I can't seem to remember what your question was," I stammered, tripping over my words.

She turned back to face me again, sighed, and rolled her yellow eyes. "I thought you rats were supposed to be intelligent creatures," she said crossly, making no attempt to hide her exasperation. "I *said*, 'For what reason are you here?'"

"My eye. I had to have my eye removed. Nuked," I replied, hoping what I said made sense. I turned my head to the side so she could see my wound. "How does it look?"

She peered at me intently and then commented as though she were critically evaluating a piece of artwork. "It looks all stitched up. Pity. I imagine you used to be quite a handsome creature when you had two eyes—as far as rats go, that is."

A bit confused as to whether this was a compliment or an insult, I was unsure whether an expression of gratitude was an appropriate response.

"Thanks. And why are you here?" I asked, hoping to change the subject.

Her reply was brief and to the point, "Spayed."

She rolled over to reveal a most impressive scar on her belly.

I was at a loss for words. "Oh … you have a spectacular scar," I said, stumbling over the words.

"Why, thank you," she replied as she turned over and then gave her back a few vigorous licks with her rough tongue.

Seeing her wash made me think about taking a bath myself. That was one of the few things that the cats and the rats had in common. We both like to keep our fur immaculate, using our tongues as washcloths. I managed a few licks to my side, but I found that the licking motion caused me to feel dizzy, so I stopped.

This whole situation was too weird. I never thought I would be taking a bath with a cat!

I suddenly remembered a book that Pops read to us when we were young. It was titled *Jennie*. A human named Paul Galico wrote it. Pops dragged it into our cage one night. He had found it lying out in the room. I think the picture of the cat on the cover aroused his curiosity.

It was a story about a boy who was metamorphosized (that means turned into) a cat and then befriended by a cat named Jennie. At one point in the story, she advised the boy/cat named Peter that he should begin vigorously washing his fur whenever he felt anxious or confused.

Jennie explained to Peter that not only did washing help cats think but that it was also a good stalling technique when one was in a tight situation.

When in doubt, wash!

Remembering Jennie's words of advice to Peter, I practiced doing the same thing, even though I was a rat. Washing my fur became a very effective way for me to deal with many an awkward or stressful situation in my life.

My feline friend's high voice interrupted my thoughts. "Lavinia, what's yours?"

I stared at the cat, startled and confused.

"What's my what?" I asked as I moistened my right front paw with my tongue and then washed the fur behind my ears a few times to cover my embarrassment.

"Your name. I said my name is Lavinia. What's yours?" Her yellow eyes twinkled.

I think she was laughing at me.

"Well, my parents named me Nicodemus, but my new family calls me Petey. It is a little confusing, even for me, but I have gotten used to being called Petey now," I explained, continuing to wash my fur as I conversed with her.

She nodded and then slowly looked me up and down, the art critic in her coming out once more.

"Petey—that suits you. Nicodemus is quite a long name for a rat," she commented, nodding her head like a wise old owl. She seemed to have an opinion about everything.

She unexpectedly looked to the left, startled by the sound of the rambunctious rabbits in the other section of the room knocking over their food dish.

"Thank you," I said again, amazed that a cat had given me not one but two compliments. "By the way, what does it mean to be spayed?"

"No more kittens!" Without warning, she started to cry. Huge tears began streaming down her face as quickly as if she had just opened a water faucet in each eye.

"I loved being a mother. I had four kittens, two boys and two girls. Two black like me and two calicos. They were such good kittens, and all went to good homes with sweet children." She sobbed, wiping her eyes with her left paw.

The tears stopped flowing as abruptly as they had started. It was like she had magically turned the faucets off. "And then my owner said, 'Lavinia, no more kittens. We're afraid that we won't be able to find good homes for them.' I wasn't sure what they meant by no more kittens, but soon after that, I came here. And now … no more." She put her head down and mewed softly.

I did not know what to say. I had never been that close to a cat or even spoken with one before. As I rummaged through my memories, I sought to find a situation from my past that might help me now. The only thing I could remember were words Pops said to his friend, Gus, when Gus's pregnant mate suddenly died. I tried using them.

"Please accept my condolences, Lavinia. Is there anything I can do?" I whispered compassionately.

"Thank you, Petey. No, there is nothing you can do," she replied.

Her eyes were as bright as the sun, burning with such intensity that I thought I had offended her. When she spoke, I understood that it was not hurt that had fueled her stare but a combination of confusion and amazement.

"I never thought I would be comforted by a rat, but having you here has made me feel better," she told me in a somewhat friendly voice.

"You know what else is really weird, Lavinia?" I asked as I tried standing up for the first time since my surgery. My legs felt weak. I was as unsteady as a newborn colt.

"No, what's that, Petey?" she asked, the black slits in the center of her eyes widening with interest.

"Well, cat babies are called kittens, and so are rat babies. I mean, it's not a big deal but just a funny coincidence. Maybe we aren't as different as we think. If you cats could just stop eating us rats, maybe we could actually be friends!" I laughed.

This was the first time I had laughed in a long time. It made me feel a little woozy again, so I sat down quite fast, but it also felt really good.

Lavinia smiled a huge Cheshire like smile, and then laughed too.

Our conversation was interrupted when Jenny walked into the room, her kind eyes sparkling as she came toward me. Then she announced, "Petey, it's time to go home."

I glanced at Lavinia and said a quick good-bye. She blinked her big amber eyes and then looked away. She was ignoring me because she didn't want the humans to know that she had communicated with a rat.

Typical cat.

Jenny stooped down beside my cage, opened the top, and held me in her hands, "You are doing great, Petey, and are going to be just fine. But remember, you have to leave those stitches alone so your eye socket can heal."

I nodded.

"Petey, you are just too cute. It's like you really understand me!" Jenny added.

I smiled.

Dr. Beed strode into the room just in time to overhear Jenny's last comment. She made eye contact with me and then winked, communicating with that wink that she knew full well that I comprehended everything that Jenny said.

It was she who carried me out to the waiting room, where my velveteen, Karin, was having an animated conversation with Ivy.

"So when I saw him, I knew that I had to take him home with me—" She stopped midsentence when she saw me.

"Petey! How are you?" she asked while she rushed over to Dr. Beed and reached out her hands, clearly indicating that she wanted to hold me.

Dr. Beed gently transferred me to her as carefully as if I were a newborn baby, and said in her doctor voice, "Petey is fine. He came through the surgery very well. If he can leave those stitches alone and he takes his medicine, he should have no problems. I'd like to see him back in a week to remove the sutures and examine him one more time."

"You can bring Petey back anytime you want," added Jenny, who was looking at me and smiling. "We all love him."

I could feel my face flushing. I was not used to so many compliments. Fortunately no one noticed since my fur covered my bright red skin.

I snuggled up to the velveteen, finding comfort in the warmth of her body. As nice as Ivy, Jenny, Dr. Beed, and even Lavinia had been to me, I wanted to go home. My body, still affected by the anesthesia, felt lethargic and slow like a turtle making its way across the sand. All I wanted to do was to curl up in the corner of my cozy den, close my remaining eye, and sleep forever.

I was more than ready to go home.

Chapter Thirteen

The Love of My Life

SHORTLY AFTER I RETURNED HOME FROM THE vet hospital, I sunk into a profound depression. The joy of being pain-free burned brightly for a brief while, but that feeling was quickly snuffed out by doubts and fears.

Is the darkest hour really right before the dawn? Is it truly better to have a half-full water bottle than a half-empty water bottle? Maybe so, but things in my life *are* pitch dark with no light in sight and my water bottle *is* half empty.

These clichés were about as helpful to me as an unfilled food dish was when I was starving. I was so negative then. My optimism had disappeared as quickly as a rat taking cover from a low-flying owl.

If at that moment some rat had come up to me and told me that the loss of my eye would be a positive turning point in my life, I would have laughed—that is, after I stifled the impulse to slam into him with my side. I would have laughed so hard that I would have rolled across the floor like a hamster in one of those clear plastic exercise balls.

I sighed. Guess I was really angry too.

If I could have seen the future back then, I would have been spared so much sadness. However, unable to see much of anything, let alone the future, I withdrew and felt sorry for myself. I knew I should be grateful that the awful, sickening pain was gone. Nevertheless, I was preoccupied with the realization that the pain was gone because the eye was gone, and for me, that was terribly depressing.

On a purely instinctual level, the loss of an eye represented weakness. Rats are prey animals and are taught from birth that any physical defect increases their vulnerability to predators. Having only one eye meant I could literally be blindsided by a predator if I were living out in the wild.

But my increased vulnerability to potential predators was not why I was upset. Although embarrassed to admit it, the main reason I was struggling so much was because the loss of my eye was a huge blow to my self-confidence.

This was so superficial!

Was it wrong to want to look normal and not look weird? Any rat would want to avoid double takes and stares. Perhaps I am vainer than most rats, but I had great difficulty accepting the one-eyed look.

Lavinia's comments about my appearance did not help at all. If anything, her reaction made me even more apprehensive about how others would react to my unusual face.

I remember seeing pictures of my namesake, Nicodemus, when Pops was reading the treasured copy of *The Rats of NIMH* that Mama had smuggled into our nest. Although we could not resist occasionally nibbling the corners of the pages, the book was one of our most prized possessions. Nicodemus was a great leader of rats. He had a strong, intelligent personality and the distinction of wearing an eye patch over one eye.

When I was a baby rat, I was intrigued by his odd, rather scary appearance. Thus, I had mixed feelings about sharing his name. I remember liking that we were both very smart; however, I took great pride in the fact that although he only had one eye, I had two.

Then there was Herr Drosselmeyer, the human toy maker in *The Nutcracker*. He only had one eye, and he also had an eye patch. As I recalled from that time when my family snuck in to watch the fighting rats at the ballet, Drosselmeyer was a rather strange character, and his one-eyed look served to accentuate his weirdness.

I did not want rats to react to me like that.

On the other hand, both Nicodemus and Drosselmeyer had eye patches to cover the spot where their eyes used to be. Now an eye patch might not be too bad. It was actually kind of cool, but I did not have one. If only I could have an eye patch, maybe that would make me feel better. I brightened at the thought and then sighed. Where would I, a tiny rat living in a cage in a human's house, find an eye patch?

Claire and Sarah seemed particularly intrigued by the fact that I now only had one headlamp. They were so interested that they went online to find out all the famous people who were missing one eye. The computer was very close to Huckle's cage and just around the corner from mine, so it was easy for me to hear their conversation as they searched the Internet.

"Hey, Sarah, look. I found a list of men with one eye! Maybe Petey will be famous too! Come and look," Claire called to Sarah, who walked quickly past my cage over to the computer, Huckle on her shoulder.

"Wow, there are a lot of them. I don't recognize any of the names, do you?" Sarah replied. I tried to get Huckle's attention without success.

"No, not really," Claire commented, sounding a little disappointed.

Just then Karin called, "Girls, come right now, dinner is getting cold. No rats at the table."

Sarah put Huckle back in his glass home and went to dinner, leaving the list on the computer screen. Huckle, who had been listening intently to the conversation, found that if he positioned himself on top of the box at the far left corner of his home, he could read the screen.

"Hey, Petey, can you hear me ... me?" Huckle squeaked.

"Yeah, Huck, I'm here. What's up?" I squeaked back, happy for a distraction from my thoughts.

"Want me to read this stuff about famous humans with one eye ... eye?" he queried, speaking quickly, excited to read what he saw.

"Sure," I answered, actually a little curious to find out.

"I can just barely make out what it says on the screen ... screen," he continued. "Wow. There are some cool dudes who had one eye. There's Sammy Davis, Jr., the actor. Get this—he actually belonged to a group of famous actor dudes called the Rat Pack, led by his buddy Frank Sinatra. Now that's an odd coincidence, isn't it ... it? And guess what else. He had a glass eye put in. Can you imagine that ... that? Then there was this other actor, Peter Falk, who played some detective named Lieutenant Columbo. He lost his eye because of a tumor when he was a little boy. Then Dale Chihuly, you know, that man who is the famous glassblower? Dang. I didn't know he had only one eye. I wonder if he ever made any really cool glass eyes like Sammy Davis had ... had?"

He paused. While waiting, I washed the fur on my left hip. This information piqued my curiosity.

"And then there's Moshe Dayan, that notorious Israeli guy who lost his eye in battle just like you did ... did." Huckle paused again. I could hear the water bottle clicking, so I assumed he was taking a drink. Then he continued, "Wait. Here's another one—James Booker. He was an amazing piano player from some rattery called New Orleans, and he had this cool eye patch with a big star on it ... it." Huckle stopped and took a deep breath, muttering something that sounded like, "Shut up, Dusty ... Dusty."

I could imagine Dusty making disparaging comments. "Are you sure he came from a rattery, Huckle? I think New Orleans might be a city."

Huckle thought for a moment and then responded, "Yeah, you are probably right, Petey ... Petey."

After a few minutes, he continued, "And then there's this comic book superhero named Nick Fury who looks so cool. Says he lost his eye from shrapnel in the war. He hangs out with other superheroes like Spider-Man, Captain America, and Iron Man. Can you imagine doing that ... that?"

Both Huckle and I were familiar with comic books from our rattery days.

"Then I'll be darned. This is too cool. This Canadian dude's eye was nuked three years ago, and he decided to have a fake eye put in that is really a camera. He calls himself 'a human surveillance machine' and plans to secretly film people out of his eye while talking to them. Get this! He calls himself Eye-borg ... Eye-borg." Huckle made a clicking sound.

"Wow, that's impressive. Having a camera where my eye was would be so cool." I thought about this for a few moments. "But all those stories you told me are about humans, Huck, and I'm a rat." I sighed, stubbornly feeling sorry for myself.

"Of course you're a rat ... rat. Listen to this then...then," he retorted, reading again, speaking faster and faster as his excitement about what he was reading grew.

"There are a whole series of books about a one-eyed cat. Can you believe it? A cat! And a book about a one-eyed killer stud horse. So why can't you be a famous one-eyed rat ... rat?" Huckle was trying his best to encourage me.

"Well, I don't need to be famous, Huckle. I just want to feel a little better about my situation. But what you just read does help. It lets me know that I am not alone. Sounds like lots of other creatures have had normal lives with only one high beam. Maybe I can too." I responded, my voice betraying a glimmer of hope.

For the first time since my surgery, I felt a little more positive and confident about my future. As the new, more optimistic thoughts percolated in my brain, I felt the dark cloud of depression beginning to lift.

For the first week after surgery, I needed to take antibiotics every few hours. In order to comply with Dr. Beed's instructions, the velveteen needed to treat me throughout the day. This schedule worked out just fine on the days Karin was at home, but it presented a logistical problem on the days she worked.

"Hey, you mousie!" the velveteen called to me, her voice cheery and light. She was so much happier since my surgery. I scrambled out of my house and climbed up to the second level. She unlatched the door at the top, lifted me up, and then held me with two hands so she could stare straight into my eye. This behavior indicated that she wanted to tell me something very important.

"Petey," she announced, "I don't know what people are going to think when they see a rat in my office, but I'm going to take you to work with me. It's the only way I can give you your medicine and make sure your eye is all right."

I did not know what *work* meant, but I was curious and ready to find out. On her next workday, she ushered me into my cage and secured me in the car, and off we went. After a relatively short drive, we parked in front of a rather oddly shaped brown building.

Karin carried me in one hand and her briefcase in the other. We stopped in front of a silver door. She pressed a button on the wall, and we waited. Suddenly the door opened, revealing a large closet. We stepped into it, and the door closed behind us like it was alive.

This was weird.

After a lurch the whole closet started moving upward with us inside. The velveteen was perfectly calm, but I panicked. I started frantically climbing up the bars of the cage. I had no idea what was happening.

"Petey, this is an elevator. It takes us up to the third floor, where my office is. You don't have to be scared. It won't hurt us," she explained, her tone soothing and her words reassuring, but I felt queasy and uneasy. This was the closest thing to an earthquake I had felt for a long time.

I had never been in an elevator before.

The door of the moving closet opened, and Karin carried me out into a hallway. I sighed, feeling relieved to be out of that thing. We stopped in front of a large wooden door. I glanced at the nameplate. There were sharp white letters with her name and Doug's name, both followed by the letters PhD. Something about these letters made me uneasy, but I wasn't sure why. I could feel a flicker of a memory activating in my brain.

The velveteen inserted a key into the lock and we entered a large waiting area. It was not what I expected. The room was carpeted and equipped with furniture, wall art, and lamps so that it looked more like a human home than a place of business.

After she set my cage down on a counter, I cautiously scanned the room with my one good eye. Close to my cage were stacks of small cards. One had the velveteen's name on it, and then underneath her name, I saw the words "Licensed Psychologist."

I froze.

Now I remembered why seeing the letters "PhD" bothered me. You see, I first learned about psychologists when Pops read *The Rats of NIMH* to my brothers, sisters, and me. As you may or may not know, the rats in the story were used in experiments at the National Institute of Mental Health (NIMH). These particular lab rats were subjected to experiments that made them unbelievably smart, much smarter than your average rat. Pops made sure we understood that this was fiction and that most laboratory rats were not so fortunate. He explained how in the real world, many rats have lost their lives while others have had parts of their brains or bodies destroyed, all in the name of science.

The rats of NIMH, furious that they had been forced to be subjects in scientific experiments, used their brilliant minds to their advantage and plotted an ingenious breakout. The escape was successful and the rats were free, however they lived in constant fear of being captured and returned to NIMH.

The psychologists, angry and embarrassed that the subjects of their experiments had outsmarted them, left NIMH in hot pursuit of the rats. This cat-and-mouse—or should I say cat-and-rat adventure unfolds in the remaining chapters.

Now it was my turn to be in the presence of a licensed psychologist. Who could blame me for expecting her office to be anything but a facility similar to the one described in the book?

Karin, completely unaware of my thoughts, nonchalantly picked up my cage and said, "Okay, Petey, let's go see my office now." Then she paused for a moment to look at me with concern. My whiskers were twitching rapidly, and my guard hairs were rising. "Why do you look so scared? I think you will like it here."

I wanted to believe her, but I felt distrustful now that I knew she was a psychologist. I expected to be escorted into an antiseptic room with spotless white walls lined with identical cages of zombielike rats.

The sound of a door opening made me jump. I knew it! A white coated, masked human is going to walk through the door, carrying a syringe filled with an experimental liquid to be injected into my brain. I stiffened and turned in the direction of the sound, holding my breath. But it was only the mail carrier, a very friendly man who looked at me with mild interest and smiled. I smiled back, never happier to see a mail carrier in all of my life.

When we walked into Karin's office, I immediately knew it was unlike the labs at NIMH. I breathed a huge sigh of relief. The most noticeable difference was the absence of rats in wall-to-wall cages. In fact, there were no signs of experiments with rats or any other animals—no syringes, no bottles of antiseptic, no metal tables. NIMH was a particularly stark, clinically sterile-looking place. This office was the opposite. It looked like a living room, and exuded a warm, friendly welcoming feeling.

My whiskers slowed down, moving much slower now, like a fan switched from high to low. My guard hairs flattened, relaxing just like a porcupine's quills do after a threat has passed. When I was a young rat, I wished I had quills and used to pretend I was a porcupine when my guard hairs stood out. Porcupines are rodents, too, with the most amazing guard hairs. Humans actually buy them to make hair roaches. Rat guard hairs are not nearly as impressive.

"Petey, look at the squirrel!" The velveteen's excited voice brought me back from my reflections on my childhood fantasy. She carried me over to the large window.

I could see the bright green leaves of a maple tree and the darker green needles of a cedar. I saw a squirrel, nut in mouth, racing up the rough trunk of the maple tree. He paused to stare into the window. I wondered if he could see me. I stared back. As if startled by my gaze, he dropped the nut and then dove back down the trunk to retrieve it again. Typical squirrel.

I looked away from the window and scanned the inside of the room. Not far from the window was a tan couch, an end table with a lamp shaped like an upside-down pear, and two soft blue chairs. Across from the window was a row of cabinets with a small black ledge on top that supported another lamp and a pile of neatly stacked papers.

Karin takes Petey to her office.

Tall bookshelves filled with books of all sizes, and a small wooden secretary's desk lined the remaining wall. A quick scan indicated that there were no books about conducting psychological research with rats, although the title of one, *The Lab Rat Chronicles: A Neuroscientist Reveals Life Lessons from the Planet's Most Successful Mammals*, made me nervous.

Karin placed my cage on the floor adjacent to a row of storage cabinets, across from a low bookshelf, and opposite the door. She gave me a dose of medicine and then said, "Petey, I need to start working now."

I soon learned that work meant talking to the people who came into the office. Each person seemed to have a favorite place to sit. Some of them noticed me, while others barely glanced in my direction. At intermittent intervals, someone would ask, "What's in the cage?"

The velveteen would calmly reply, "Oh, that's my rat, Petey. He is here because he just had surgery and I need to watch him closely for a few days."

A few simply nodded, clearly uninterested in pursuing the topic any further. However, most of the people were intrigued by the idea of a rat in the office and wanted to know more about me.

I listened as the velveteen told the story of my eye surgery and explained about my medicine. Some of the people wanted to pet me while others preferred to observe me from a distance. I was content to stay in my cage or sit on the top, quietly observing the comings and goings of the office, my nose and whiskers absorbing new information like a sponge.

A stream of people flowed in and out of the office all day. There was a rather predictable pattern of behavior. Karin would escort a person into the office, and they would both sit down, the most common configuration being one on the couch and the other in a chair. Then they would begin to talk. I learned that this phenomenon was called *a session* and it lasted a long time.

Sometimes the people were very sad and tears ran down their faces. Other times they would laugh, or yell, or become very animated. Periodically more than one person would come in, and sometimes a whole family engaged in animated conversation would be there. These were my favorite sessions.

It took me a long time to comprehend what was happening because I was at the office during the day when it was a struggle for me to stay awake. Even though I was very interested in the discussions, I became so tired by about ten o'clock in the morning that I couldn't keep my eye open. I would doze only catching bits of conversation until about four o'clock in the afternoon. Then I would wake up for awhile, listen a little more, have a snack, and go back to sleep until we went home. Despite these logistical challenges, I eventually developed an understanding, appreciation, and fondness for psychotherapy.

I soon finished my course of antibiotics and received a clean bill of health from Dr. Beed. My incision was healing nicely and I was feeling healthy and strong for the first time since that dark night when ER 002, Sketch, and X-Con ambushed Hoover and me.

One morning as she was getting ready for work, the velveteen paused, looked at me thoughtfully, and then said, "Petey, it has been really nice having you at my office. Would you like to continue coming to work with me?"

I nodded, and then smiled. I had just landed my first job.

When at work, I spent most of my time in the velveteen's office, but sometimes I stayed out in the work area with Julie, the office manager. Julie had brown hair with red highlights that made it similar in shade to the rat fur color called cinnamon. The work area and the waiting room were one large room partitioned by a wooden divider that served as a desk and worktable for Julie.

In the waiting area, there was a couch the color of mushrooms that was big enough for two humans, several chairs with pinkish cushions, and a small gray box that played music, the classical kind like we heard that time we snuck in to watch the ballet.

Julie let me run around and explore the cubbyholes above her desk. I found a special place behind a pile of CDs where I liked to sleep during the day: however, I never slept for very long because I was always interested in what was going on in the office and who was coming to visit. Every morning around 11:00 a.m., the mail carrier, who startled me the first day I had gone into work, handed a pile of envelopes to Julie.

Then Julie would hold out an envelope toward me and say, "Petey, want to help me open the mail?" I would take the envelope in my teeth and drag it to a cubbyhole where I would proceed to chew off the edges. Julie would retrieve it before I got too carried away and then handed me another one. We would carry on this way for quite awhile. Some of the envelopes actually tasted pretty good!

One particularly interesting visitor to the office was a woman whom Julie called Hanah. She delivered office supplies on a regular basis. Her sparkly blue eyes and light, straight hair, which was the same fawn color as mine, caught my attention. Hanah took a particular interest in me, so she and I had extensive conversations. I liked it when she picked me up and stroked my fur.

Hanah came in soaking wet one day because it was raining so hard outside, but she had a huge smile on her face. I wondered why she was so happy and then she explained. Karin had just come out into the waiting area, so joined in the conversation.

"Karin, Julie, and Petey! Guess what? I adopted a little girl rat yesterday. I am so excited!" Hanah could hardly contain her enthusiasm. "She looks so much like you, Petey! Her fur is a pretty fawn color just like yours but her eyes are a little lighter. Would you like to meet her?"

I nodded.

Hanah looked at Karin and added, "If that is okay with you, Karin."

"Of course," Karen said, smiling at me. "I think it would be so nice for Petey to have a friend."

I actually forgot about this conversation until the momentous day when the little girl rat came to visit. I was sleeping in my tissue box den, snuggled up with some remnants of food and shredded paper, when I heard the velveteen's voice.

"Petey, Petey, can you wake up? I have a surprise for you."

I woke up quickly, responding to the excitement in her voice, poked my head out of my box, and yawned. I expected some banana yogurt.

"Hanah wants you to meet somebody," she continued, scooping me up in her hand as she was talking to me. She swept me into the waiting room and we sat down on the couch next to Hanah, who was holding something ... or someone in her hands as well.

I began to squirm with excitement. I turned my head so that my eye could focus on Hanah, and I gazed at her hand, trying to catch a glimpse of the doe.

My heart started to beat faster. I sensed the presence of an awesome creature. Instinctively my whiskers started twirling like the blades of a fan on high speed.

I raised my head so that I could get a better whiff of her scent. Then I was close enough to see her. I squinted to sharpen the image and saw her beautiful creamy beige fur outlined against the fabric of the couch.

I gasped. She had rose-colored eyes that took my breath away. I had a definite weakness for does with those light pink peepers.

For just a moment, my thoughts traveled back to that day at CarPet World when Hoover told me that Willow was attracted to me and thought I was handsome. I remembered helplessly staring at the girl rat, transfixed by her beauty, wanting to talk to her. We finally figured out how to communicate with each other even though we were in separate bins. The frustration of always being separated by glass seemed unbearable at times.

I also remembered the sadness I felt the day she was adopted, even though I knew that she was going to be well cared for in a loving home. However, it's not in a rat's nature to remain loyal to one mate and not pay attention to an attractive new partner. Just as I would move on, I knew Willow would as well. It's just the way we are.

"Petey, Petey, can you hear me?" the velveteen was speaking again. "Petey, I would like to introduce you to Bailey."

She stood up and placed me on the couch. The rough fabric felt odd on my paws. The beautiful doe was sitting next to Hanah, washing her face, carefully smoothing her delicate, pinkish ears with her paws.

Then she began washing her golden fur that was tipped with light orange highlights. It looked silky and smooth, obviously groomed daily with great care. My heart accelerated instantly.

I inhaled, holding my breath as I watched her. Her tail, which was long with a slight curl at the tip, moved in a slow side-to-side motion. My head felt funny. I must be either hypnotized or dizzy. Breathe, Petey. Breathe. I exhaled and felt better.

Suddenly a series of awful thoughts assaulted me like a pack of hungry cats. What if she does not like me because I only have one eye? What if she laughs at me? What if she thinks I am ugly or stupid?

I felt a wave of insecurity envelop me, deflating my confidence as quickly as a balloon loses air when stuck with a pin. I hesitated and took a few steps backward, vigorously washing my face to stall for time. What was I going to do?

Then I remembered something. It was that conversation I had with Pops when I was a young kitten. The sun was shining in the window and we were eating hazelnuts. I was dreaming about being a show rat.

I could hear his deep, strong voice as clearly as if he were sitting right next to me, munching on his hazelnut. "You are a very fine rat, Nicodemus. Your looks are good, but even more than that, you are very smart and lots of fun. Remember, appearance is not what is most important. It is what's inside that counts!"

On that day so long ago when he first spoke those words, I was too young to fully understand what he meant, but I understood now. His words quelled my fears enough to restore my confidence. I needed his viewpoint to help me put my self-doubt and irrational thoughts into perspective.

It was almost as though I could hear him saying to me, "If Bailey rejects you because you only have one eye, she will miss the chance to know an honest, compassionate, and caring rat. That will be her loss."

It did not take long for me to realize that my uncertainties were groundless. From the moment our three eyes met, there was magic in the air. We greeted each other and exchanged sniffs as is the custom for rats upon first introduction. Then Bailey began to dance around the couch.

Bailey mesmerizes Petey.

At first I just watched her, transfixed by the gracefulness of her movements. Then I began chasing her. We played with each other for a long time, running around the cushions and up over the back of the couch and then around the cushions again. In my excitement I completely forgot there were humans in the room with us until Hanah spoke.

"Bailey, we have to go home now," Hanah uttered the words I dreaded hearing.

I wanted to stomp my foot like a little rat and say, "No, you can't go!" but I controlled my kittenish impulse.

Bailey looked at me with a mixture of sadness and merriment in her flirtatious pink eyes. She squeaked in her very high, musical voice, "Petey, thank you for a fun afternoon. Will I see you again?"

I stared at the girl rat, my heart melting as quickly as a yogurt drop accidentally left in the hot sun. I could not bear to see her go. I knew that my life had been changed forever.

She had just asked me a question. What was I going to say? I wanted to say something romantic like, "Of course, nothing can keep us apart," but in reality, I had little control over whether I would see her again.

My emotions were so strong that I was dumbstruck. I opened my mouth as if to speak, but much to my dismay, nothing came out. It was as though a mute button had been pressed on my voice box so that I could not make a sound.

"Petey," Bailey called as she was going out the door, riding on Hanah's shoulders. "Don't worry. I'll come back!"

I just stood there, staring, feeling stupid for being so inarticulate. She must think I am an idiot!

I sighed.

So preoccupied was I with my own thoughts that I hardly felt the velveteen place me back in my cage in her office.

I lived the rest of that day in a dream state, totally oblivious to everything going on around me. Even though I was very tired, I could not sleep. My thoughts of Bailey stimulated my mind as much as if I had just consumed ten cups of coffee. (I knew what coffee was because

I had tipped over a cup the velveteen was drinking last week and had tried it. My body felt jittery and I ended up staying awake all day without even trying.)

My mind was like a video stuck on auto repeat. All it could do was replay everything that had happened during my time with Bailey over and over again.

When Karin walked toward me and said, "Time to go home, Petey," I jumped, once again so preoccupied that I was not paying attention to my surroundings.

She picked up my cage and turned off the music and the lights, and we exited from the same door that Bailey had passed through a few hours earlier. The girl rat's scent lingered. I inhaled deeply, not wanting to ever exhale again.

Although we arrived home in the early evening when I should have been ready to wake up, I was exhausted. I had not slept at all. For a rat, staying awake all day is like a human pulling an all-nighter.

Just as the last rays of sunlight streamed through the window, I retreated to my tissue box house to try to catch a few winks. I was just drifting off when snatches of the conversation the velveteen was having with Claire and Sarah caught my attention.

"Hanah, the delivery person, at the office brought her rat in today, and Petey seemed so happy to play with her. Do you think that Petey is lonely?" Karin asked, curious about her daughters' perspective.

I smiled knowingly. Loneliness was not what motivated my interest in Bailey.

"Well, I think he is," commented Claire, who had been curled up on the couch next to my cage, avidly reading a thick book. She looked at me, her brown eyes warm and friendly. "I think rats are happier if they have a companion," she added with the confidence of one who had just stated a well-known fact.

Sarah, her mind leaping one step ahead, asked, "Can we go to CarPet World and see if there is a rat we want to bring home to live with Petey?"

"Sure, let's go," said the velveteen, reaching into the refrigerator for some leftovers to warm in the microwave. "It's only 6:30, so let's eat a quick dinner and then run over there. I need to buy some rat food anyway."

I was alert now. As I peeked out of my den door, I could see them scurrying around and making dinner. Soon I heard the clanking of dishes followed by the familiar whirl of the dishwasher. It was not long before they were ready to go. As they disappeared from my sight, Claire yelled excitedly, "Wait until you see what we are going to bring home, Petey."

I heard the door slam shut behind her, and then I chuckled as I heard Doug mutter, "I keep telling them to not slam that door."

Well, I sure did not expect this. Given that my track record with male rats was quite pathetic, I simultaneously relished and feared the thought of a new cage mate. It seemed like other bucks and I either got along really well or not at all. I did not have a problem with them, but quite a few, notably ER 002, Sketch, X-Con, and now Dusty, definitely had issues with me.

I tried to alert Huckle to this new development; however, the radio was on, and the dishwasher was still whirring, making it impossible for him to hear my squeaks.

Even though my mind was swirling with thoughts of Bailey and the possibility of a roommate, I was so fatigued that I did manage to doze off until the familiar sounds of the garage door opening and the family shuffling in roused me.

My eye widened when I saw Sarah carrying the unmistakable white cardboard To-Go box with the familiar CarPet World logo on the side. They had actually adopted a new rat from CarPet World.

Sarah and Claire had huge smiles on their faces. "Petey, Petey! Come out and meet your new friend!" Claire exclaimed with so much excitement that her voice sounded as high as a rat squeak.

Karin took the box from Sarah, set it down next to my cage, and then opened it. I could hardly contain myself. Claire carefully lifted out a small male rat with dumbo ears and a white possum face.

If I had not already been lying down, I would have toppled over out of shock. I was sure that I was dreaming, so blinked my eye really hard and opened it again just to make sure I really was awake.

The velveteen was showing me the new rat and saying, "Petey, come and look at this cute little guy we just bought at the pet store. Do you like him? We also bought you a new cage so you would have enough room for a friend."

So focused was I on the newcomer that her words sounded far away as if someone were speaking to me from the other end of a long tunnel. I honestly could not believe my eye. I stared at the new rat, and he stared back at me. It was Hoover!

"Hoover, you scoundrel, how did you end up here?" I exclaimed, hardly able to contain my excitement, speaking in such high-pitched squeaks that the humans could not hear me.

"Nicodemus, you rascal! I can't believe it's you. How in the blazes are you?" Hoover squeaked back, his whiskers swishing back and forth in excitement.

"Mama, let's put them together and see if they like each other," Claire said while she was fashioning a hammock for the new cage out of blue and green plaid fleece.

"Here's the new water bottle and food dish," said Sarah as she brought the gray plastic cage bottom filled with fresh litter into the room.

"Okay, I hope they don't start fighting like the last time we put Petey in with another rat," the velveteen said, a little worried. "I've read that male rats can be very territorial and fight when meeting a new rat for the first time even when in a neutral cage. I wonder if we should put vanilla extract on their rumps to cover their scents."

"Petey." She was looking at me intently now. "I hope you are nice to this new rat. I think he will make a great companion for you. We named him Eddie. When I held him, I had this feeling that we should bring him home to meet you."

I grinned.

She turned to Hoover and spoke with the same serious voice, "Eddie, this is Petey. I hope you two will become good friends."

By now the much more spacious cage was ready. Karin picked me up while Claire held Hoover. They put us into the new cage at the same time. We immediately tousled and rolled around in the bedding

Petey and Hoover (soon to be known as Eddie) are reunited.

on the floor, patting each other on the back, rolling over and over. Although it could have looked like we were fighting, we were roughhousing, playing our traditional game of tag-and-tackle because we were so happy to see each other.

Sarah was standing right next to the cage, watching our every move. "Mama," she said in alarm. "Do you think they are fighting?"

The velveteen scrutinized our behavior very carefully. "No," she replied. "I think they are playing. It seems as though they like each other. I have a feeling they are going to get along just fine."

She watched us for a while and then walked over to the kitchen. I could hear the familiar clanking of the dishes as she began to unload the dishwasher. She looked over her shoulder and added as an afterthought, "It's weird, but it's almost like they already know each other."

After Hoover, aka Eddie, made the game-winning tackle, we settled down and began washing and smoothing out our ruffled fur.

Eddie paused midlick and stared at me as though he had just truly seen me for the first time. "Hey, Nicodemus, I mean Petey, what happened to your right head lamp? It's not there anymore."

I sighed. I knew that sooner or later I would have to tell the story of my eye. "Well, it's a long story, my friend," I began, not particularly relishing the prospect of recounting the details of what happened.

"Well, I've got the rest of my life to listen," quipped my buddy, patting me on the back and smiling.

That night Eddie and I talked and talked. I told him the story of my surgery and of the experience at Dr. Beed's veterinary clinic. He was supportive, sympathetic, and encouraging—all qualities I had come to love about him.

After we had thoroughly dissected all that had happened to me, we shifted subjects, and he told me the latest news of CarPet World and then explained how he ended up coming home with the velveteen and her daughters.

"Well, Petey, not too much has happened at CarPet World since you left. A really nice family adopted Sugar. Same with Templeton. Fred and Joe, arguing as usual, brought in a new shipment of rats just the other day. I was the only rat left in the exotic rat bin from the days when you were there, and I was starting to get worried that no one would want me. I thought it might only be a matter of time before I would end up in the feeder bins if I did not go to a home pretty soon. I think Mr. Jaguar was getting concerned too because every morning he would shake his head and say to me, 'ER 17, I just don't get it. You are one of the most likeable rats in here, and you still haven't been chosen to go home. Well, don't feel bad, buddy. When I was a kid, I was always the last one picked to be on the baseball team, but look at me now. I'm doing just fine. Your turn will come.'

"Then he would smile, scratch me behind the ears, and walk away. I would just stare at him. I think he liked me." Eddie was talking really fast as he always did when he was excited about something.

"So today I was sleeping in the corner of the bin. You know, just like we used to do. I heard some voices, so I looked up and saw Mr. Jaguar talking to the same human who came in and took you home. When they moved closer, I could hear her saying, 'He is doing much better now, but we thought he might not make it.' They paused. 'Yes, we are so glad we adopted him, but we think he might be a little lonely, so we came back to see if we could find a buddy for him.'

"Well, I knew they were either talking about you or Harry or Snake Eyes. By the way, what are their names here?" Eddie asked detouring the conversation right in the middle of recounting his story.

"Oh, Harry is Huckle, and Snake Eyes is Dusty," I replied. I shifted my position a little as I spoke.

"Huckle and Dusty. Got it," Eddie commented and then jumped back into his narrative. "I figured it was probably you because you were the only one who had a problem when you went home. I mean your eye looked pretty bad. Actually it really did not matter to me who was sick or hurt. All I knew was that this was my chance to go home with this velveteen lady and see my friends again. So I walked over to the side of the bin and stood up on my hind feet and looked at her. Have you ever noticed how humans think it is really cute when we stand up on our hind feet?"

I nodded. He went on, "Yeah, me too. So I thought I would see if I could get her attention."

I started laughing as I imagined him standing on his hind legs, trying to get the people to look at him. "You know, Eddie, you are right about that. I hadn't thought about it before, but humans really like it when we stand on our hind legs."

Eddie's story was interrupted again, but this time it was because the velveteen had approached our cage and announced, "Petey, Eddie, time for dinner." It was about 10:30 p.m. This was when we were fed what was called "special food."

"It looks like you boys are getting along quite well. I hope you like your first meal here, Eddie," she said as she opened the door to our cage and filled our dish with the food I loved best.

"Hey, man, this is good stuff. Is that a banana? And what about this? Is this lettuce? Yum! It's got something on it that tastes really good." Eddie smacked his lips as he spoke. Then he grinned as though he was in paradise. He relished each bite, eating like he had been on a restricted diet for days.

Well, I guess he had. The food at CarPet World is nothing like what I was fed here.

"I think that's olive oil. I heard the velveteen telling someone that she puts it on because she thinks it's good for our fur," I explained between bites of the rice and my favorite frozen pea mixture.

"Wow! Look at this, Petey. Here's some sweet potato. She must have cooked it because it's still warm. Ah. Did I just die? Is this heaven?" Eddie had a dreamy look in his eyes.

I laughed again. Eddie could make me laugh harder than any other rat I knew. It was so good to be reunited with him.

Eddie's eyes closed as he savored the flavors of the different foods just like a gourmet chef tasting a spoonful of one of his delectable creations.

While we were still eating our unbelievably delicious meal, Karin came over to our cage, said good night, and turned off the light.

Following our excellent repast, we took turns drinking from the water bottle and then began washing our faces, an after-dinner ritual all rats perform. Having any food particles on our whiskers not only dulls their sensitivity but feels terrible and is very irritating.

When we felt adequately cleaned up, Eddie and I decided to explore our new home. Normally we would have done that immediately after we moved in, but we were both so distracted by our unexpected reunion that we actually forgot.

Eddie and I explored every surface with our whiskers. Our cage had two levels. The maroon bars of the cage matched the metal flooring on the first and second levels as well as the ramps that helped us run up and down. There was a huge exercise wheel in the cage that was much bigger than the ones at CarPet World. I tentatively stepped on it, and then I jumped off immediately when it moved and threw me off balance. I was not much of an exerciser, but I thought I would give it a try.

Eddie was more determined. He stood on it, struggling to maintain his balance, and then he tried to walk. He staggered left and right, trying to stay upright, his dumbo ears pointing straight out from his head like wings on an airplane.

I began to laugh.

Then with a look of determination I had seen many times before, he began to run on the thing. The faster it turned, the faster he ran until finally he stopped running and spun all the way around like he was on a ride at a fair. Then he flipped off and landed on his side at my feet.

By this time I was doubled over from laughing so hard. Once he had regained the wind that had been knocked out of him, Eddie joined in the laughter, rolling on the floor with amusement.

For the next hour or so, the story he was telling momentarily forgotten, Eddie practiced on the wheel, determined to master it, and he did, becoming quite proud of his ability to run on it without falling off. I tried a few times and then watched when I found that observing Eddie's antics was more fun than running on the wheel myself. When he tired of practicing, we finished exploring the furnishings in the cage.

I was happy to see that my tissue box den had been transferred to the ground floor. But there was something new, a hammock made out of fleece attached to the ceiling bars of the cage with safety pins. Eddie and I tried the hammock and found it very comfortable. We were pleased with our new home. As we settled down on the upper deck, a great vantage point from which we could survey the household happenings, Eddie continued telling his story.

"Now, where was I?" Eddie asked as he absentmindedly washed behind his ears with his front paws.

"I think you were telling me that the velveteen and her daughters had just arrived at CarPet World and that you were trying to get their attention by standing up on your hind legs," I reminded him, smiling as I imagined him in the exotic rat bin, practically dancing to catch their eyes.

"Yeah, that's right! Well, I was standing on my hind legs, slowly shifting my weight back and forth in a gentle swaying motion when Mr. Jaguar noticed me.

"I think he was helping my cause when he said, 'Hey, look at this little guy. Isn't he cute? Looks like he can dance! He has the nicest dumbo ears, a sleek long tail, and great markings on his back, don't you think? Besides, he has a very warm, friendly temperament! One of the best rats we have!'

"I thought he overdid it a bit," Eddie added an editorial comment and then continued recounting the tale.

"'Yes, he is really cute. He looks kind of like an opossum.' Karin studied my features, her green eyes surveying me carefully. I smiled.

"'Exactly right!' Mr. Jaguar explained. 'He is called a possum rat because of those markings on his face. Would you like to hold him?'

"I held my breath as I waited for her answer.

"'Well, actually, I think I would rather hold this little guy over here, the one with the black head and black spots on his back,' she answered while she was pointing to a male rat who had just moved in last week.

"I sighed. Boring! I thought. Exactly like the two she already has, except for you of course.

"'Sure. Here you go.' Mr. Jaguar handed ER 38 to her. He shrugged his shoulders as he looked at me as if to say, 'Hey, buddy, I tried.'

"This had happened to me before. It seemed to be the story of my life, one rejection after another. Usually I would go over to the

PETEY THE ONE-EYED RAT

corner of the cage and lie down, feeling quite dejected, but this time I decided to keep looking at the woman in the hopes that she would appreciate my perseverance and reconsider. It worked, but not in the way I expected. It was her daughter who spotted me."

"'Excuse me, Mr. Jaguar.' It was Claire. 'That little possum rat keeps looking at my mom. Would it be okay if I held him?'

"'Sure, kid.' He reached in. His large hand scooped me up as effortlessly as if I had been a cotton ball. 'Here you go.'"

"Mr. Jaguar placed me in her small warm hands. I immediately liked her. The big question was whether she would like me. My thoughts raced ahead like a stallion taking the lead at the races. If she wanted to adopt me, maybe she could convince her mom to take me home."

"I watched Sarah walk over to Claire. Winning the hearts of both girls was essential to guarantee my adoption. I looked up at Sarah and smiled. She bent down so that her small face was even with mine, scrutinized me like I was a creature from outer space that she had never seen before, grinned, and then started petting me behind my ear.

"'Wow, this rat *is* really nice. He has such a cute face and funny ears. I think Petey will like him.'

"I grinned.

"'I like him too,' said Claire, scratching me behind the other ear. "Let's see what Mama thinks.'

"I shifted my gaze to the velveteen. She and ER 38 seemed to be having difficulty. The velveteen would put ER 38 on her shoulder, but every time she put him there, he scampered down her arm. This happened five times.

"After I had watched this sequence repeat, I realized that it was of utmost importance to her that the rat she takes home is content to sit close to her neck. It was almost like this posture was a prerequisite for her to adopt him. This was exactly what I needed to know. I felt like a detective who had finally found the most important clue needed to solve a puzzling mystery. If she would just hold me for a minute, I knew exactly what to do."

"'I don't think this little guy is the one I want for Petey,' she said thoughtfully as she handed ER 38 back to Mr. Jaguar.

"Claire tapped her mom on the shoulder to get her attention and then immediately began talking about me while Mr. Jaguar was placing ER 38 back in the exotic rat bin.

"'Mama, look at this rat. He is really nice, and he has the cutest markings on his face. I've always wanted a possum.'

"Her face took on that special disarming expression she reserved for very important occasions when she wanted to convince her mother to see her point of view. Claire held me in both hands and extended them out toward her mother. I tilted my head, displaying my dumbo ears, and then walked boldly onto Karin's outstretched hand.

"She smiled at me. I knew that the moment I had been waiting for had finally come. With the single-minded determination of a bee filled with nectar flying back to the hive, I scooted up her arm and made a beeline for her shoulder and sat there.

"'Wow. This little guy must be a shoulder rat. Look at this, girls. He climbed up on my shoulder all by himself.'

"I grinned again.

"She stroked my fur, and I took that as a good sign. Determined to stay on that shoulder even if there were a serious earthquake, I braced myself so that I balanced without digging my claws into her skin as she walked around the rodent pavilion at CarPet World.

"She picked me up, held me up right in front of her face, and then looked at me, her green eyes sparkling with delight.

"I looked back at her with my friendliest expression, moved my ears slightly in a hopefully endearing gesture, and then licked her hand in an attempt to communicate that I liked her. She must have understood because the next thing I knew, she turned to Mr. Jaguar and said, 'Mr. Jaguar, this little guy has won me over. I should have listened to you when you first pointed him out to me. I would like to adopt him.'

Mr. Jaguar looked at me and winked, his open deep brown eye twinkling with happiness. And then the oddest thing happened. Remember that jaguar on the pendant around his neck?

I nodded.

"I could have sworn that it winked at me!"

I smiled knowingly.

Eddie spoke excitedly as he remembered this moment. "I was ecstatic. At last I was going home, and best of all, I knew that I would see you again, Nic—ah, Petey."

Eddie finished his story with a flourish and strode around the cage as if he was checking to make sure he was really here and not back at CarPet World. Then he took a spin on the wheel.

We talked for hours. By this time it was very dark in the house. All of the humans were asleep, even Doug, who stayed up into the wee hours of the morning. I liked this time of the night because it was quiet except for the sounds of us rats moving about our cages, drinking out of our water bottles, or running on our wheels.

Eddie and I had just eaten a snack from the food dish and were about to go to the water bottle for a drink when all of a sudden, Eddie stiffened.

"Hey, Petey, did you see that?" he asked in a hoarse whisper, his voice dripping with trepidation.

"What?" I asked, puzzled by how quickly his mood had changed from casual and calm to extremely anxious.

"On the wall over there." He pointed to the white brick wall of the fireplace to the right of our cage, his paw trembling. There was a dim silvery light shining on that wall, giving it an eerie glow. The moonlight was shining in through the window, casting its spell over the room and apparently over Eddie as well.

"I don't see anything. What is it?" I asked, squinting into the semidarkness, scanning with my one good eye to try to distinguish what he had seen.

"It's gone! Maybe I imagined it," said Eddie, rubbing his eyes with his front paws. "Man, was that creepy!"

He just sat there, shaking his head as though he was trying to delete the memory from his mind.

"What did you see, Eddie?" I demanded, persevering in my questioning, unnerved by his abrupt mood change and frustrated with his lack of responsiveness to my questions.

Eddie sat there for a few minutes longer, still shaking his head. I waited, my breath shallow.

"It was a shadow, Petey. Of a rat walking slowly outside that glass door right over there." He was pointing to the door to the deck that was across the room from our cage.

"Oh, Eddie, I know exactly what you mean," I replied, speaking quickly to cover my emotions. "There are a lot of wild rats out there. I think they come for the birdseed that drops onto the deck. You can't see it from here, but there's a bird feeder hanging in front of the kitchen window. I bet one of those wild rats happened to walk close to the glass door. I've seen one or two since I've been here. Also saw a raccoon one night, and there are three or four squirrels that run by looking for food on the deck during the day. Take it easy, buddy. Those wild rats aren't going to bother us." I patted him on the back reassuringly.

Eddie's fur started to lay down flat again as he relaxed. "Yeah, you're probably right, Petey. It was just some wild rat running by."

His reaction puzzled me, but I forgot about it as we continued updating each other on the events of our lives during the time we were separated. Eddie was particularly interested in hearing about Bailey. As the morning light began to stream in through the window, a wave of exhaustion swept over me. After all, it was bedtime for Eddie and me.

"Eddie, what do you say we take a nap?" I asked as I made my way up the ramp toward the fleece hammock.

"Good idea, Petey," Eddie agreed, yawning widely as he followed me.

We settled down next to each other in the hammock. It was nice to have a companion—not just any companion but my best friend. I felt happier than I had for a long time; Eddie's total acceptance of me even though I only had one eye was so reassuring. It was obvious that the change in my appearance had no effect on our friendship.

Even though I knew it was silly to worry that he would not like me as much if I did not have two eyes, I had been concerned about it anyway.

Eddie fell asleep right away, his breathing slowing as he relaxed into a deeper sleep so that it made an odd, syncopated rhythm with the ticking of the nearby grandfather clock.

I took this opportunity to review all that had happened since the velveteen and the kids had headed out to CarPet World. It had turned out to be a great night because of the totally unexpected reunion with my good friend. The only unsettling thing that occurred was Eddie's odd reaction to that shadow.

Why was he so scared? The only viable explanation I could think of was that he had not seen a wild rat for such a long time that it unnerved him. Yes, that must be what happened.

I was satisfied with my reasoning, so I dismissed the incident from my mind. I yawned twice. I was getting drowsy.

The warmth of my friend's body felt good, and soon I felt as relaxed as a lion sleeping in the sun on a warm summer day. It was not long before his rhythmic breathing lulled me to sleep.

Chapter Fourteen

The Omen

IT SEEMED LIKE I HAD JUST CLOSED MY EYE when the velveteen's voice woke me. "Hey, you mousie! Time to go to work! Eddie, it's your first day on the job!"

Eddie's head popped up, a quizzical expression plastered on his white face. "Do I have a job?" he asked me as he absentmindedly scratched his left ear with his foot.

"Well, sort of. Karin takes me to her office with her, so I guess you are coming too. We don't do very much. Just observe human behavior, eat, and sleep," I replied, stretching my hind legs as I tried to rouse myself from a very short sleep.

"Sounds like my kind of job," Eddie commented as he stretched and yawned.

Karin opened the door to our cage, petted each of us, and then put two rectangular rat blocks in our food dish while she announced, "Breakfast!"

Eddie ran over to the dish and grabbed a rat block in his teeth. As he held it in his paws so he could eat it, he asked, "How's the grub at this place during the day, Petey?"

He paused to swallow some of the rat block. "Yuck. Tastes just like the ones at CarPet World. Is this all we get until dinner?"

I began chewing my block and then responded between bites,

"Other than the breakfast bars, I think the food is great. This is it for the morning, but it gets better as the day goes on. I actually had a stash of these blocks in my old cage. They make great building bricks. Made a small fort one time."

"Really?" asked Eddie, gazing at the half-eaten block with new respect. "I always wanted to build a fort. Can we make one?"

"Sure," I answered, brightening at the idea of having a friend who wanted to do some fun activities with me. I stopped eating, dedicating the remainder of my block to the construction project.

Returning to our favorite topic, food, I went on, "At lunchtime the velveteen gives me some of her grub. So I have a tiny sandwich and a small glob of yogurt. The yogurt is the best! I'll bet you'll get some too. Then at night we get a mix of table scraps and some rat food. Sometimes the velveteen or the girls serve me a corn wheel just like we used to have at CarPet World, or if I'm really lucky, I get a piece of cheese."

I paused to wash my whiskers and then added, "The most special treat is at the office. Candy! It is delicious. I'll show you the secret stash when we get there."

Eddie was just staring at me in a trance, speechless, mesmerized by the idea of all the delicious delicacies to come.

While I was explaining our varied menu, the velveteen picked up our cage and took us to the car. Once at the office, she placed the cage on the floor and then opened the door and let us out.

Eddie was a lot more adventurous than I was. Running on the floor and climbing on the couch were enough for me but not for Eddie. He was determined to climb to the top of the bookshelf. This was not as easy as it might sound given that the supports were round metal pillars.

My friend's first attempts were totally unsuccessful because he kept slipping. He could climb about six inches off the floor and then would lose his grip and slide down to the carpet again. It was like watching a cartoon of a rat on TV. I began chuckling.

Eddie, not easily dissuaded, tried jumping onto the top of the bookcase from the back of one of the chairs. The first three attempts were unsuccessful. He missed his mark and landed on the floor! I could not help laughing out loud. On the fourth try, he made it.

After a few minutes of exploring the books and knickknacks on the shelf, he realized that the fastest way back to the floor was to wrap his paws around the pillars and slide down the metal supports. It was actually quite funny to watch. He looked like a little firefighter with a white face and big ears sliding down the pole at a firehouse.

Eddie so thoroughly enjoyed this routine that he repeated the cycle eight more times before he slumped down next to me, exhausted. I was laughing as hard as I laughed last night when he was practicing on the wheel. My sides hurt, and tears started streaming out of my eye. I wanted to say something to Eddie, but I was so hysterical that the words would not come out of my mouth.

Eddie stared at me, standing on his back legs, front paws on his hips, feigning a look of outrage as if to say, "What's so funny?" Then the familiar warm glow returned to his shiny black eyes, and he started laughing too.

At this point the velveteen poked her head in the door and said, "Petey, you have a visitor."

"What did she say?" I had to ask Eddie because I was still too distracted by my amusement to pay attention to her words.

"Something about you having a sister, I think," Eddie replied, trying to compose himself.

I was in the middle of telling Eddie that she had no way of knowing I had a sister when Karin picked me up, placed me on her shoulder, scooped up Eddie, and then left Eddie behind in our cage.

"Eddie, we will be back in a few minutes!" the velveteen stated as she and I waltzed out the door.

I glanced back to see Eddie watching me, a perplexed look on his face, obviously disappointed that he was being left behind. I shrugged my shoulders. Remembering that the last time she took me out of her office like this was when I met the beautiful amber doe named Bailey, I began washing my face and smoothing the fur on my head, struggling to maintain my balance with my hind legs. I wanted to look as presentable as possible just in case she was taking me to see my new love again.

Karin walked out of her office, turned left, and moved toward the waiting room. I was scanning the area, hoping Bailey might be there. When I saw Hanah, my heart started beating faster. By the time Karin and I reached the couch, I could sense Bailey's presence, but I did not see her until she poked her golden head out from behind one of the stiff pillows.

Karin set me down on the arm of the couch. Bailey immediately pulled her head out of sight as though playing hide-and-seek with me. She was so irresistible that I immediately felt drawn to her. Although I wanted to just sit on the arm of the couch and wait until she poked her head out again, the force of attraction was too strong. I found myself moving toward her as if I were a tiny piece of iron being helplessly pulled toward a giant magnet.

Her flirtatious gaze melted my heart as quickly as a flame dissolves a tiny candle on a birthday cake. I felt suddenly awkward and self-conscious. I was hyper aware of my every move as her beautiful pink-lemonade-colored eyes looked me up and down.

For a fleeting moment, I worried about what she thought about me only having one eye, but her warm, coy smile told me that for her it did not matter at all.

"Petey." Her voice was high and musical. It sounded like a flute being played by a skilled musician who could trill the highest notes with elegance and skill. "Bet you can't catch me!" she teased as she ran behind one of the pillows on the couch.

I raced after her; however, she was as agile as a deer, and she eluded me for a long time. Finally she took a moment to rest, and I gingerly approached her.

As I came closer, her ears began to wiggle back and forth so fast they became a blur, a sign that she was interested in me as more than a friend. She raced under the pillow, and I followed her like a moth drawn to a flame, unable to resist her magnetism. I was so enamored with her that I was convinced that she had cast a spell on me.

"Bailey, I have never met a girl like you," I began in my most handsome-princely voice, but she just smiled, seemingly uninterested in my words. She ran off again before I could finish expressing my thoughts. So what else could I do but chase after her once more?

I heard Hanah's voice, "Bailey, come here."

Bailey ignored the call. She gently nipped my ear.

"Bailey!" It was Hanah's voice, more insistent this time, persisting after she saw no response from the girl rat. "Time to go home."

It was very clear to me that Bailey had no intention of going home. She kept darting around on the couch, eluding Hanah's grasp for several minutes.

Finally Hanah resorted to enticing Bailey with a piece of a peanut butter cookie. That worked. Hanah managed to pick her up, and Bailey retreated to her shoulder to indulge in the delicious treat.

I stood in the middle of the couch and stared up at this doe named Bailey, my one dark ruby eye focused on her like a tractor beam, noting and observing even the tiniest of her movements as she ate her cookie and washed her face.

I was transfixed, and try though I might, I could not move. Even my tail was motionless, drooping on the fabric of the couch, seemingly paralyzed.

For the second time that day, I wondered if she had cast a spell on me. Finally I was able to slowly put one foot in front of the other, but it was like I was walking in a pool of thick, gooey caramel.

Even my senses were dulled. I could hear a voice, a human voice, but it sounded muffled as though it were coming to me from a distant place.

"Petey, Petey! Can you hear me?" it called.

I recognized that voice. It was the velveteen's. Slowly the sound became louder, and the room came into sharper focus. My legs started to move a little faster, although I was unsteady at first, and I staggered over to her at a snail's pace. She picked me up, her touch anchoring me.

I started to feel like myself again, which was very reassuring, as I feared that I had been permanently changed into a confused, lovesick rat. As the numbness left, I felt tingly all over. It was as though not just a leg or a paw but my whole body had fallen asleep.

The entire experience left me a little dazed.

The velveteen took me back to my cage, and I tried to explain to Eddie what had just happened; however, I was still too disoriented. I felt confused, like a cat that abruptly stops in his tracks when the rat he has been chasing suddenly disappears from sight.

Embarrassed by my discombobulation, I mumbled something about talking after dinner. Then I lay down, hiding my head under my paws, and tried to sleep.

When I woke up, I desperately needed a distraction, so I decided to spend the remainder of the day observing human behavior. All rats study humans very carefully with the primary purpose of determining how to elicit what the humans call "positive reinforcement."

There is one simple reason for this. Positive reinforcement means food, and if you have not figured this out by now, rats love food. Did I mention that the highlight of my day at the office was lunchtime?

I do not remember exactly how our lunchtime routine began, but I quickly learned that I would receive positive reinforcement if I performed certain acts that the velveteen found highly entertaining. If my memory serves me right, it all started when I accidentally wandered out of her office into the adjacent hallway at the same time that the velveteen was ready for lunch. Because my instinct told me to slink along the side of the hall rather than run out in the open, I ended up in front of the refrigerator door. The smell of food caught my attention, so I faced the door and began sniffing.

The velveteen squealed in delight, exclaiming, "Petey, you are so smart! How did you know that my lunch was in there? I am going to give you a special treat today! Now move aside so I can open the refrigerator door." The admiration in her voice told me that this fortunate coincidence pleased her.

I scooted over by the water cooler and then heard a creaking sound when she opened the small brown door. A whoosh of cold air blew in my face, so I ran back into the office to my cage and waited. There was a rustling sound as she grabbed a brown paper bag from the refrigerator.

I learned to recognize the sounds of the door and the lunch bag.

When the two happened simultaneously, I knew it was lunchtime and my cue to climb out of my cage and walk or to be more honest, run in the direction of the refrigerator. I watched as she opened the lunch bag and extracted a sandwich and yogurt.

Once she closed the refrigerator door, I would run back to my cage and wait to be served. This is when Karin would give me the small piece of sandwich and dollop of yogurt that I had mentioned to Eddie when describing our time at the office. Banana yogurt was my favorite treat!

The velveteen enjoyed this routine so much that she frequently invited other humans to watch. They would say things like, "Oh, he is so cute!" or, "What a smart rat!"

For me, it was operant conditioning. This voluntary behavior was rewarded with food, so I kept it up. However, if I had started salivating to the sound of the refrigerator, I would have stopped running out there immediately! Dogs might stoop to such a level, but not rats!

Unfortunately the reinforcement menu was rather limited. I had yogurt and a sandwich every day. Oh well, it was food, so I was not going to complain. I loved positive reinforcement.

After lunch I usually slept for the rest of the day, but today I had difficulty staying asleep. Eddie, on the other hand, was lying beside me, snoring away.

Thoughts of Bailey kept percolating in my mind, jarring me to consciousness each time a new one bubbled up. I dreamt of chasing her around the couch and having long conversations with her as we snuggled under the pillow. I would rouse with a start and look for her, feeling terribly disappointed when I realized that the other rat in my cage was Eddie, not Bailey.

There was one time, however, when Eddie woke up suddenly after I, still half asleep, put my paw on his back and called him sweetie. He glared at me with glazed, sleep-laden eyes and a confused expression on his face. Then he carefully removed my paw, left the hammock, and went downstairs to the tissue box den to sleep.

He still teases me about that incident to this day.

The rest of Eddie's first week passed rather routinely. The

following week, however, brought some exciting news. It was a workday for the velveteen, so Eddie and I went to the office. Just after our lunches of sandwich and yogurt, the velveteen bounded into the office with a big smile on her face. She opened the door of our cage, picked me up, cradled me in her hands, and held me at eye level.

"Petey, guess what? You are going to be a father! Bailey is pregnant!" She was grinning with pride.

I felt my jaw drop open. It really should not have come as such a surprise, but I had not even thought about the possibility.

My thoughts immediately went to Pops. I thought about our last conversation before I moved to CarPet World. It seemed like such a long time ago.

I sighed.

I remembered exactly what he said. "You will be successful in life and will make a fine father when you grow up. I bet you will be Best of Show just like we talked about the other day."

Well, the Best of Show dream would never happen, but it looked like I was going to be a father. I wanted to be a good father just like Pops had predicted.

That night after the humans had gone to bed, Eddie and I played a rousing game of tag-and-tackle. This time I won. We each took a long drink from the water bottle and then settled down for our usual evening talk in which we discussed the events of the day and reminisced about old times.

I glanced around the room. There were dying embers spluttering in the fireplace to the right of our cage, adding a warm orange cast to the silver white moonlight streaming in the window.

I told Eddie about Bailey and how enjoyable it was to spend time with her. When I finished my story, all he said was, "I wonder if she has a sister."

We were speculating about this and how much fun it would be if we could double-date when Eddie suddenly stiffened just like he had done the other night.

His voice quieted to a hoarse whisper that was barely audible.

"Look!" He could barely speak as he pointed to the wall, his paw trembling.

I followed the line of his arm with my eye and squinted to sharpen my vision. This time I saw it too. A chill ran up and down my spine.

There was a diabolical shadow of three rats outlined on the white bricks of the fireplace. They looked huge because of the way the moonlight projected their images onto the wall. Moving in single file past the glass door, their pace was uncharacteristically slow for wild rats walking in the moonlight. Wild rats normally dart from place to place to avoid being exposed to predators by the bright lunar light.

At first I looked with casual interest, thinking it was just some wild rats out scrounging for morsels of birdseed scattered on the deck by careless songbirds, but then my attention was riveted to those shadows.

I gasped.

The rats had ceased moving and were standing on their hind legs as though they were trying to peer into the window in our direction. It was the leader of the pack, the third rat in the line and farthest to the right, that caught my attention.

My body reacted instinctively, becoming rigid as my guard hairs poked straight out like the quills of a threatened porcupine. Eddie and I shivered simultaneously as if an invisible choreographer had orchestrated our movements. The shiver ran from my neck all the way down my spine into my tail, which began shaking like a leaf.

I could not believe my eye, so I blinked hard and looked again.

There was no mistaking it. That rat had a W-shaped nick in his left ear. I knew only one rat that looked like that. It was my nemesis, ER 002, Ratzilla.

Eddie and I stared at each other, shocked. We knew what this meant. ER 002's parting words came flooding back to me. "Don't think this is the last you'll see of me, Romeo. I'm not finished with you yet!"

Just then Doug, who was staying up late as usual, flipped on the light and walked into the kitchen for a snack of chips and salsa. After he had assembled his snack, he left the room and turned off the light.

The diabolical shadow of the rat with the W-shaped notch in his ear appears on the wall.

I immediately focused on the wall, looking for the shadow, but the rats were gone.

Before Eddie and I had a chance to speak, I heard faint high-pitched squeaks coming from the other room. It was Huckle. He had seen ER 002 and his cronies too.

About ten seconds later, I became aware that a rat was sitting on the table outside of our cage. My guard hairs stiffened further, becoming like steel spines. I was ready to defend Eddie at all costs and fight to the death if necessary.

Then the rat spoke in a loud voice, "Boo ... boo!"

"What in the Sam hill?" I screeched. I jumped two inches into the air and whacked my tail on the wheel, expecting to see ER 002's beady black eyes glaring at me.

Suddenly I realized who it was. The mysterious rat's habit of repeating his words gave away his identity in an instant.

"That was not funny, Huckle! How did you get over here?" I exclaimed, my voice about an octave higher than usual.

"I found a way to open my cage door and sneak out. Dusty doesn't seem to care. I was practicing going in and out all afternoon, just waiting for the right time to surprise you guys ... guys," he explained apologetically.

"Yeah, you just about gave me a heart attack. I thought you were ER 002, you scoundrel!" Eddie said. He was panting, trying to catch his breath.

"Yeah, me too!" I chimed in as I checked my tail to make sure it was intact. It looked fine. As my heart rate slowed, my guard hairs began relaxing. They certainly had quite a workout that night.

"Well, since you're here, let's talk," I suggested, now able to laugh at Huckle's prank.

And talk we did. All night. Nonstop.

Exploring all of the possible ramifications of the fact that ER 002 now knew where we lived was very stressful. Our washing behavior dramatically increased in direct proportion to our anxiety about seeing those three stooges again. By the end of the night, we were the cleanest rats around.

"How could he have found us ... us?" Huckle asked, as mystified by their appearance as I was. Huckle seemed to be very interested in meticulously washing every inch of his tail.

"I have no idea," I replied, trying to think of a probable explanation for the unforeseen appearance of ER 002 and his two cronies. I found myself vigorously licking my paw and washing my ears and face with unusual enthusiasm.

"He must live in the area somewhere, but I don't know why he would be roaming around outside at night. I wonder if he and Sketch and X-Con are still with those kids," Eddie chimed in, scrupulously grooming the thick gray fur on his back.

I shrugged. "Well, I guess that really does not matter. The fact is that he has found us, and it looks like he is going to try to figure out how to enter the house. It will probably take him one or two nights to do that since it's really not that hard. Wild rats have been doing it for centuries," I commented, still reeling from the recent turn of events.

I craned my neck so that I could clean my stomach fur for the fourth time.

"Well, maybe he just wanted to see if we live here, and now that he knows we do, he'll leave us alone," Eddie began, but he trailed off when he saw us both staring at him as though he had completely lost his mind.

He covered his embarrassment by fastidiously cleaning the toenails on his left rear paw.

"I wish we knew where Sugar was living. He would for sure have some good ideas about what to do ... do," Huckle mused as he twisted to wash his back. He seemed unusually interested in smoothing the stripe of black fur that ran down the middle. Then he added, "Now that we know they are sneaking around our home, we have to be prepared for an attack ... attack."

We all agreed. The three of us decided that it would be best for Eddie and I to come up with the strategic plan and then communicate it to Huckle at a time when Dusty was not around. His allegiance to ER 002 when he lived at CarPet World and his initial hostility toward me made us cautious and untrusting, suspecting that if push came to shove, he would join forces with ER 002.

"You know, guys, Dusty was not bothered when ER 002 and his friends showed up. It's weird, but it was almost like he was expecting them ... them," Huckle observed and then shivered.

"That really worries me," I responded, my distrust for Dusty growing stronger. "Listen to me, Eddie and Huckle," I spoke in a hushed tone. They moved in closer. "Like Huckle said, we must be prepared. There is no way I will ever be ambushed by ER 002, Sketch, and X-Con again. We must be ready for war. Are you both prepared to defend any one of us to the death if necessary?"

They shook their heads up and down.

"Good. I am too," I said in a grave voice. I was dead serious.

Eddie, uncomfortable with the somber direction of our conversation, lightened the mood a bit by asking, "What do you say we spit to seal the pact?"

"Great idea," Huckle and I said in unison with Huckle tagging on an extra *idea*. It sounded like an echo, but we were used to his unusual manner of speaking.

Then the three of us spit. Eddie was first. Huckle was second, and I was third. As silly as it may sound, this simple ritual made us all feel significantly more safe and secure.

The strength of the friendships I had with Eddie and Huckle gave me confidence. I was determined to stop ER 002 from negatively affecting my life or the lives of my friends again.

But I had another reason to fight for my life, and this was Bailey. She and I had a future together, and I wanted to survive so I could spend time with her. Besides, I was going to be a father. I was determined to live long enough to share what I had learned about life with my sons and daughters just like Mama and Pops had done for me.

"Looks like the sun is coming up," observed Eddie. His simple statement jolted me out of my deep thoughts about fatherhood and the meaning of life.

"Huckle, you'd better head back to your home before the humans start moving around," I commented, concerned that his cage would be secured if someone saw that he had gotten out. I wanted him to be able to come and talk with us as often as possible.

"Right ... right," Huckle replied. "See you guys later."

He jumped down from our table, slinking along the wall in customary rat fashion. He paused in front of the glass doors to the deck, peered outside, and swept the deck with his eyes. Then he turned toward us and indicated by a shake of his head that the coast was clear.

The three visitors were gone.

"Hey, Eddie. What do you say we catch a few winks before breakfast?" I asked. Then I washed my front paws a few times, betraying the fact that I still felt a little nervous.

"Good idea, Petey," Eddie replied. He licked his right foreleg and then reached up over his head to scrub his dumbo ears. Eddie was nervous too.

We trudged upstairs to the cozy fleece hammock and settled down for a good rest, lying side by side and on top of each other. Typical rat behavior.

I saw Eddie's eyes droop shut. I glanced one last time at the fireplace wall to make sure no ominous shadows were dancing there. All was still. I closed my eye, knowing that soon the velveteen would get up and greet us by saying, "Hey, you mousies! Time for breakfast."

I was right. The velveteen did greet us by saying, "Hey, you mousies! Time for breakfast," but then, after feeding us our rat blocks, she added something completely unexpected. "Petey and Eddie, you will never believe this, but I just finished talking on the phone to a woman named Linda from Port Orchard."

We continued munching, not finding this particularly interesting. I assumed this lady had something to do with apples or pears, not my favorite foods, so I was only half listening.

She continued. "Turns out she owns a rattery. I had never heard of a rattery before. Can you believe it? Humans actually breed rats as a hobby in their homes."

My ears perked up a little when she mentioned rattery. I smiled, remembering my days living at Annabelle's rattery with Mama and Pops and my brothers and sisters.

Then she added, "Well, listen to this. She went on to tell me that she is a member of a group called RatsPacNW. Turns out this group is putting on something called a rat show."

My heart skipped a beat. She had my attention now. I glanced at Eddie, wondering if his dad had ever talked to him about being a show rat.

"And guess what?" she asked, looking at us expectantly.

Eddie and I, standing side by side, looked up at her in unison as if to say, "What?"

She continued, her green eyes sparkling with excitement, "We're going to go! To the rat show! Port Orchard is only about an hour away from here."

I could not help running up and down the cage ladder with excitement. I even took an awkward spin on the wheel. Eddie dropped his half-eaten rat block and stared at me, his black eyes wide with surprise.

I could hear Pop's deep, confident voice saying, "You are going to be a show rat, my son."

What do you know? When I lost my eye, I gave up the dream of ever going to a rat show. Maybe through some strange twist of fate, despite having only one good eye, I am going to be a show rat after all.

Afterword

Petey was my little friend for two short years. The hardest thing about loving a pet rat is that the life span of a rat is so brief. However, during the fleeting time he was with us, Petey impacted my life and the lives of my husband, my son, and my daughters so significantly that we will never forget him.

For ten years, my two daughters and I operated 3 Girls Rattery where we bred exotic rats, standard size and dwarf, for people to adopt for both show and pets. We chose "When you adopt a rat, you adopt a best friend!" as the slogan for our rattery because it is true. There is a very strong symbiotic bond that develops between rats and the humans who nurture them.

As you may have noticed, *Petey the One-Eyed Rat* contains a strong message about the plight of the feeder rats. This is why the members of the United Federation of Feeder Rats worked so hard to improve their sordid living conditions. After we began breeding rats for show and pets, we became aware that there were other breeders who sold rats to pet stores as food for snakes. These rats often received inadequate care or were neglected. We also became aware that some people adopted rats as pets, decided to try breeding, tired of the responsibilities that came with this hobby, and then no longer wanted the rats that they had. These homeless rats needed a new place to live.

Rat rescue organizations were established that are dedicated to finding homes for unwanted or abandoned pet rats so that they do not die of starvation or disease, or become food for snakes. These organizations need our support. A percentage of the proceeds from the sale of *Petey the One-Eyed Rat* will be donated to help fund the work of rat rescue organizations.

In addition to awareness of some of the injustices faced by rats, we learned that there are people all over the world who love rats as pets and that rat shows are an international phenomenon. We have made many good friends because of our involvement in the world of rats, including Lynn, the exceptionally talented illustrator of *Petey the One-Eyed Rat*.

About the Author

Dr. Kim Lampson Reiff is an animal lover, author and psychologist. She has a private practice in Mercer Island, Washington and is professor of graduate psychology at Northwest University in Kirkland, Washington. In her free time, Kim loves being with her family – her husband Dan, and her three children: Chris, Krisanna, and Stevie. She also enjoys taking ballet classes, bird watching, writing, and sitting by a cozy fire.

Kim currently has one cat, although over the past 15 years, she and her family have nurtured and loved more than a hundred rats, seven guinea pigs, six chinchillas, three cats, one degu, one frog, and one dog. Although no longer breeding rats, she remains active in RatsPacNW and attends rat shows twice a year.

About the Illustrator

Lynn Rosskamp is an animal lover, artist, web cartoonist, and graphic designer. She graduated from Reed College with a bachelor's degree in visual arts and currently owns Those Bad Girls Greetings, Pingi Hats, and a rattery called Rodents of Unusual Sweetness, which specializes in exceptionally friendly pet rats. She is a longtime member of RatsPacNW, and she is the coordinator of Ratapalooza, Seattle's pet rat expo, which has been going strong for more than a decade. She lives with her husband, a whole lot of rats, and several cats in Seattle.

Cast of Characters

Here is a guide to help you understand the name changes of rat characters in *Petey the One-Eyed Rat* due to moving and adoptions. The animals themselves have their own ways of referring to one another. Pet store caregivers often bestow names on the animals waiting to be adopted. After adoption, people who love animals carefully choose the names for their new pets.

A listing of the main human characters follows this guide with their hair (fur) colors described from Petey's perspective.

First Name In story	Fur Color/ Type	Ears	CarPet World Name Among the Rats	CarPet World Name(s) Given by Humans	Adopted Name Given by Humans
Pops/ Whiskers	Agouti	Standard			
Mama/Iris	Agouti Berkshire	Standard			
Nicodemus	Fawn	Standard	Nicodemus	ER 22/ FR22	Petey
Templeton	Agouti Berkshire	Standard	Templeton	ER 23	
Rose	Fawn	Standard	Rose	ER 24	

First Name In story	Fur Color/ Type	Ears	CarPet World Name Among the Rats	CarPet World Name(s) Given by Humans	Adopted Name Given by Humans
Peony	American Irish Black	Standard	Peony	ER 25	
Stuart	Shiny Black	Standard	Stuart	Adopted by Mr. Jaguar	
Willow	Pink–eyed Seal Point Siamese	Dumbo	Willow	ER 12	
ER 002	Shiny Slate Blue Fur Long Tail, Lightning Blaze	Standard	ER 002	ER 002	Ratzilla
ER 4	Agouti Bareback	Standard	Sketch	ER 4	Hank
ER 19	Blue Berkshire, Short Tail	Standard	X-Con	ER 19	Drover
ER 17	Blue Possum	Dumbo	Hoover	ER 17	Eddie
ER 89	Black-eyed White	Standard	Sugar	FR 89/ ER 89	
ER 54	Black Hooded	Standard	Fritz	ER 54	Raspberry
FR 76	Black Hooded	Standard	Harry	FR 76	Huckle
ER 51	Black Hooded	Standard	Snake Eyes	ER 51	Dusty

First Name In story	Fur Color/ Type	Ears	CarPet World Name Among the Rats	CarPet World Name(s) Given by Humans	Adopted Name Given by Humans
Big Tommy	Fawn	Dumbo			
King Pin	Agouti	Standard			
Papa Joe	Albino	Standard			

People	Hair Type from Petey's Perspective
Sarah	Cinnamon Satin
Claire	Agouti Velveteen
Karin	Fawn Velveteen
Doug	Chocolate
Charlie	Agouti
Fred	Agouti Double Rex
Joe	Lilac
Arnold Jaguar	Hairless
"Cat"	Beige
Moose	Blue and purple – no comparable fur color
Ivy	Red- no comparable fur color
Dr. Beed	Agouti Velveteen
Jenny	Mink
Julie	Cinnamon Agouti
Hanah	Fawn

CPSIA information can be obtained at www.ICGtesting.com
Printed in the USA
BVOW05*2230110416

443563BV00001B/2/P